THE RETURN

A Novel by Inelia Benz

Published by Inelia Benz 2018

© Inelia Benz - All Rights Reserved

No part of this book may be reproduced or transmitted in any form or any manner, electronic or mechanical, including photocopying, recording or by any information storage and retrieval system, without written permission from the author.

Author contact details:

www.inelia.com

Cover by: Laura Uribe

http://laurauribeart.com

ISBN: 978-1-387-76342-9

Disclaimer: Although based on actual events, this is a work of fiction. Names, characters, organizations, places, locales, and incidents are either the products of the author's imagination or used in a fictitious manner.

Novels by Inelia Benz

The 13th Mage

Interview with an Alien

Interview with a Psychic Assassin

Interview with an Angel

Other books by Inelia Benz

Are you a Witch?

Personal and Global Ascension 2012-2017

Weekly Empowerment Workbook

The Essential Guide to Spiritual Events

Table of Contents

Chapter one 1
Chapter two 10
Chapter three 22
Chapter four 33
Chatpter five 40
Chapter six 51
Chapter seven 64
Chapter eight 78
Chapter nine 88
Chapter ten 102
Chapter eleven 115
Chapter twelve 126
Chapter thirteen 139
Chapter fourteen 149
Chapter fifteen 161
Chapter sixteen 171
Chapter seventeen 182
Chapter eighteen 193
Chapter nineteen 204
Chapter twenty 221
Chapter twenty one 234
Epilogue 248

CHAPTER ONE

Anin took his three personal use hours per light cycle very seriously. These hours were, by all accounts, precious.

He moved quickly and with purpose through the stone alloy corridors on his way to the observation bay.

At times Anin would be overcome by a compulsion to be at a certain time and location, this was one of those times. Not knowing exactly why until after the fact and often when the compulsion came in this strongly, whatever was about to happen would be life changing not just for himself but for many others. This was not a usual characteristic of his genetic lineage, but a side effect of some combinations involving a highly developed sense of what might be called, "connecting the dots". At least that's how his family explained this strange phenomenon. Other lineages such as those involved mostly in spiritual matters, would say that the person had Divine Guidance or channeled Source Wisdom.

His robes rustled and clicked as he walked. They were covered in gems and symbols which spoke of Anin's lineage, his job, his social status, marriage status, personal achievements, age and rank, among other important facts. It made his progress through the long corridor slower than he would have liked.

His headdress lay firmly under his left arm, a sign that at the moment he represented "himself" and not his job, position, family, race or species.

By Anunnaki standards, Anin was barely an adult and still very fit, yet his heart was beating hard from the effort of carrying such heavy garments. He made a mental note to start using the artificial satellite's gyms to build some needed gravity muscles.

This particular observation bay was rarely occupied, which made it one of his favorite places in the entire complex. Anin did not enjoy idle chatter and the thought of having casual conversations with inferior species or staff members repulsed him. His job was socially interactive in nature but Anin had managed to minimize all interactions and made sure that his personal hours were allocated to the times of the light cycle which were least populated on the Anunnaki section of the artificial moon. The observation bay lay in his line of sight now, although distant still. He hoped it would be empty as usual but as he got closer, the distinct shape and form of a person became apparent. The bay was not empty. His heart sank. He couldn't change his mind however, the impulse had guided him to the bay and it was now too late to turn back.

He entered the waiting area and stood still while the room scanned his genes and placed him firmly next in line for the bay's control panel. Anin actually didn't know if he was supposed to use the bay controls or simply sit and wait. He did know for certain the location he had to be at, at that precise moment in time and space was the observation bay.

It took him a few minutes to become interested in the person at the bay controls. It was a female Rumni, a reptilian humanoid. Like all Anunnaki, Anin found the reptilian species to be repulsive. They had a strong odor and a disregard for cross cultural social etiquette.

Her attire revealed her to be a high ranking, and highly regarded, scientist to her species as well as to many alliances. Her brilliant white scaled skin, and almost luminescent blue eyes, indicated a royal bloodline.

It didn't make much sense to Anin that his own government would be so accommodating of this particular species sharing and observing the same planet. Their intentions and actions on the planet's inhabitants were at best considered hostile and genocidal at worst.

He looked at the timekeeping device in the bay area and wondered if the Rumni female would ever leave but she seemed deeply engrossed in her observation of the planet below.

His attention moved to the image on the large bay screen and saw that the Rumni had carried out a methodical multi-frequency scan of the planet.

The result was quite beautiful. It had been two years since starting his commission here, it occurred to him that the thought of doing such a thing had never crossed his mind.

Anin's heart slowed down and the telltale energy and feelings around his head and body that told him the moment in time space he had been compelled to be at was about to come to pass. His body tensed to keep him aware and awake. Whatever was about to happen was very important and he must not miss any details.

The image of the planet they were observing went progressively dark, the colors turning from a very dark purple, to a very dark blue. It was beautiful.

And suddenly it happened, and he gasped. Between the darkest of shades, a tiny bright, pure white light, surrounded by slightly grey lights. And then it was gone.

His gasp made the Rumni aware of his presence. She cocked her head very slightly in his direction communicating her awareness of him.

She moved her hands on the holographic control panel, and Anin could almost sense her mind guiding the observation bay lens. She found the light again, this time she kept the frequency and location stable, and zoomed in.

The infinitely small light occupied most of the screen now. She moved the dials and the image moved back to a spectrum visible to the naked eye.

In front of them the bright light turned into a very young human female. She sat in what looked like a garden. She wore human attire and there were a few toys laying around her. His mind scanned his intimate knowledge of the human attire communication system, the information indicated her to be around 3 years old. Her greenish hair tied in plaits on each side of her head. A frilly white dress, socks to match, shiny red shoes, big silk ribbons in her hair, the nature and appearance of the toys around her told of a wealthy or middle class, Western family.

And then it happened. The girl paused, suddenly looked up, her big brown eyes filling the screen, and looked right into him.

She smiled, and told him her name was Cecilia, and, to his utter shock and surprise, her Anunnaki Lineage and Rank.

As Anin received the correct genetic vibrational signature for her family, he fell to one knee in respect, and his body filled with Source Bliss. This happened automatically, it was a program built in to all Anunnaki when greeted by a Source carrier, a King, or Queen, of their people.

It took a few seconds for his logical mind to take over and tell him that this lowly, badly designed, genetically polluted humanoid, could not possibly be what she had communicated she was.

He stood up quickly, looked over at the Rumni and realized she had not yet seen the human female on the screen, the Rumni's eyes were still focused on the controls. At that moment, the reptilian looked up directly at the screen, her lizard tongue twitched in and out of her mouth and her vertical pupils became hair thin, a sign of extreme excitement.

She looked at him, released the controls and strode quickly toward him, breaking several cross-cultural taboos.

She put her hands together in the sign of universal peace, and said, "Shylar, First Ranking Ultra-Dimensional Biologist sends greetings to the Humanoid Male in front of me. Human female, of young age, is claimed by the Rumni. She is Rumni property. Stay away".

He searched his Rumni vocabulary for his rank and Genetic lineage, and responded to her in the same casual format she had introduced herself, "Anin, of the Anunnaki Empire, Accountant Stock Problem Analyst and Resolver Ambassador to the Solar System, 110th descendent of..." The reptilian rolled her eyes. Anin paused. She actually rolled her eyes at his greeting. He didn't know reptilians could roll their eyes, but apparently, they could. Anin decided to forfeit the rest of his introduction and see what this creature wanted. He too could be rude to others. "...greets you. What is the basis of your claim?"

"My search found her, and I was the first person here to see her."

His mind raced. Anin knew, beyond any doubt, that he could not let the human girl be claimed by this murderous race.

"I agree that you executed the search that found her, but I do not agree that it was you who saw her first. I was here when her life force signature first appeared, and also the first to see her three dimensional projected image. And I can also state that the technology used for the search is Anunnaki in design and ownership." The thought that the human child had greeted him first and only him, crossed his mind. But this information Anin had to keep very close to his chest.

The Rumni considered him for a split second, then, shockingly, projected her mind into his, and tried to command him to conform.

This would have worked if Anin had been three ranks lower, but his genetic coding did not allow for it to happen.

He logged the amount of protocols broken, and said, "I protest your attempted interference of my mind and free will."

She blinked, surprised at her inability to influence him, then stood to her full height, towering a full head above him, and projected a full force wave of fear and deadly threat toward him.

He felt the wave go through his energy field and oratory senses, his rank allowing him to bypass any physiological reactions this might have in an ordinary humanoid, and again stated his protest at her war provoking actions.

It was, indeed, a very serious matter.

He was about to place her in war advisement but realized that he had his headdress by his side therefore, to be fair, her actions were a personal assault and not an interspecies one.

He quickly reached for his headdress, which once in place took this out of a personal matter and into a governmental one. But before he could reach it, her hand shot out and again breaking all known protocols, she touched him. Glands in her hand released a paralyzing compound into his skin, and Anin found himself unable to move.

"Agree to my ownership of this human female, or I will terminate the person you are."

His garments were more than a communication system to let others know of position, lineage, specialization and rank. It was also one of the most sophisticated survival Artificial Intelligent pieces of equipment in the known universe.

Having detected the telepathic and vibrational attacks, it had already gone into high alert, and as the paralyzing compound worked its way through Anin's body, his robe released an antidote.

Feeling the release of his body from the compound's effect, Anin quickly reached his headgear and put it on.

She stood back in surprise and for the first time, he thought, she realized that Anin too held a high ranking office among his people, and that she was in deep trouble for her actions.

He merged his mind to the communications channel of the collective mind of his people and sent out a quick summary of what had just transpired between himself and the female Rumni.

A call went out to the Rumni hierarchy, demanding immediate punishment and banishment of the female named Shylar.

He received an apology from her superiors, telling of the female's genius status, Royal blood, and documented allowance for "strange, aggressive and antisocial behavior", which had been agreed upon by all present cohabiting species on the Solar System.

Anin sighed in frustration. They too had some loose cannons running around in the known universe, genetic mishaps that contained enormous skill in their lineage, but were completely unruly, unpredictable and non-conformist.

Cross Cultural Mediators from both races took control of the interaction and decided that all facts would have to be cross checked before ownership of the human girl could be established or any actions taken regarding the alleged assault.

He knew this meant the Observation Bay cameras, genetic records and a full memory scan of both parties would be downloaded and analyzed by both species.

As the communication arrived to all concerned, two armed Rumni arrived at their location. They were much larger than the female, and highly skilled in armed combat, as Anin witnessed during the scuffle that followed when the female was removed from the room against her will.

His heart racing and a metallic taste in his mouth, the side effect of the poison and antidote, made him aware of the extreme danger he had just been in, and as his robes worked to physically and emotionally stabilize him, Anin remembered Cecilia.

The bay's timekeeping device showed he still had two hours left of his personal use time. Anin took off his headdress, made his way to the bay controls, sat down, closed his eyes and breathed deeply. His thoughts needed to stabilize, and a personal course of action needed to be decided upon.

The perceived communication from the human girl, and his reaction, were heretic. The mere thought of what she had said, and his reaction to it, was an abomination. As he scanned her claimed genetic lineage in his races memory banks, Anin found it to belong to an ancient Throne Bearing line, direct descendants of the Gods. This particular lineage had been declared lost. And the present King and Queen were but distant surviving cousins in comparison. The purity and light from the signature was unmatched in present records. If this human pursued her claim, she would, by all rights, become Queen to all Anunnaki. She could potentially become the absolute ruler of his species!

The words formed in his mind before he could stop them:

THE RETURN

Anin felt his body shiver. His heresy could be declared punishable by death. He wondered if a claim of genius insanity could be logged before it was too late, it might save his life. He was, after all, a highly skilled genius in his own lineage. Unfortunately, Anin was also very, very sane.

"The Return" belonged to a religious belief among his people. It stated that the Original Source would one day return to them. The Queen of the Anunnaki throughout time and space, would come and release them from their linear time-space shackles. She would open up the portal to higher dimensional physical experiences and colonization.

She would heal the sick, cure the poor, and expand his species' skills, capacities, awareness and power.

What genetic lineage she would come in through was a highly contested topic. As were other claims of what she would bring to the Anunnaki. This formed a truly rich and varied, within reason, cultural and religious spectrum across the known Galaxies.

In one of those cultural religious variations of Her Return, it did state She might arrive in a low level, enslaved, genetically polluted, humanoid species. Recently, many heretics had been spreading word of this prophecy among his people. They were crazy, militant, righteous maniacs who forced his government to make this particular branch of heresy, punishable by death. Yes, he would be executed for even thinking this was true.

But every time Anin tried to logic his seeing and memory away, her eyes seemed to pierce his, and Source Bliss would return.

He had to see her again. A way to get in touch with her had to be found. She must also be removed from the planet and away from the reptilians. The child needed protection, and she needed it now.

No. What Anin had to do was to get psychologically evaluated, maybe his sanity was not what the genetic engineers had told his family it would be during his petri dish conception. If insanity could be proven, the financial compensation to his lineage would be tremendous.

Turning his mind back to the present moment, Anin connected with the bay control system, then switched the recording apparatus off and removed the evidence of his spontaneous response to the girl from all devices and databases. But instead of deleting it completely, he placed it in a mobile storage device designed for top secret communication transport. After checking that the dangerous footage and recordings were deleted, he focused the lens back to the child. She sat on the ground cross-legged now. It felt like she was connected not just to himself but to the entire universe. This time, she did not look up toward him but simply sat, eyes closed and smiling.

Anin swiped one of the holographic dials, added a genetic filter to the formula and scanned the planet again. If the girl was who she claimed to be, her next stage would be to find and activate her Guards. If he could find them first, there might be a way to get the girl into protective custody before the reptilians found her. There was no doubt in his mind that that Rumi female had already sent an extraction team to Earth.

Due to a very regrettable decision several thousand years earlier, the Anunnaki superior genes now run in the blood of millions of humans. It was a disgusting fact, but one that might come in very handy in this situation. Anin searched for the signature of the Guardian lineage attached to this particular Royal Family. All high ranking families had Guardian lineages who were programmed and designed, at a genetic level, to protect and serve them. Anin hoped against hope that the Queen Returned had Guards on the planet.

He found one.

CHAPTER TWO

Francisco had been ordained into the Enlightened Brotherhood Order at the age of 6. It was now 1969 and it had taken him 30 years of intense training to become a Senior Brother. He was in charge of the most secret of their mystical works, The Hat Monitor Room. Also known as The Room. Which, in turn, lay in the innermost chambers of the Brotherhood HQ, a large medieval castle complex in the Southern coast of France. Given a choice, he would have preferred a lesser role in the general running of the HQ.

He had a fondness for researching everything related to physical fitness and for years had tried to get a fitness routine going for the Brothers. But the brothers, especially the Senior Brothers, wore tired of his ideas and fitness interests.

His title and status in the Order was coveted by many younger Brothers. Francisco had worked hard to get where he was. But no matter how much he meditated, studied and struggled to understand their role within the larger spectrum of the world, none of what the Order did made any real sense to him. Not really. Nothing seemed to fit with what he felt life was really about. The Senior Brothers spent years trying to make him fit in and surrender to his fate. When that didn't work, they had taught him to simply have faith. Faith will see us through, they taught him. So, he had spent a good part of ten years learning all about faith. It helped.

The name The Hat Monitor Room was not very imaginative, but accurate. Inside, was a hat. An elaborate, bishop-like, highly adorned hat, that only a handful of individuals on the planet could put on without going crazy or dying.

Francisco was one of those individuals.

It was no secret, for those with access to The Room, that the Hat had originally belonged to an extraterrestrial race of huge power and scope. Various cultures around the planet had rich and elaborate origin myths which mentioned this race and considered them to be the race of God the Creator.

For his Order though, there was no God involved. Simply a highly sophisticated and technologically superior extraterrestrial race of humanoid appearance. The Order's bolts contained a large number of artifacts and technology from that particular race, as well as many skeletons.

The beings from this particular species, whom the order called Anunnaki, seemed to average eight and a half feet in height, their skulls were elongated, and their features resembled that of a human being. In fact, apart from their height, elongated skulls and a few other anomalies, they seemed to be otherwise identical to any human on Earth.

The job in The Room was simple. After daily meditation, bilocation, remote viewing, and astral projection exercises, Francisco would simply go into the Room and put on the Hat, which was connected to multiple measuring, reading and detection devices. After putting the Hat on, it was a matter of simply sitting there, with it on, for the next seven hours. At which point, someone else would come in and take his place.

This had gone on for hundreds of years. The transferring of the Hat had been designed to take them half a second to get it from one person's head to another. And this, every seven hours, was the only time the Hat was not monitored by a Hat wearer.

No one knew what exactly would happen with the Hat if it ever became active. There were myths and rumors of course, but nothing concrete. The only scripture on the Hat hinted at it being a type of telepathic radio receiver.

"And the Wearer Will Hear the Word of God, as if it is his own thought, and the Word will announce his Return".

The Brotherhood analysis had established that the Hat was indeed a telepathic radio receiver type instrument, and that when the race that had created it returned to Earth, it would pick up their signal and whomever wore the Hat at the time would receive a direct transmission.

Francisco didn't mind wearing the Hat for seven hours every day, it gave him time to simply BE. His mind silent, his entire being in present time, and no distractions. Plus, the rest of the time belonged to him to do whatever activities he wanted or felt inspired to. Hiking, exercising, and creating tasty nutritional snacks that his Brothers would fight over, were his favorite personal activities. A few years earlier Francisco had been very interested in pursuing a romantic relationship with a local girl, but the Brotherhood had a strict no long-term relationship in place. Most Brothers retired when they turned fifty, at which time they could leave if they wanted to, to pursue a relationship or whatever else they wanted to do. But that was an eternity away for Francisco. He had enjoyed casual relationships for a while, but after his first taste of love, nothing else seemed enough. He followed news of the girl's whereabouts for a few years. The last piece of news he had received some time back, was that she had gotten married and had had her first child.

The thought that perhaps she had forgotten about his existence occupied his mind when the flash came, the perfect vision of a tiny young girl's face, a distinct vibrational signature, and a name "Cecilia" and the words, "find Cecilia". The signature was so high, so filled with light, that it sent him into a complete state of Bliss. Francisco felt his body jerk forward as he fell off the chair onto his feet, his left arm across his chest, his right fist in front of his stomach.

Gasping for breath, he took stock of his situation and quickly regained control of his body, he reached for the red button and pressed it.

A rush of activity ensued.

Although everyone in the department had learned the drill and practiced it a thousand times, it had never been used before. It seemed it would never be used. But here they were, and it had been him who had heard it. It had been Francisco himself who heard the transmission.

Three of his colleagues entered the room, one of them wearing nothing but his underwear and still soaked and soapy from a short lived shower. They stayed silent, pulling up desks and switching on monitors which were connected to computers that were so advanced, the general public would not see them for another three decades.

The readings were clear, something had happened, but no one could work out exactly what.

They waited, their excitement palatable even though no one had said a word. Keeping verbal and mental silence was a key requirement while in the Room.

But Francisco could not keep his mind quiet. All the years of training and practice had not prepared him for this moment. Looking around at his Room Brothers, he signaled for someone else to take the Hat, something not part of the protocol, as that half a second could mean missing a vital piece of information. But there would be no more communication today. That there would be no more communications coming through the hat had not formed part of the protocol or projections planned for by the Brotherhood. Now it was a fact Francisco knew to be true and permanent. He needed to leave the room and analyze what had happened, go back through it, and write his report. He needed to trace the girl's energy signature and find her. The urge to find her overtook all other priorities.

The other men looked at him in surprise, and Francisco signaled again, they looked at each other, reading their collective decision on how to proceed, then one of them nodded and got up to put on the Hat.

It was David, the youngest of the Room Brothers and one of Francisco's closest friends. A brother among brothers. For a split second a darkness flowed through the younger Brother's eyes. But as Francisco looked closer, his eyes were filled with kindness and trust. Yes, David could be trusted to take over.

The transfer complete, Francisco left the Room, and returned to his bedroom.

His heart thumped against his chest and his hands and legs were shaking ever so slightly. He lay down and closed his eyes. The astral plane would be the best and fastest way to find the girl. But the usual breathing method to go astral didn't work for him this time, his physical body was too emotionally heightened for it to work. His body had been sent into a state of bliss, from which Francisco had pulled out very suddenly and violently in order to press the red button.

He decided to let his body return to the state of Bliss and come back to normal at a natural pace. Not only would this provide him with valuable information about what had happened but would also help him to really fine tune the girl's vibrational signature.

It didn't take long, all he had to do was to picture her face, and the moment of Bliss returned. The girl had looked right into him, into his soul, his very essence, his entire eternal being. To be utterly and completely seen, recognized, allowed to exist fully and completely, to be acknowledged, known, was something all human beings strived for, but few had the opportunity to experience. The urgency to find and protect her took over his mind and all his senses.

The moment of her eyes looking into him stayed and became stronger. He allowed it to exist and grow but this time from the space of the Observer. His awareness extended throughout the world, but there was no individual at first to zoom into, it was more like looking into the eyes of Source, like being looked back at by the entire Universe.

"The return of God", Francisco thought out loud and smiled at the thought that the ancient scriptures had gotten God's gender wrong.

The girl felt like she was the entire Universe. Like she was also, in fact, himself, Francisco.

He zoomed into her human appearance, and after a few seconds found what he was looking for. Her individual vibrational signature. The girl, Cecilia. Tuning into that individual signature, it locked it into his own vibrational memory. After making sure the signature was fully recorded, he slowly let his body come out of Bliss.

He would find her. No matter where she was in the world, he would find her.

When Francisco opened his eyes, he was greeted by Master Lo. Francisco tried to get up, but his body did not respond as it should, his head and shoulders barely lifting off the pillow. Master Lo held up his hand and motioned for him to lay down again. Francisco looked over at the clock on his wall and made a mental note that ten hours had gone past since the incident. It explained why his body felt so sluggish.

"Can you speak?" Master Lo asked him.

"Yes. I have found what I was looking for," he responded, and went on to describe his experience in minute detail.

"How old is the girl?"

Francisco quickly analyzed the girl's features and attire, "she's between 3 and 5 years old," he said.

"Interesting. We thought this communication would come from an alien race, and that the expression of God would be male, but here we are, with an infant human female instead."

Master Lo was the most senior of the Brothers. His age undeterminable, the younger Brothers would often joke about him being one of the Order's original founders. Something which, disturbingly, Master Lo never denied.

"There has been no more activity with the Hat, but you know about that?" He stated more than asked Francisco.

"Yes."

"Tell me, why do you think your physical body stood like that when he sensed the girl's presence?"

Francisco had not thought about this. It bothered him that he had missed that detail. But thinking back on it, it felt like a compulsion. Like something that could not be helped. His body had not just stood to attention to her image, it had saluted in reverence.

Master Lo reached over and handed him two photographs. One of Francisco at the moment the incident had happened. He was standing in a very odd position. Then Master Lo handed him a photograph of an ancient pre-Egyptian wall sculpture showing two Anunnaki, one obviously on a throne, and the second in front of the throne, standing in the exact same position as Francisco had been in the Room.

"Francisco, have you ever wondered why you can wear the Hat, and others cannot?"

"Well, yes. I have. We all have. There are theories..."

"It is because you carry active Anunnaki genes," Master Lo cut in.

Francisco's mind did a cartwheel, "excuse me?"

"Yes, there are various families who carry it on the planet, and part of our Order's job is to keep records and monitor these genetic lines. Occasionally, the Anunnaki genetic sequence surfaces. And when that happens, we recruit the child."

Francisco felt sick to his stomach at these words. There was nothing to pinpoint what it was about this information that made him feel sick. It reminded him of the feeling that would overtake him when someone found him out on a lie. The feeling of having information taken from him against his will.

"Now, this child, this child is obviously also Anunnaki, and her lineage is probably hierarchically superior to yours. She is not wearing any of our temple garments for that age, so she is not in our system. It must be a hidden lineage. Or a hybrid."

The new data spun inside Francisco's mind, it felt as though a whole new aspect of reality had opened up and must be made to fit into what was real and true for him.

A lost lineage would be hard to hide, but not impossible. He himself had stayed out of the Order's radar until approximately six years old, which was six years older than most kids who had been recruited for the Room. On the other hand, the possibility that the girl was a hybrid meant that someone, or a species already on the planet had created her. That disturbed him more than he cared to admit.

Master Lo watched him with the analytical, observer look. The look that read every twitch, every eye movement, dilation of his pupils, every muscle in his body, and even the tiniest sweat bead.

He felt himself desperately trying to hide his thoughts and conclusions from the Master and felt like a traitor at the same time.

"You feel conflicted." Master Lo stated.

"Yes, I don't know why, but I feel walls going up. And also like I want to hide things from you. Defensive too. Tell me Master Lo, have I had access to everything the Brotherhood knows, or has, regarding the Anunnaki?"

"No. But I think that now is the time to learn about them. I will give you access to the Chamber, everything we have gathered about this species is there. There is also information about other species there, ones that are the subject of investigation to other Brothers."

"Why is your Order made up of just boys? Why are there no girls here?" The words came out of Francisco's mouth.

Master Lo stood up quickly, and was across the room in a split second, reaching up and pressing the alarm before Francisco had a chance to listen to, or hear, what had just come out of his mouth. "Who are you?" Master Lo asked Francisco.

Francisco scanned his field, his body and his mind, "it's not a possession Master Lo, it's something else."

Master Lo's voice changed, he used Command.

"Reveal yourself to me."

Francisco felt his vision double, just for a split second, and something left his personal energy field. He had not sensed it there, but now it was gone, he knew it had been there. Not possession but quantum travel, the borrowing of another's viewpoint and awareness to explore different locations in time and space.

Master Lo fell back against the wall, his features contorting, then collapsed on the floor unconscious.

"I'm sorry," Francisco heard the same childish voice say to him inside his mind. "He's too fluffy, I think he's broken."

"Cecilia?"

"Yes?"

"Can you fix him?"

Silence.

"Yes."

Master Lo stirred. Then opened his eyes.

"Am I in trouble?"

"I think so. Don't do that again OK?"

"OK."

"How old are you Cecilia?"

The answer came in the form of a visual of three chubby fingers being held up.

"Where do you live?"

"With Mommy and Daddy. But they are not my real Mommy and Daddy."

Master Lo managed to get himself up and sat on one of the meditation chairs in the room.

"What country do you live in?"

There was a long pause.

"What is a country?"

It felt so strange to him that a three year old girl had such a large vocabulary, and obviously had huge analytical capacity, but also knew very little.

"What can you tell me about the Anunnaki?"

"What is that?"

"Tell me what you can see where you are right now."

"I can see my brother sleeping."

"Is it night time?"

"Yes."

That ruled out a huge portion of the planet. If only more data could be found, searching her physical location would be very easy.

"Do you know what the time is?"

"It is the end."

"The end of what?"

"I don't know. But it's not nice. I don't like it here. Can I go home now please?"

"Where is home?" He saw the night sky, stars shining brightly above him. He made a mental photograph of it and planned to compare the constellations with the present time to calculate an accurate location for her. "Are you seeing those stars right now?"

"Yes. Is fluffy ok?"

"Yes."

"Is he a bunny? I like bunnies."

"No. He's a man. Do you know how he broke?"

"He's too fluffy. You are not too fluffy."

Francisco thought of the Hat, and how it would kill anyone who didn't have his genes.

"That's mine. That's my hat."

Francisco was taken aback, of course the girl could see and hear him too. And apparently in a more direct way than he could hear or see her. He wondered how she did that.

"Many bodies, one mind," she said.

He had heard this before, it was a Buddhist concept of unity of intention and thought among many varied and unique individuals.

Master Lo put his finger up to his lips. The building would go into mental and verbal silence.

"Fluffy wants us to be quiet now." The little voice said.

"Yes, I have to be quiet, but you can carry on talking if you like."

"Who are those people?"

"What people?"

"They are looking at you. They are like us."

Francisco saw the faces of his Room Brothers in his inner vision.

The other Room Brothers, he thought.

"Why do you just have brothers? I have a brother. But I have a sister too."

"I have sisters too, but they live somewhere else and they come here when it's their turn."

"How come they are not home all the time? My brother and sister live with me all the time."

"This is a workplace, not a home. And we take turns because otherwise we would get tired." He thought how in previous centuries men and women worked together, but it resulted in a lot of complicated and unnecessary relationships.

If Francisco could get more personal information from her, it would make his search that much easier.

"What are your brother and sister called?" He asked her.

"Maria and Roberto. I'm sleepy now. Can I sleep with you? My brother and sister pushed me out of their beds and Mommy's and Daddy's room is locked. It's not nice to lock rooms."

"Yes, you can stay and sleep here if you like."

Francisco's mind went quiet, closed his eyes and scanned his entire energy and awareness field.

There was nothing. She was gone.

He had noticed, however, that when she asked very basic questions, her energy signature became stronger, and the Source light within it, weaker.

"She's gone," he said out loud.

"We will be traveling to the Andean research facility, where we can monitor this situation more precisely." Francisco sensed an emotional charge behind Master Lo's words, it was very subtle, but certainly there. This was the first time Francisco had detected any charge in Master Lo. It was fear.

Chapter Three

Shylar, the female Rumni hissed and spat. She had demanded presence at the investigation board, as was her right, and had to be shackled and restrained on the second day into what appeared to be turning into a long drawn data gathering and analysis of facts.

"I would like to speak to Shylar alone, if the Board agrees, in a personal capacity."

Anin's words had been projected to have an effect, an emotional and mental effect to all present individuals. It was his right to use Command in times of emergency, but it could be argued that as no lives were at stake at that precise moment his actions were illegal. It felt to him that whatever actions they took against him were unimportant. And that, not finding the thought of being reprimanded for an illegal action important, shocked him.

Shylar calmed down and stared at him. Her demeanor and body language shifting quite dramatically to one of interest.

The Board conferred for a few seconds.

"Denied."

Exin, the Anunnaki Chief of Security and a close friend of Anin, shifted uncomfortably in his chair. Of course, the chief's role was more than security, his lineage had a strong genetic diplomatic background. Anin and Exin had known each other since childhood, and his reaction was clearly based on the out of character action Anin had taken just now.

Anin had not revealed the nature of his encounter with the human child to his people and wondered if the insanity card could still be used to save him. His behavior was definitely odd even to himself.

After the day's investigations were concluded, Anin retired to his quarters. As the artificial satellite lay mostly uninhabited, he had chosen an out of the way location that, in his usual home spaceship, could house several dozen high ranking individuals.

Anin changed for dinner, taking his time as usual. He left his official headdress behind and proceeded to the dining room.

Dinner had been served a few seconds before he made it to the room. This made him happy, as interacting with his servants was not his favorite activity. His servants had figured this out a long time ago and would give him two hours of privacy. Which was unusual for his career, rank and age.

Anin knew she would come but didn't quite expect her to simply materialize in front of him while in the middle of his second course.

One moment he was alone in the room, the next moment Shylar sat across the table from him, heavily hooded, and not easily recognizable.

"What is that, some sort of cloaking device?"

"You wanted to speak in private. I am here."

His mind raced to catch himself from using any and all protocol. He had read and watched everything there was to read and see about Shylar through official and questionable channels, and knew that if he fell into protocol, she would simply clam up and leave.

"I... eh, know of your religious beliefs."

He sensed the in-breath at his words. But no violent reaction.

"My beliefs are not your concern. The female human belongs to me. I found her. You have to release your claim or..."

She paused, then continued in a friendlier manner. "I implore you to do this. You do not know what this means to my people, it is very important that we conduct scientific investigation of this female human."

"Shylar. I know that you believe she is your Savior. Please don't humor me with scientific claims."

Shylar took off her hood, revealing her scaled humanoid face and bright blue eyes, "do not speak this! You, and I, would face death if these words are known outside of this room. Not official of course, it is... it is something which some individuals of my race will kill over, us if we speak of it."

"I understand. But here we are safe. These quarters are private, in my world this means that I am able to use technology which blocks any known type of surveillance or recording. We take our private time very seriously."

He also knew that most of the major moments in his races history had been decided in a private chamber.

"Shylar, I want to tell you something, but I need you to Promise me to not repeat it at any point in the future to anyone, do you understand what I am asking?" He accentuated the word Promise and then repeated it in the Rumni language. This particular pronunciation and accentuation of the word, meant it was not an ordinary promise, but a particular action that was regarded as impeccable and unbreakable to the Rumni.

He knew that the Rumni would die before breaking a Promise. Rumni honor was paramount and held above all other personal and social characteristics.

Shylar sat back on her chair, her hands clasping the armrests.

"You ask for my Promise, but do not give a hint of what it is I am putting my life on the line for?"

"You know what we are discussing. There is something I want to share with you, tell you, but will not do so unless a Promise is formally made not to repeat it, or discuss it with anyone but me in my private capacity."

Shylar's pupils narrowed, she was agitated.

"What I have to say, will further your cause, it will give... corroborating evidence to something you want to scientifically prove."

Shylar hissed a non-aggressive hiss, it was one that he had come to know meant a form of "friendship" of sorts. The closest type of friendship Shylar could express to a member of a different species. In simple terms, it meant she wouldn't hurt him and would listen to what he was saying.

"Receive my Promise, whatever we discuss from this moment forth in these chambers, I will not repeat to anyone but yourself, in your private capacity, in the future. As a return, you will not make any mention of my religious beliefs to anyone but myself."

"I Promise."

"We will seal the Promise after the conclusion of our conversation. I take it you are familiar with the ritual?"

"Yes."

Indeed, he had researched this thoroughly. The Promise had to be concluded with a bloodletting and sharing ritual, where the participants would inflict a superficial wound onto the other, and then mix it with their own blood. A barbaric and extremely ancient ritual. Probably dangerous too, as diseases and pathogens could easily be transmitted through the blood. He had made sure Rumni normal blood didn't carry anything that could hurt him. Yes, they could excrete deadly substances through their fingertips, teeth and tongues, but their blood was harmless to Anunnaki.

He got up from the dinner table, and motioned Shylar to follow, leading her into the library.

"What I am about to show you," he said, taking a book from his desk, "is something that has been spoken about by my people for millions of years."

He opened the book, letting the holographic imagery fill the room. The mythological play of The Return. The time when the Queen to all Anunnaki would be returned, opening up portals to new dimensions for them to conquer and profit from. But of course, the book had the Queen as a beautiful, pure blooded Anunnaki.

"If I declared that the human female child is The Return, to my people, I will probably be terminated."

Shylar laughed. She reached the closest chair and collapsed into it.

She then put her head in her hands and made noises that sounded very much like sobs or crying.

Anin looked in his robes for a handkerchief, which is what one would do for an Anunnaki female in distress. But then couldn't be quite sure if the Rumni had tears, or other secretions, when they cried.

He decided to simply stay present. He pulled over a chair and sat in front of her.

It took a few minutes for the sounds to subside.

"My people originated from Earth. We were there when the mammalian humanoids were brought to Earth. And we were present when your people genetically manipulated some of the mammalian humanoid races for your own ends. Your people used some of our genetic material for these creatures. Yours too, I believe."

Anin nodded. He knew this planet's history and his species' role on it like the back of his hand. It was his job to know it.

"Shylar, one of my main roles is one of Problem Solver. I think we have a big problem here, you and I, and we need to solve it."

"This problem you speak of, it is not just ours, it is both our species' problem. Our species who have played with genes for millions of years, have purified ourselves so much that now… now we are stuck in a small and barren Third Dimension. Anin, I am the best Geneticist in my species. I am a genius among my people and yours too. I far surpass any Geneticist in your species or any other species we have encountered. This is a fact."

Anin nodded.

"Genetics is more than a way to create a master race Anin. It is the key to ultra-dimensional travel and awareness. Do you understand?"

He did not.

"This is a not religious matter. It is a matter of physically being able to embody several dimensions, so we can travel from one to another with our bodies. Your race and mine, are stuck in the Third Dimension. We are stuck because it is all we care for, all we strive for, all we care about when we create new Rumni or Anunnaki."

Anin felt the sign of something about to happen, something that would change things forever.

"This human female," Shylar began, "this child, is not God or Goddess, or anyone's Queen. She is the key to our liberation because, as you saw in that Observation Bay, she physically exists in more than just our dimension. The scans I carried out, the vibrations I observed, were not of our dimension alone. I had the Observation Bay altered to my specifications. In layman's terms, I was looking into the multiverse."

Anin sat back.

"We need to examine her, get her genetic blueprint, we need to investigate her, so we can replicate it. I can do this, I can keep her alive long enough to get the answers we seek."

Although Shylar, like any good scientist, had turned the entire scenario into a research and development one, there was one piece of information that she did not have.

"Shylar, I do understand what you have just told me. I, myself, among my people am considered to be of genius capacity. And, it makes perfect sense that the Queen of the Anunnaki is a being that physically exists in more than the third dimension as our legend clearly states that she comes to open other dimensional portals for my people."

Anin stopped speaking. If he verbalized what he wanted Shylar to hear, there would be no going back. There would be no way to deny it to himself even or claim insanity.

"Go on, please."

"As you mentioned before, these Humans carry genes from many species, including both of ours. Their building blocks are of the planetary soil, water and air, yes, but their genes can certainly be contested among our people. Shylar, this female's Anunnaki genetic blueprint belongs to a lost Royal family among my people..."

"How do you know this? You seem certain beyond doubt. Have you taken samples already? That would be a breach of our treaty!" Shylar interrupted.

"No, the girl has not been touched. Among my people, there is, as you know, telepathic communication which can span several planets in distance. We are wired in such a way, that our physical bodies will recognize and react in set programs to every family line we have. This human child greeted me in the Anunnaki way that day on the Observation Bay. She used the correct protocol, and sent the correct vibrational signature corresponding to this lost genetic lineage."

Anin waited for Shylar to respond. Now that the truth was out, he felt much better. But also, very grave.

"I have studied the communication records since our encounter. I also know that you believe what you just told me to be true. But I did not see it. Nothing in the recording indicated that she sent that greeting, or that you saw or experienced any communication with her at all."

Anin got up, and opened a door, revealing a large screen. He went back to his seat and telepathically commanded it to play the last showing, giving his personal vibrational signature within the command.

The familiar scene played out. They had watched it in the investigation procedures many times. But this time, at the crucial moment, it showed the female smiling at Anin while Shylar was looking at the controls, and Anin falling to his knees into a very awkward position. Anin then played another film to her, one from the holographic projection of The Return. Where millions of Anunnaki kneeled in front of the Queen, in that same awkward position.

"How did you manage to remove this from the Observation Bay? How come you have taken it? This is illegal, it is cheating!"

"The technology you used for the scans belongs to us. It is Anunnaki. My rank allows me access to all Anunnaki technology, whether it has been cordoned off or not. It would be cheating if I had not shown it to you in person. But for me to have this shown publicly, it would mean the possible immediate death of the human female child. And possibly yours and mine too. Would you like that to happen?"

"No, of course not. If she dies before I can take samples, and do tests, it would be useless. A corpse doesn't hold multidimensionality. Play it back... please."

The Rumni played the scene over and over. After several hours, Anin felt a nudge from his personal assistant. It was time to get ready for the next work cycle. They had been up all night.

He wasn't sure how to get Shylar out of his chambers, and there was no way she could stay there unattended. He decided a direct, non-protocol approach to be best under the present circumstances.

"Shylar, it is time for you to leave. My work cycle begins in two hours and I need to get ready. I would like, if possible, an assurance from you that you will not capture, detain or cut into this little girl... or kill her." There was no other way to put it, "I think that if we work together, we can both get what we want without involving our governments. You know as well as I do now that if she enters the system, she will be taken away from us and disposed of quickly and quietly. And probably also know that we might be disposed of in the same way."

The Rumni sat back and sighed. He realized she had taken painstaking effort to mask her odor from him. The masking of odor was indeed a diplomatic protocol among their people as both found the other to be repugnant. During conflict, the Rumni would intensify their personal odor. And during peace talks, they would minimize it and expect the other species to do the same. For him to notice this just now might seem to be random, but it was in fact crucial.

"Our cooperation, and the peace between us, is very important to me." Anin began, "the hearings are going my way, which means you will officially lose all rights over this human child. I think that you already know this. My reaching out to you is not based on winning or losing, but on understanding and deep desire to work with you and not against you. This places me in great personal and political danger, but the greater good of both our species is at stake, and I think you will agree with me that it is not something we can trust our governments to handle."

Shylar nodded. She regarded him closely. His mind raced to analyze her body language, she communicated friendship, trust and guarded confidence. There was also a hint of smugness which he attributed at his asking her for cooperation rather than simply disposing of her in the usual manner both their species dealt with enemies.

"Anin, I am not without social protocol, although my previous actions might indicate otherwise. I know the risks involved in asking me to meet with you. I also do understand and appreciate that because I came here in secret, and there are no recording or monitoring devices in your chambers, you could have killed me at any time, yet I am not dead. I am not certain why you want to collaborate with me, and this brings me pause. But I can sense and feel the truth behind your words."

Considering that the Rumni saw all Anunnaki as lying, deceitful, greedy marketeers, what Shylar had just said was a huge compliment.

"My goal is to remove this child from government investigation and eyes as soon as possible," he said. "We cannot let this case escalate any further. You have been very careful to mask your personal reasons for searching for this child. And I have not shared my knowledge of who she claims to be. We need to get her off the radar, as it were. After this incident is logged and forgotten, we can coordinate a way in which we can proceed in our investigations that does not involve our governments and also does not involve physical harm or stress on the child. My reaching out to you has to do with that too. I really don't want her placed in a lab and systematically pulled apart limb by limb... or cell by cell in this case. I'd like to get a chance to investigate the validity of her claim and I also feel a very strong compulsion to protect her. Once I win this case, I plan to allow you supervised access to her."

"This compulsion," Shylar responded, "could it be considered mind control? And if so, would being under this human's control not affect your judgment and decision making capacities? Could we not define this compulsion as a form of manipulation on her part?"

Anin had thought the same things over and over the past few days. It was both a manipulation and proof that what the child claimed was real. How to explain this to a Rumni?

"The compulsion is in itself proof of her claim, and the reason why we must keep our governments out of it. Can you categorically say that as you looked into her eyes, you felt nothing but curiosity and a desire to cut her up?"

The last sentence lacked friendliness, in fact it was charged and aggressive. But it was too late, he had already uttered it filled with unchecked emotions and he could not take it back. Then remembered that the Rumni often reacted spontaneously and without etiquette and then apologized for their words. An unfiltered show of emotions was perceived by them to be proof of honesty.

"I am so sorry Shylar. That was rude and uncalled for. I am finding it difficult to contain my emotions and inner knowing."

Shylar's pupils were dilated, and her tongue flickered in and out.

"Anin is the strangest Anunnaki I have ever met. You are either very, very clever, way more than our intelligence department knows about, or are truly honest, a trait unknown to your species. Anin of the Anunnaki, Accountant Stock Problem Analyst and

Resolver Ambassador to the Solar System, 110th descendant of the Great Nactarel, Third in Line to the Throne of Pratanikous, I will take your words and consider them deeply. We will conclude our official dispute and meet again to plan a course of action. Please know that I am not without power, and that if pushed, I will eliminate the person you are and take the child regardless of what the council decides, but time is on my side and I find your words to have merit."

She saluted him as her kind would salute a fellow friendly high ranking official, by embracing him and touching his forehead with hers, then she vanished.

It did not escape Anin that Shylar had left without answering his question, did the girl have any effect on the Rumni? It appeared that she had.

Anin smiled at the thought then felt something on his forehead. He wiped it and looked at his hands, it was blood. The Promise ritual did have a linking of blood, but the data didn't say anything about sharing blood and disappearing like she had. Plus, some notification would have been preferred. He moved quickly and purposely to his private office and saved the blood for later analysis. If he was right, it would contain the Rumni's genes. Genetic samples from Rumni were hard to come by and one day it might come in handy.

CHAPTER FOUR

Master Lo accompanied Francisco to the Andean facility. Neither of them had slept since the incident at the Brotherhood HQ. Francisco kept falling back into an altered state repeatedly but had so far managed to stay fully alert.

They had taken several airplanes and were now in a military grade vehicle traveling through unpaved mountain roads somewhere in the north of Chile, South America. The last town they had driven through was called La Serena. The Serene. It was a good name, very descriptive of the area.

The vehicle came to a stop and he heard conversations in Spanish. A gate opened, and they proceeded forward. Soon, they entered a large cave and the sound of personnel and machinery brought him back to full consciousness.

"Brother Francisco," Master Lo shook him gently by the shoulder.

Francisco opened his eyes and found himself strapped onto a semi horizontal bed. His arms and body were attached to various machines. He looked at the straps and pulled on them.

"What happened?"

"You appear to have lost consciousness."

Master Lo nodded to one of the attendants who then proceeded to remove the straps from Francisco and give him some water.

Francisco scanned his own body and clearly felt dissonant chemicals present within his circulatory, nervous and muscular system. He masked his body scan with a sigh. He had lost consciousness alright, but it had been chemically induced.

He looked over at Master Lo and detected inconsistencies in the other man's body language. On the one hand, and to anyone who hadn't taken the time to train themselves in the art of reading another person, Master Lo appeared to be calm, concerned and working with Francisco. On the other hand, he appeared frightened, on edge and unsure on how to proceed.

"Very accurately perceived Francisco. I can say I have underestimated your skills and capacities. Please don't think of me as your enemy. We are very concerned about the creature that borrowed into your body. We mean no harm and simply want to establish a good communication protocol with the creature."

"She's not going to hurt you again Master Lo. She was only trying to communicate with you directly, but like the Hat, only certain people can hold her frequency. She did not attack you. She was saying hello."

Master Lo considered Francisco's words carefully before responding. He held Francisco's hand and said, "please understand that we have no way of knowing if this is you talking or the creature. You removed the Hat from yourself against protocol, and none of the Brothers can reach or scan you anymore. Not in any dimension or plane. The Hat has not been active again, it's completely dead. We have always been able to perceive energy in the Hat. Now it is almost like the circuitry inside of it has been destroyed. We tried it on various individuals and there was no effect. Not even on ordinary humans."

"You tried the Hat on ordinary humans?"

"Military volunteers. They knew the full risks."

"The military are involved? From what country?" The Brotherhood prided itself in being independent to all other organizations and governmental bodies.

"Let's concentrate on what's important here. We want to establish a healthy communication channel with the creature and insure your safety Francisco." Master Lo replied, gently squeezing Francisco's hand in an attempt to comfort him.

Francisco thought about this. He really wanted to cooperate, he really did. His entire life was based on serving his Brotherhood. But now it seemed impossible for him to prioritize the Order's precepts and goals above his own goals. And his goal was to get out of here and find and protect Cecilia. There were no other options. Master Lo, who until that moment had been like a father to Francisco, someone who could be trusted completely and the person to go to about any issue, now felt poisonous and dangerous. Francisco saw a clear image of a man shaped snake and shuddered. He gagged and coughed to mask his true feelings.

"The chemicals will clear from your body very soon. Do be warned that this facility is top secret, as well as fully weaponized. If you try to leave here, you will be disabled and possibly killed."

"He's not very nice. He's a nasty man."

Francisco closed his eyes and relaxed back into the bed.

"Cecilia?"

"Yes?"

"How long have you been here?"

After a long pause, three chubby fingers appeared in Francisco's inner vision. He had to reword his question.

"Yes, I know you are three years old sweetie. What I'm asking is, how long have you been in my body, listening to the nasty man and I talk."

"Oh. I never left. You told me I could stay with you."

"Yes, I did. Cecilia, listen to me very carefully. I need to get out of this place and find you. This is important, do you understand?"

"Yes. I don't like that nasty man. He's not a good person."

Francisco thought how sophisticated Cecilia's vocabulary was for a three year old and wondered what language she spoke.

"I can speak all languages. I take them from the..." She paused for quite some time. "I take them from everywhere."

He analyzed her answer and it appeared to him that she downloaded languages directly from the human collective. That ability fascinated him. He had studied various religious and scholarly theories of the human collective being accessible to all people, a field where a person could search and tap into all the wisdom and knowledge ever created through time and space. Although he had met individuals who could and did tap into this field, this was the first time he'd met a person who could literally download complete data, such as a language, into her own personal field of knowledge.

He felt Master Lo releasing his hand and leaning back on his chair. It was important Master Lo not know that Cecilia was chatting to him right now.

"I'm going to scan for the girl in the astral plane Master Lo. Please don't inject any more chemicals into my body, it makes my work very difficult."

"I will not inject any more chemicals into your body."

The response sounded robotic. Francisco opened his eyes and saw Master Lo staring into the distance, pupils dilated, expression nondescript. He'd seen that look before, but where?

"Are you feeling OK?"

"I am not feeling OK, I am feeling fearful and suspicious of your actions."

That was not a response Francisco ever expected to hear from Master Lo.

"Why are you fearful and suspicious?"

"Because you are a second rate mystic, and what you have been able to do, including the direct communication with a creature that I cannot hold the energy for, far exceeds your skills or capacities."

"What kind of things, apart from communicating with the creature, are you referring to when you say they far exceed my skills or capacities?"

"Neutralizing the sedatives to begin with. They are still being delivered into your body yet here you are, conscious and aware.

And the excruciatingly frustrating power you have over me right now that makes it impossible for me to lie or withhold information from you."

"You are being honest because you can't help it?"

"I feel compelled to answer truthfully. You are using 'Command' on me to a skill and degree that far surpasses mine."

"Cecilia, are you doing something to the nasty man?"

"No."

"Why is he unable to disobey my command?"

"You said you wanted to leave that place. So, I..." Again, she was silent for quite some time. "I switched on the light. You are my ..." Another silence. "Guard. My mommy says that we have to use our words when we want something and that we ask with the magic word. If you ask people nicely and use 'please', they will let you leave and then you can come and find me. I made sure that you have the magic word when you want to ask people for things."

Francisco laughed. And Master Lo laughed. Francisco found this disturbing.

"What are the chances of you overcoming your compulsion to obey me Master Lo?"

"There is less than 5% chance that I will succeed. But working on it."

"Stop working on it."

"There is a 0% chance that I will succeed."

"Good. Keep it that way."

Francisco pulled the IV drip off his arm. He had noticed the drip on his arm when he woke up but assumed it to be for hydration or to bring him back to full consciousness. It had never occurred to him that they were giving him a sedative. He felt instantly better, and disappointed at his Brothers.

"Master Lo, you will escort me out of the facilities in a safe and friendly manner. You will behave as though everything is normal and communicate with anyone who interacts with us that I am back to myself and we are working together to address the communication with the alien creature. You will explain that we are going to confer with experts in a secret location, and that only we are qualified enough to make that contact. You are to behave to others within the parameters of how they know you to be. At no time will you tell them you are under my command."

Master Lo stood up. His robotic stare now replaced by his usual calm and collected expression, and he helped Francisco off the bed.

"Cecilia, when you say I am your guard, what exactly do you mean?"

He saw the image of a picture book, there was a princess dancing with a prince in a palace full of people, the image of the dancing couple faded out of focus and instead, the figure of a fully armed guard standing unnoticed in the background, zoomed in.

"Are you making me do things against my will Cecilia, are you commanding me like I am commanding the nasty man?"

"No."

Before the question formulated in his mind, Francisco already knew the answer. He knew that he acted from his own desire and volition and not because Cecilia was commanding him. Yet, his actions were driven by such an intensity that he didn't feel in charge of his will at all. Something else definitely drove his actions, but what?

As these thoughts crossed his mind, he could sense and feel Cecilia wondering the same thing.

Master Lo had already managed to get them out of the most secure area of the facility, and now they had an armed guard escorting them to the garage. They would take a nondescript vehicle out of the building.

"My brother wants to meet you too. Can you see him?"

"No sweetie, I can't see your brother."

He saw the face of a boy appear in his inner vision. He looked about ten years old, and Francisco could tell the vision was a live feed. He could now see what Cecilia was seeing. The boy opened his eyes wide and smiled, waving at Francisco.

Back to his present location, Francisco noticed that both himself, Master Lo, and their armed escort had come to a dead stop. He instantly animated himself and animated the men around him. It had been no more than a split-second pause but if anyone was paying attention, they would know it was not normal behavior. He hoped no one was paying attention.

"Cecilia, I need you to be super quiet for the next few hours. No more visuals. I will talk to your brother later OK? I need to concentrate on leaving this place undetected and for that I have to stay focused on what I am doing here."

If one could physically feel or hear a pout, he definitely felt it and heard it at that moment in time.

"I promise I will be able to talk to you very, very soon. But for now, be as quiet as a mouse."

"Mice make scratchy noises and squeak."

"I know you understand what I mean Cecilia. Ask your brother what 'radio silence' means."

He felt and heard the pout again, then absolute silence. He felt overcome with a sense of abandonment, but quickly processed the reaction and continued his so far undetected exit from the top-secret Andean facility.

CHAPTER FIVE

Anin received an urgent personal communication request from his friend Exin the Anunnaki Chief of Security, in the middle of his morning administrative staff meeting. It was a very unusual and unorthodox request. Particularly poignant were the words URGENT COMMUNICATION in flashing neon red capital letters within the request. Exin could be very exuberant at times but had never used neon capital letters in his communications before. Anin tried to postpone the communication but the postponement was refused, and now the entire message flashed bright, red and loud in his inner eye. Anin excused himself from the meeting and left for his office, his secretary close behind him.

"Firstly, are you in your personal capacity at the moment?" His friend's voice entered his mind as Anin sat down at his desk, making sure his secretary closed the door behind her, he opened the holographic communication device in front of him.

"No, I'm in the middle of my morning work shift."

"Take off your headdress immediately. We don't have much time."

Anin felt confused, his friend had never behaved like this before. He took off his headdress and told him he now represented himself. His friend appeared in the holographic image before him, and said, "first of all, congratulations on your win over the Rumni's claim over that human child." Anin was about to give the casual response but Exin, shockingly, cut in, "however, it is highly unusual, unorthodox, and not something you would do. I refuse to believe that you would bring your personal issues into a cross-species government incident. I cannot believe this is something you did, so I am now calling to see if my inner knowing is correct."

Anin felt more confused than he had ever been in his life. His friend read him and said, "thought so. You have no idea yet. You know nothing about it. In fact, you probably think I have gone insane or something."

"Well, now that you mention it, I have no idea what you are saying, and your comments and present behavior do sound rather disconnected and insane."

"In about ten minutes, a co-joined force of interstellar authority will go into the Lunar Base offices and take you into protective custody."

"Excuse me?"

Anin immediately thought about Cecilia and his reaction to her claim. If he could swear out loud he would have. But swearing was not part of his vocabulary.

"Oh... for God's sakes." His friend said as Anin's expression radically changed. "Please tell me it is not true. You really did? OK, just hold tight. I will get you out of this my friend."

"I couldn't help it. It just happened. I do not believe for a second that it's real or true. It has to be some sort of trickery or charm that overtook me."

"Yes, we can totally claim mental manipulation. That's a brilliant idea."

Anin held his head in his hands. This was the end of everything he had ever held precious. It was the end of his career and social standing. Whatever happened next would seal his fate and that of his offspring. In fact, he would probably be denied the right to have offspring.

"What's going to happen to her? The girl?" He asked his friend.

"Well, I've never heard a Rumni of such status called a girl before, and it shocks me that you care, but I guess you are still under her mental influence. She's going to be held in protective custody too and has applied to be held with you until the birth of the child."

Birth of the child? Anin's eyes widened in confusion. The child had already been born. When he asked for clarification, Exin stared at him in silence for what seemed to be an eternity.

"Anin, what do you think we are talking about here?"

"The human child and her claim to be Queen of the Anunnaki."

"The what?" Exin's expression went from worried to shock in a split second.

Anin realized Cecilia's claim to the throne was something Exin knew nothing about and wondered how to backtrack. But it was too late. Backtracking or lying were not in Anin's box of tools. The withholding of information, now that he was an expert in. The dots came slowly together in his mind, making him feel very sick.

"Exin... what are you talking about?"

"The Rumni female Shylar has claimed that you are lovers, and that you are so in love with each other that she has become pregnant with your child. We put her through a full medical examination, genetic testing, and she is definitely carrying your child who is now in his second month of life. Yes, it's a boy. This puts us in a very bad political situation. Although there have been other incidents of our people breeding with other species, and yes two incidents a few thousand years apart of Anunnaki and Rumni mating, this type of thing is unheard of in our modern age. How are you even fertile? You are not meant to be activated for another seven hundred years."

Anin felt like someone had just punched him in the gut. He felt violated to the most extreme levels. Shylar had obviously collected some of his genes and created a hybrid she could carry. He didn't even know reptilians carried babies, he thought they laid eggs. She must have accelerated the fetus' age in the lab to reflect conception weeks before the incident at the observation bay and then transplanted him into her body.

Anin started to lose composure. He was going to vomit anytime now. His robe took control and stabilized him.

"Anin?" Exin began, "I can see the news is as shocking to you as it is to me. It is as I suspected, you know nothing of this child or your affair with the Rumni. As you know, in our society every single trick has been used to gain political, economic and social power. This is nothing new. It is extraordinary that a Rumni is doing it, which makes me think that she would make an excellent ally, but it's nothing we can't deal with. We need to make a plan of action, what to do with the child, for example. I will make sure you do not physically meet the mother, you know what will happen if you do."

Anin knew what would happen. Anunnaki males were genetically programmed to bond and make a lifelong connection with the mother of their children. During the second month of pregnancy, the mother would create the necessary chemical compounds in her body that transmitted the child's parentage. It only took one touch, or one sniff of the pregnant female and the father would be claimed by the child's mother forever. It was one of the reasons why male Anunnaki's were kept artificially infertile until a mate was chosen for them. And even then, the embryo would be created in a lab, the child's genes altered to maximize both lineages. Once the embryo was altered to perfection, he or she would be implanted in the woman's uterus. The Joining Ceremony would take place on the second month of pregnancy. Marriages were political and social bonds in Anunnaki society and had huge consequences in both parent's lives as well as the social standing and lives of their families.

When an Anunnaki man or woman, created such a bond outside of social agreements, they were sometimes outcast and isolated from the rest of society. Most of the time, if it involved high ranking individuals, their families would take matters into their own hands and kill both parents before the child's birth. Thus, the need for protective custody.

Anin was still putting his thoughts together when his secretary's loud protests began outside the room, with a male authoritarian voice demanding entry into his office. He grabbed his headdress, switched off the holographic communications system, and opened the secret escape door behind his desk. No Ambassador had an office without an emergency escape route. Which also meant whomever had come for him, would not take long to find it. Still, it would buy him several precious minutes, more if his secretary switched on her military training. He tried to get in touch with her to give her permission to do so but was surprised to find that his personal communication system had been switched off. Only his top secret channel still worked, but unfortunately his secretary's rank didn't have access to it.

He ran down the stairs, and into the escape pod. Escaping would be used as proof of guilt, but he could not risk meeting the woman. He entered a flight and landing trajectory to an isolated area of Earth onto the pod controls and pressed the launch button.

Nothing.

He pushed the button again.

Nothing.

The pod's communication screen came alive, and a man in religious robes appeared. "Now what," thought Anin. Anin looked at the screen, there was something eerily familiar about the man that greeted him.

"Excuse my boldness Anin, but I do not have the time to make the formal introductions. I am Anteriz, Leader Supreme of the Church of Our Lady, Queen Eternal. Our system has detected a communication between you and Exin, the Chief of Security, which indicates you know of our Queen's Return?"

Anin did not remember the religious man's name, which he felt to be very odd because remembering names and all personal details was one of his strengths. There was no doubt in his mind, however, that he'd met this man before. His face was extremely familiar. But Anin's memory banks came up empty.

"Did you by any chance deactivate my escape pod?"

"Yes."

"This could not come at a worse time. You do realize that the nature of escape pods is that of escaping the area in an emergency, correct?"

"Do not despair. Our undercover agents are at this moment disabling the interspecies retrieval team sent to detain you and will be escorting you to a safe location."

Anin closed his eyes. Could this get any crazier? He did not think so.

"It is imperative that you cooperate. I have personally reviewed your recent history, not in great depth of course and I've only had a few minutes to do so and I have many questions. I will not risk your capture by sharing the location we will be taking you to, but please know that you are safe with us, and that you won't be claimed by the Rumni female while under our protection. Formally and officially speaking, I can tell you that you have no choice in the matter, and that you are in fact being kidnapped. You are of course required to resist, and I totally understand this. However, please use your higher functions to decide not to resist as this might cause personal injury. Our agents are altered to not react to or follow orders from any being. They are independent agents who answer to their higher consciousness only. Any attempt at controlling them, or resisting them, will be met by strong force."

Anin sat back and let his analytical mind take over. This man was very clever. He had in fact told Anin that his rescue was a kidnapping. This would allow Anin to return to his life, position and work without the negative results of having worked with or allied himself with criminals and heretics. He would have to think on some form of resistance that didn't result in his actual escape from these people or injury to himself.

Having allies, even within an illegal heretic organization, gave him a much better chance of success in his present predicament. The pod door opened. He turned around and saw five armed men wearing full black body coverings. They entered the pod and stood to attention.

One of them took a step forward, "Most Elated Messenger of Our Queen Returned." He said and then proceeded to prostrate in front of him. He then stood and said, "I am ordering you to come with us. We have the technology and means to make you comply, but we also want to avoid any assault to your sovereignty or status. Please do not resist."

Anin stood up, picked up his headdress placing it firmly under his left arm, and followed the man into the secret passage. The rest of the men followed closely behind.

After a reasonable amount of time, and just as they entered a corridor with full surveillance, Anin used his military training to attack the leader. His combat training had not gone very far or very well, as his body type had not been built for it. But it was good. It actually felt very good. He used his full force, frustration, anger and instinct for survival to take the leader by surprise and took him down for a full two seconds before losing consciousness.

When Anin woke up, he found himself to be practically naked, wearing only his undergarments and favorite house tunic. He blinked wondering if it had all been a bad dream and that he was in fact at home, in bed. He looked around, this was definitely home.

Not his own home but one of his family's many homes. This was his parent's ancestral house on Pratanikous. Confused and dumbfounded, he scanned his surroundings. His senses became aware of the familiar smells, sounds and sights that had greeted him so many times during his youth. The house felt peaceful and welcoming. Outside the slightly pink light from their native star indicated midday.

He heard a gentle yet assertive knock at the door. It was his mother. He could recognize that knock anywhere.

"Enter."

"My dear boy. How happy I am to see you back at our humble home."

As second in line to the throne, his parents' home was anything but humble. He wondered at the choice of words. He did not respond.

"You are probably wondering why we brought you home, and why you are still alive after your little indiscretion with that horrendous creature. A baby. Honestly my boy." She sat on the bed and held his hand. "Rest my child, I will watch over you." She continued and touched his forehead. Anin fully expected to lose consciousness again, in fact, he should have. His mother's voice carried the energy of Command to put him back to sleep, or at least that's what appeared to be happening. He closed his eyes expecting the Command to take over any second.

His mother whispered, "I have much to tell you my son. The cameras are now broadcasting a recording of you fast asleep while I sit next to you. We need to discuss what is happening and you need to know about your true lineage and reason for existing."

Still conscious and aware, Anin opened his eyes to the sounds of another person entering his room. It was the religious heretic leader. His mother smiled broadly. "Meet your uncle Anteriz."

"My uncle? I have no uncles, mother."

"Anteriz is part of our lineage, he is my brother by another father."

Anin gasped in surprise, "another father?" He thought. That meant that his grandmother had had two husbands.

"Perhaps the thought of how my mother could have two husbands might be crossing your mind. I know they crossed my mind when I heard all this. For thousands of years now, our family has led a double life. One branch of our family is the official Nactarel lineage. The other is our true and secret pure lineage of Spirit. Our role, the Nactarel lineage's role, is to keep our status and fortune safe and protected so that it can support the existence of our pure lineage through time and space. My brother and I will hold your hands now and will open the secret knowledge and programs within you that will reveal and explain everything."

Anin jumped out of bed so quickly his mother nearly fell off it.

"It's ok," his mother said raising her arms in a show of peace. "It is a natural response to protect yourself from mind or program alterations."

"You should have seen me the first time I heard I was a Nactarel!" The heretic exclaimed.

"Mother, I don't know what this man has done to you. But I have to warn you, I am no child now. I can and will resist your command. This, all this, is absurd..." He felt the telltale sign of something important and significant happening and felt his body tense up in anticipation.

"Anin?" A little girl's voice sounded in his mind.

Anin fell awkwardly to his knees.

The heretic and his mother observed Anin. Surprise then joy exploded in their features.

"She is here! Our Queen Returned is here!" The heretic said.

Both his mother and the heretic prostrated in front of him. And stayed there.

"Why are they lying down on the ground? Mommy says it's bad to lie down on the ground."

His mind struggled with the illogical situation he found himself in right now, and his deep desire to comply with the girl's voice, and the physical state of Source Bliss which overcame him.

The desire to comply won.

"For crying out loud, stand up!" He shouted at them.

His mother and the heretic stood up and came over to him, holding his hands. His mother stroked Anin's head lovingly. He desperately tried to stand up but couldn't.

"They are so pretty."

Suddenly Anin felt afraid. Maybe this creature was too powerful. Maybe it could harm and destroy at will. It could, if it so wished, destroy them all. And Anin didn't just think it could just destroy everyone in the room but destroy every Anunnaki in existence.

"That's mean. I don't like that. I don't like hurting people."

The state of Source Bliss returned full force and Anin realized that without his official robes, overcoming the Bliss was practically impossible. As the feeling that the Bliss had needed to be turned down drowned all other thoughts in his mind, it turned down.

"Anin don't like hugs. My sister don't like hugs either. I'll not hug you Anin if you don't want hugs."

Anin could hear his mother and uncle talking to him but could not work out what they were saying. He then realized that no words were being spoken, they were in fact intoning an elaborate chant. An ancient, chant which they were accompanying with movements and also putting pointed pressure on certain areas of his skull, neck, face and chest.

He felt like a stream of water started flowing through his body. It was cool, crystal like water, sparkly and alive. His eyes rolled back making him fall down, his back arched, and body tense. The water was flowing upwards now, toward his head, it felt like it was filling up his head, washing it, then leaving through his nose. His eyes back in his control, he saw his mother wiping his face, her hands covered in blood.

"Just a little nosebleed my son. It will soon be over." With the help of his uncle, his mother lifted him off the floor and lay him back on his bed.

"I don't know what sort of reaction this will have since The Returned is already in his field and he is barely an adult, not fully formed yet. I have never seen so much blood loss before." The heretic said.

"Anin?" The small girl's voice said his name over and over in his mind.

"I'm here."

"You are a bit fluffy. Would you like me to fix you? I know how to fix you."

Anin thought for a moment. He felt it important to remember that this was a very young child of a very unevolved species. He assumed that fluffy meant weakness.

"Yes, do fix me if you can. I think I'm dying."

From the look that had taken over his mother's face, Anin really thought he must be dying.

"OK. I fix you."

Anin felt the stream of water change, it became less of a flow and more of a circulation. He then saw the entire Universe appear in front of him, and thousands of lives, faces and situations flow through his inner eyes and ears.

"He has stopped bleeding," his mother stated more to herself than anyone else in the room.

He looked over at his uncle and saw that the man was crying and smiling at the same time. These Spiritual people could be so dramatic.

Taking a deep breath, Anin's life became complete. Everything that had ever happened to him, every decision he had taken, the extraordinary rise in his career and social status, every moment of unexplained precognition, it all made perfect sense to him now. He was Anin of the House of Nactarel, Spiritual Servants and Protectors of The Queen Returned, or as they called themselves, The Protectors.

"Are you Complete?" His mother asked him.

"I am Complete." Anin responded and saluted her with the secret sign of The Protectors.

CHAPTER SIX

Francisco grabbed the water canteen and took a big gulp, put it down and continued scanning the horizon with the army grade binoculars someone had equipped the truck with. This was one big desert. He didn't know South America had deserts, but here he was, and here it was.

"Any luck?" He said to Master Lo who sat inside the truck busy examining a map.

"Luck has nothing to do with it my son. We should have at least brought a compass. As it is, there are no discernible land markings for me to figure out where we are."

Francisco shook the canteen, there wasn't much water left. They would be able to survive at least a day. Back at the Order HQ one of the boys he grew up with had told him deserts had their own spirit and that if a person could connect to that desert's spirit, they would be able to borrow the desert's body and know where all directions were, and where all directions they led to. Francisco tried to remember the boy's name, but he could not. All he remembered about the boy was his place of origin, a native tribe in North America. "New Mexico," he thought out loud.

"Sorry, what did you say?"

"Nothing important."

He wondered how the spirit of the desert could be connected to without releasing Master Lo from Command. The previous night Francisco had fallen asleep for a few seconds and woke up with Master Lo about to stab him. The thought about abandoning Master Lo had crossed his mind more than once, but he couldn't. The old man wouldn't survive a day out in the desert. This was a fact. Mystics were often very good at ultra-dimensional travel, battles, exploration and survival, but not so good at surviving on the three-dimensional physical planet itself. Most of the Order

Brothers wouldn't even bother eating if the food wasn't placed in front of their faces three times a day. Francisco was the odd one out, working out regularly and actually feeling hungry if he didn't eat. He was also the only Brother who had bothered to learn to cook. In fact, spending time cooking felt great. For him it constituted physical support alchemy which also tasted delicious.

Food. They needed to get food and they needed to get it soon.

All directions looked identical. Dry hills, mountains, more dry hills and more mountains. Francisco leaned against the hood of the truck and closed his eyes. Geography had never been his forte, but from what he remembered of their trip here, Chile was located on the West Coast of South America, and therefore, if they traveled West, they would eventually hit the Pacific Ocean.

The sun was to his right and they had been driving for about 7 daytime hours, so it must be coming up to late afternoon. Although to be fair he didn't know how far from the Equator they were located, therefore there was no way for him to know at what location or angle the sun rose at this time of year here. In his mind Chile had opposite seasons to France as they were now South of the Equator and France was North of the Equator. France had entered Fall already, which meant Chile must be in Spring. His mind struggled to remember at what time the sun rose in Spring back home but came up blank. It was not a detail that had ever been important to him and therefore had never crossed his mind.

They would stay put until he could figure out what direction the sun was traveling, and then they would simply follow the sunset. Francisco put the binoculars back in the truck and climbed onto the roof where six gas tanks, three of them now empty, were tied securely to the roof rack. He untied a full one and jumped down to the ground with it. After emptying the gas into the truck, he climbed back up on the roof and tied it securely again.

Master Lo had given up on the map and now sat silently, probably frustrated and tired, looking out of the passenger window.

"We wait here for the next hour." He told the old man.

It didn't take an hour to figure out what direction the sun was traveling. Once they figured it out, they made note of the mountains ahead of them and started driving. Four hours later they were sitting in a small roadside family rest stop. No more than a small shack with homemade wooden tables and chairs which the owners had arranged in a line under a canvas canopy, but a huge relief for both Francisco and Master Lo. The young couple who ran it didn't speak English, but they were happy and enthusiastic enough to communicate with hand signals and drawings. After a hot soup of potatoes, corn and beans, some fresh made bread and a bottle of soda each, Francisco and Master Lo parted company.

Francisco knew that leaving Master Lo behind, and alive, was a big mistake. Master Lo would not rest until he found the girl, nor would he rest until he found a way to stop Francisco from controlling him. And it was probably only a matter of time before he worked both of these things out. Francisco also knew that Master Lo would not hesitate for a second in killing him the first chance he got. Yet Francisco could not kill him. He just couldn't. A decision, he hoped against hope, he would not live to regret.

For two days he traveled South, North, back South, and often going East for a while, checking out small towns and cities in the mountains, and spending time analyzing the stars looking for that precise mental image he had of the night sky Cecilia had sent him. He wasn't knowledgeable enough to figure out exactly where to go from the stars alone. It was impossible for him to figure out if the image he remembered was from the same country, or even continent. When he first saw the image, he assumed he would be able to study star charts and other relevant material at HQ. But now had nothing to compare the image to except for what he could see above him.

There were hundreds of countries that were at night when he got the first message. She could be in so many different countries. But, against all objective proof, his feelings were that he was relatively close to her now. And he also felt that he was in the right country. The decision to bring him to the Andean facility had been taken very quickly by Master Lo and, in Francisco's opinion, the Andean facility was not the best one to do the observation and investigation which Master Lo said he wanted to do. There were other facilities which were better equipped and situated. Either Cecilia had influenced Master Lo's decision to come here in some way so that Francisco could find her more easily, or Master Lo knew more than he cared to share about Cecilia's location.

If only Master Lo would work with him and not against him, Francisco could ask him the reason behind coming to Chile and use the Brotherhood's resources to find the girl.

Even though Francisco's thoughts that Master Lo had been influenced in his decision to bring him to Chile to find Cecilia was just a theory, it resonated deeply within Francisco's own compass of reality. The whole thing felt as though it was orchestrated by a higher source.

Every now and then Cecilia would communicate with him, ask him things, mostly childish things about fairies and tell him of her different dolls and other toys. Sometimes she would talk about her siblings or her parents. But mostly, she would ask him where he was and how soon before he would find her and take her home.

Francisco had decided that he would concentrate on finding her for now. The taking her home part he would deal with after the girl was under his protection.

The thought that she was a hybrid would often occupy his mind. It didn't make any sense that an alien species, or even a government agency, would create a hybrid like her, then leave her alone and unprotected with a human family.

He also wondered about his own ancestry, his lineage and his future. His entire life up until now had been the Brotherhood. His knowledge of the world strictly limited to the books at HQ, his remote viewing and astral travel. There had not been any real interaction with regular people, or real experience of what life was like outside the Order. Traveling through all these cities and towns, commanding his own days, choosing when to eat, rest, drive, and not having to wear The Hat day in and day out, felt both destabilizing and energizing to him.

At times, he felt elated and free, like he could do and be anything he set his mind to now. At others he felt sad, frightened and depressed. The loss of everyone he had ever known, the stability and continuity he had known all his life. Missing even the familiar smells of the place he had lived and worked in for most of his life.

Maybe now he would meet a woman, start a family, get a job. He wondered what type of job he could get with his skillset. And what if he had to adopt Cecilia as his own daughter? How would he provide for a little child? He would need to find her a mother to take care of her during the day while he worked. But, how could they even have a normal life when the Order were after them and would not stop looking for them? They would not be able to settle anywhere.

These and more thoughts ravished his mind day and night. He felt mentally and emotionally exhausted.

He heard the telltale sign of barking dogs that accompanied his approach to small towns and cities in the area. Sunset had come and gone a few hours earlier and he needed to rest. He drove around the town until he found a bed for the night. He had found that towns and cities of a certain size had many worker's lodges. Private houses that had rooms or a separate building with a communal bedroom where seasonal workers or miners stayed during the week.

By now he had picked up several words in Spanish and managed to rent a bed with dinner that night and breakfast included for the morning without much difficulty. In the morning, he would see about finding a library and perhaps locate one with star charts. He also bought a notebook and some pencils from the lodge owner.

After a dinner of chicken and rice, Francisco sat at the dining room table and started drawing the stars he remembered from Cecilia's mental projection. The little voice chatter in his head started soon after. She liked notebooks and pencils very much. And every now and then she would look out of the window correcting any errors in the placements of the main astral bodies.

He had a photographic memory, so the corrections he felt must be the planetary movements from the time of the first vision to today. At the end of the drawing session, he had two star charts. One with the original vision, and one of the original vision with the corrections Cecilia had sent him. He still didn't know how stars were used to pinpoint locations but felt the two charts would make things much easier once he found a book that taught him how to navigate via the stars.

The owner's wife came over and looked at his drawings. She smiled broadly and started speaking to him fast, pointing at the charts. He communicated that he didn't know what she was saying. She called her husband over, and he looked at the charts and smiled too. The woman pointed to the door and to her chest, talking to him at length. He picked up the words Doctor, and "estrellas", which meant stars in Spanish. Eventually, the wife and husband spoke to one another, came to some sort of agreement, the husband put on his coat and hat and left, waving and communicating that he would be back soon. The wife tapped Francisco's shoulder and smiled.

About an hour later, the husband arrived accompanied by another man.

"My name is Jorge." The new visitor said.

These were the first English words Francisco had heard since leaving Master Lo. "You speak English?"

"A little."

"Parlez-vous français?" Francisco asked.

"No French. Only Spanish, and a little English." He said and pulled Francisco's drawing toward him.

"My sister say you like stars like I do."

"You are familiar with the stars?"

"Yes, I have PhD in Astronomy. I am part of team building La Silla Observatory. It is big telescope we built ten kilometers from here. It is new and best in the world."

Francisco looked at the small, dark Native looking man in front of him. He wore a white shirt, jeans and cowboy boots. He had seen dozens of men dressed like him the past few days. Never in his wildest dreams would he have thought this man was a Doctor in Astronomy, or that there was a modern telescope in the vicinity. They were in a small wooden house with no floors, no bathroom, one faucet, and one light bulb for the entire house and the town was sparsely populated, the other houses being no different to this one.

"This map, is it completed?"

"Finished? Not yet." Francisco pointed to several places in the drawing and told Jorge the brightness of the stars that went on each. "I need to find out where on Earth the stars look like this."

"Well, esto es Southern Hemisphere for sure, see these ones? They are called the Southern Cross. That's good start because the Southern Cross can only be seen Southern Hemisphere. Now, these stars here you can only see in Winter and Spring. This one here is Sirius, and this Jupiter, very close to moon, yes? I need comparison with maps at our Observatory, but I say this is South from where we are."

Francisco felt elated. The thought that all this had been orchestrated from a higher source came back to him.

"Is it Chile? Are these star maps what one can see from Chile?"

"My first opinion is yes. These maps are very familiar to me. But there is much data here, and to be sure of the city we need compare to official maps."

Francisco felt like he would cry. But of course, he did not.

"Can I come with you to the Observatory to check out the star maps?"

Jorge looked at him and smiled.

"It is not open to public. But you foreign, so I say you are visiting scholar. No one will question. We go in the morning." Jorge then started talking to his sister and brother-in-law in Spanish. They were very animated and happy. Every now and then he would hear his own name in the conversation.

After a while, he turned to Francisco and said, "I come tomorrow morning. Be ready I say my sister get breakfast at 4am."

"Thank you so much Jorge! I am so grateful."

The next day, after a hearty breakfast, Jorge arrived to collect Francisco. It was still dark out, and very cold. Jorge offered to drive Francisco in his Volkswagen, but Francisco chose to follow him in the truck instead. He didn't know how close behind Master Lo might be and needed to be prepared to leave at a moment's notice.

The observatory was bigger and more modern than anything Francisco had ever seen. Not that he had seen any other observatory before, still, the technology and buildings took him by surprise. There was no security to speak of, and Jorge and he walked right in without anyone questioning their presence.

Jorge asked him where he, Francisco, had gotten the maps from. Francisco told him he had seen them in his mind's eye, something which Jorge didn't find as interesting as he did about the fact that Francisco had a photographic memory.

Jorge wanted to know all about photographic memory, it wasn't something he had come across in his life before and it filled him with curiosity. At the same time, compared Francisco's drawings to the large and detailed maps stored in specially built drawers inside one of the buildings. Francisco thought they would be using one of the telescopes but was disappointed to find out that it would not help him to do so. Plus, the observatory had not officially opened yet, and the telescopes were already fully booked and scheduled for the next few months.

After making calculations from the dates the maps were seen by Francisco, Jorge concluded the stars had been seen from somewhere in the neighborhood of 500- 600 kilometers South of their present location. And were more likely to be in Chile than Argentina. But most certainly in one of these two countries.

Jorge made him a list of some of the cities and towns he thought were the most probable locations, and then they spent the rest of the day touring the observatory and talking about astral travel and remote viewing. Topics which Jorge had heard about but called by different names in his own culture.

On the way south, Francisco stopped at Jorge's sister's lodgings to pay his bill. They gave him sandwiches and fresh water for his trip, on the house. He searched the truck for something to give back and found an emergency kit with various items he knew he would never need. He handed it to the couple and was met with tears and many "gracias" and "dios te bendiga", which he learned meant thank you and god bless.

The trip south was uneventful. The towns and cities became larger and more populated. Modern houses and suburbs started to line the road. Gas and water were easier to find, as were lodgings and food. The further south he went, the happier he felt.

The little voice in his head told him of a friend travelling to Earth, someone called Anin. And also told of a lady who was apparently very scary, that Anin was afraid of her too and that she looked like a snake.

Francisco didn't know if what he was hearing were flights of childhood fantasy, nighttime dreams or real people. But he listened carefully and analyzed everything that Cecilia said regardless. The image of a snake shaped like a person reminded him of the vision he had had a few days earlier while talking to Master Lo.

The next morning, he woke up to the sound of heavy traffic. He got up, ate breakfast, paid his bill and left. He had arrived in Valparaiso. The main port in Chile and probably of all of South America by what he could see from his location. The city and the port were bigger than anything he had seen in Europe. But there again, he wasn't a widely traveled person so there might very well be bigger ports in Europe. When he arrived the night before, the sky was overcast, so he had not been able to check the night sky against his maps. He would wait in the city until he could see a clear night sky. Cecilia had told him she could see many houses, streets and cars from her living room window. She lived in a city.

"What's a city?"

"It's a place where a lot of people live, it has houses and buildings, and lots of roads."

"Francisco?"

"Yes?"

"I'm frightened."

"What's making you frightened?"

"They took my friend Anin very, very far away. I don't think he can make it in time."

"In time for what?"

"I don't know. Something bad is coming. I think it's the snake lady."

Francisco noticed that her voice sounded clear, almost audible in real life. She must be close. He looked toward the port, then the ocean.

"Cecilia, can you see the sea from where you are? From your house?"

"Only if I stand on the garden wall."

"Can you go out into the garden and stand on the wall please? I need to know what you can see."

There were several minutes of silence.

"I can see two little ships far away."

Francisco saw two large carriers in the horizon. His heart jumped.

"Can you see any other ships?"

"No."

"Can you see the beach, or the port?"

"What's a port?"

"Like a place that has big cranes and lots of buildings, and ships and boats anchored…" he knew she didn't know what anchored meant, "ships and boats standing still in the water near the buildings."

"No. I just see the houses, and then I see the sea far, far away and two little ships."

Francisco looked inland. There were hills after hills covered in houses as far as the eye could see. It would be like looking for a needle in a haystack. But he was close. He was very close. Then he had a thought, a game he played with his Brothers when they were little.

"Cecilia, I need you to do something else for me. We are going to play a game."

"OK."

"Do you know what a mirror is?"

"Yes."

"I need you to find a mirror you can carry, can you do that? And bring it to the wall?"

"Yes. Mommy has a round mirror I like to play with. It's in her bedroom."

"Go fetch it."

The minutes stretched to eternity before he heard the little voice again. He spent the time calculating which way Cecilia would have to point the mirror so as to make it reflect the sun toward him.

"My brother is here. He says he wants to play too. Can he play?"

"Yes, of course he can play too. Listen, I need you to place the mirror so that it points toward the bigger of the two ships, but it has to be turned more to the sun ok?"

"My brother wants to know if we are playing light signals."

"Yes! Tell your brother yes, we are playing light signals."

"He says can you send one first."

Francisco looked around the truck, then saw the side view mirror. He jumped out and kicked the mirror off the truck being careful not to break it. He then started to direct the sunlight toward one hill at a time.

"We can see it! We can see the shiny little light far away. You are real!"

"Yes, I'm real Cecilia, tell your brother to point your mirror toward mine."

A few seconds later, a small bright light appeared near the top one of the hills. Then it started blinking. It was Morse code. "Are you real."

Francisco laughed, and made his own mirror blink, "yes, are you real."

"Yes. We are real. Are you an alien?"

"No, I am human." As he blinked the response, Francisco realized the statement was not actually accurate.

"I am part alien." He added.

"Cool."

"I will be driving over. Be there in half hour."

"Roger that."

"Roberto won't give me my mirror back!" Cecilia's voice shouted in his head.

"It's OK. We don't need it anymore. I'll be there soon."

He would be there soon, but what would he do next? Explaining to the parents that their little girl might be an alien was not going to be easy. Or perhaps they already knew. He realized that if he just took the girl, he would be considered a child kidnapper. The entire country would then be looking for him. If the family already knew of their Anunnaki lineage, he would be able to explain the present situation, and why she had to be protected from the Brotherhood.

Then he wondered why he felt he needed to protect her from the Brotherhood. The reason came to him as clear as day. Master Lo was afraid of her. If Master Lo was afraid of Cecilia, Francisco didn't know how he would react or how the rest of the Brotherhood would react toward her. When people are afraid, they tend to kill and destroy what they don't understand. The way they had treated Francisco was indicative of what they would do to her were they to find her and take her before Francisco did.

He jumped in the truck, threw the mirror on the passenger seat and set off toward the children.

Chapter Seven

The news of the Rumni Anunnaki child occupied the front cover of every news outlet in the known galaxies. Anin scanned the titles and sped read through the main networks and social forums. The great majority believed the situation to be an attempt to manipulate the Nactarel lineage, and in particular Anin, to do something he had refused to do.

A minority thought that Anin had been having an affair with the Rumni for his own political ends, and that the affair had backfired, leaving a poor unwed Rumni to raise his child on her own. The Rumni official stated that no comment would be forthcoming until the situation had been fully investigated. Shylar's family, however, released an official statement disowning their daughter and publicly condemning her to death. If, they stated, she had been the subject of rape or manipulation, they could forgive her, but in her own admission she had entered this relationship willingly and was madly in love with the Anunnaki Diplomat. Madly being a key component to the whole situation. They also stated that Shylar was indeed registered as mentally and emotionally unstable, having had a long and arduous history of unconventional and heretic practices and beliefs.

Anin's personal communication device blinked. It was Shylar again. He had ignored her long enough, it was time to answer her call.

"Anin? My beloved? Is that you?"

"Shylar, enough. I am shocked and surprised at your actions. I know that you are trying to make me your slave. You know very well that if I detect my prodigy inside of you, I will be joined to you in honor and loyalty forever."

"Anin, why are you speaking to me like this? It's your family isn't it? They put you up to this. I have no one Anin. I am alone and desolate without you. They have me imprisoned on a planet I do not recognize. My family has placed a high reward for my execution. They will kill our baby Anin!"

He felt a tinge of protection toward the abomination in Shylar's body.

"Anin, please! I saw our child in my dreams. He looks like you."

Anin knew her last statement meant she had genetically engineered the child to look like him. He sighed heavily. She still thought that meeting him in person would create the Joining. She had no way of knowing that he was now Complete. That all the lesser control programs were now gone from his genes. Although her rhetoric was annoying, he also understood that she had to play the role she had created for herself, or the consequences would be much worse than being imprisoned on an unknown planet. He could not have a real conversation with her unless they met in person, unwatched and unheard by cameras or other people.

The only reason she had become pregnant was to control him. Once she realized she could not control him even though she carried his child, she would very likely abort it and try something else instead. If her Rumni pregnancy hormones, if she had any, had taken over and had indeed driven her completely insane, making her believe the terrible lies she had concocted, things would be somewhat more difficult for him and his lineage. She was officially insane after all, so it was a strong possibility that her madness had overcome her.

"Anin, are you still there?"

"Yes. I am. Listen Shylar. I will not be partaking in this game. Not in any capacity, personal or professional. However, your insanity has created this new being, part of whom belongs to my lineage. My family stands behind me, they know what has happened Shylar. They know. They have promised not to kill you or the child. My family is progressive and wise, they see opportunity where others see damnation. A representative will be sent to discuss your welfare as well as the child's future, and possible gene harvesting for medical research."

"You would cut up our baby?"

"Shylar, he's not our baby, he's a genetic creation you made in a lab. I know you would not think twice of cutting up babies for research. Our representative has been instructed to be open and willing to negotiate a proper course of action. He will wear my seal."

Shylar was silent for a while, "send the representative." She answered and closed the call.

She didn't know he would be representing himself.

His mother, his uncle and the rest of The Protectors were informed of Shylar's reasons for creating and carrying this child. His lineage had never been as geno-phobic as most Anunnaki. They were fully aware that The Return was in a human child's body and it had not affected their loyalty to her in the least. For them, genetic exaltation and supremacy was not linked to the purity of Anunnaki genetic lineages. They also felt, from a spiritual standpoint, that the conception and age of the Rumni Anunnaki child being carried by Shylar was not a coincidence. It was too unusual and too connected to The Return to be a coincidence.

If Shylar decided to abort the child, they would take the fetus and mature it to full term in an artificial womb. That would be the optimum solution going forward, as far as they could see. Alternatively, they would adopt and protect Shylar until the birth of the child, at which point she would become obsolete and could be disposed of quietly and permanently.

Shylar had done this from a place of fear and control, but the result was the creation of the first Spiritual Servant and Protector of Rumni descent in history. When the child was old enough, he would be Completed. The gifts and abilities inherited from his mother would enhance the perfect and pure genetic blueprint passed down to every Nactarel child by design and default.

Anin inwardly smiled. Outwardly he looked distraught and stressed, as a victim of these kind of crimes should be.

He summoned his mother and got up. The time to act had arrived.

Shylar was secretly held on an Anunnaki planet of few inhabitants, Garenidan. The co-joined force of interstellar authority that had taken upon themselves to protect the alleged lovers, had decided that a Rumni planet was out of the question, and a neutral location would be too difficult to guard. Therefore, the obvious choice was a quiet, out of the way, heavily armed Anunnaki planet of alleged insignificant meaning or status.

The cogs of power had been fully activated by the highly respected and influential Nactarel to protect the Rumni woman and the child. Ownership of the genes was of course a big deciding factor, especially as the woman's lineage had decided to disown her, thus disowning the genes she carried.

Officially, Garenidan was one of the Nactarel's many holiday homes. Unofficially, it was one of the main headquarters for The Protectors. Anin arrived a day later accompanied by the man whose features he had recognized during his attempted escape from the Lunar Base in the Solar System, but whom he had never met before this incident, Anteriz Leader Supreme of the Church of Our Lady, Queen Eternal. Or, as he preferred to be called, Uncle Anteriz. He had never had an uncle before, in fact the only male authority figure he had molded himself on had been his father, and his father was not Complete. Which made his uncle the only blood related man he could start emulating from now on.

This fact had not escaped Anteriz, and Anin knew it. Their relationship, although brand new, was deep, trusting and respectful.

Because they owned the planet, and every person there was a secret Protector, his meeting with the Rumni would not be witnessed or recorded. Anteriz and some of the other Protectors wanted to go in the room with him, but Anin dissuaded them. Shylar would respond better if they were alone. Plus, there was no need to put unnecessary pressures on her body, which by now might be struggling with the unnatural pregnancy.

He entered the room after a long and arduous pause. Intellectually he knew that Shylar's condition could not affect him, that he would not be bonded to her, yet an entire life of living according and subject to his genetic programming was hard to overcome.

Shylar sat facing away from the door looking out into one of the property's manicured gardens. Her odor felt amazingly pleasant to him, alluring even. He detected his own child in the scent and felt an overwhelming sense of love wash over him. He stopped, knowing that this would be the moment when the joining occurred, but it did not. He could feel his body's reaction, but the programs that were supposed to activate when those reactions happened, never came.

The Rumni woman turned, her eyes tired and her complexion without luster.

"Anin? Is that you? I can't believe it, you came?"

"Yes. I'm here."

She tried to get up but her left arm was handcuffed to the chair and held her in place. She looked at her arm confused, then sat back down defeated.

"Anin, I'm not doing well. My body and mind are not stable. You are here now, do as I say, tell them to release me, tell them we are bonded now…" she said.

"Shylar, I am sorry to see you in this terrible condition. The bonding will not occur, it is impossible for me to bond. Your plan could have worked with another, but my lineage does not carry the bonding program. You have gone to all this trouble for nothing."

Anin moved forward and sat next to her. Her pupils were dilated, and she looked confused.

"Where am I? Who are you?"

The words arrived from her directly into his mind. They were telepathically connected, Anin was startled as interspecies telepathic communication was not something he had experienced before.

Shylar looked out to the garden again, her eyes becoming absent and distant again. He remembered the sharp minded, crazy reptilian he had met so many times the past few weeks and felt disheartened. He had come here to do battle with the creature who had violated him and instead felt saddened and sorry for the pitiful state Shylar was in. She deserved everything she got, but losing her mind, social status and probably her life, were things no one deserved.

He took her hand in his and held it. He felt the child's energy field become stronger. Of course, he thought, if the mother wasn't doing well, the child would not do well either. Could the child sense him here? Could that be why he was becoming stronger?

"Anin? Is that you?"

Shylar was speaking out loud again, looking at him.

"Yes, it's me."

"I'm so sorry. I did something very stupid, and disgusting, I am disgusted with myself. You won the case and then didn't contact me, I had to see you. I needed to do something, but I can't remember what it was."

"It's going to be fine."

Anin got up and strode out of the room, slamming the door behind him. He put out a call to his mother and the doctor in charge of Shylar, they were in one of the many garden rooms waiting for him.

"Yes, her condition worries me greatly." The Servants and Protectors' head doctor started saying, "she seems to have lost all lucidity. Not only that, but it appears her body is breaking down. I am not an expert in Rumni biology and bringing in an expert might compromise our position. It is almost like whatever she did to herself to carry this baby is altering her in ways we cannot understand."

"Is there any way to at least stabilize her mind?" Anin asked.

"You were able to hear her telepathically even though you don't carry the ability for interspecies telepathic communication?"

"Yes."

"This might be a way we can stabilize her. Her own species does have extraordinary telepathic abilities. We might be able to create a stable frequency pattern and overlay it over her own mind. We do have her memories and personal frequency stored from the case investigation. We could use those to create a stable frequency field for her."

"Won't all this go away if we simply take the child and place him in an artificial womb?" His mother interjected.

"That is a possibility, but we have to understand that this is not an Anunnaki baby. Our technology would not take into consideration Rumni biology, and less so a mix of the two, plus we have to take into consideration that the mother's own biology is changing, terminating the pregnancy at this point will probably kill them both." The doctor responded.

Anin struggled with the information. Ending the pregnancy would probably kill both mother and child. In a way, this was the most logical and best result for him. However, although he was not bonded and didn't much care for Shylar, he cared for the baby. Like the order believed, he also believed it was no coincidence that the child had come at this time, and in the manner in which he had come. Shylar's motives were self serving and manipulative, but the result was a child who was linked to The Queen Returned. They would have to find a way to stabilize Shylar and keep the child alive.

One of the guards in charge of Shylar entered the room and approached the group. Anin's mother nodded, giving the guard permission to speak.

"It's the Rumni, she appears to be lucid and wants to talk." He was addressing Anin.

The lack of protocol and ritual exhibited by the guard took Anin by surprise. It was as though he was speaking to a group of common folks. It seemed the guard picked up on Anin's surprise, "Sir, I apologize for the lack of courtesy in your presence. I am, as you are,

Complete and here of my own volition to do the greater work for Her Return." He explained.

Anin expressed his understanding and followed the guard back to Shylar's room.

Shylar was still restricted to her chair, but this time her eyes were alive, present and alert.

"Anin!"

Anin also felt the energy field from his son, it was strong and powerful. Healthy.

"Anin, please help me. I'm so sorry, this whole thing was insane. I'm officially insane as you know, but this was too much even for me. I don't know what took over me. It felt like I was under some crazy mental influence. I would never do that to you on purpose Anin, we had a deal and I know you would honor it."

Anin had wondered why Shylar had gone to such an extreme action when they were already in speaking terms and under contract to collaborate. Yes, he was doing everything possible to undermine their agreement, and had ignored her calls, but had every intention of contacting her once he had succeeded in securing the human child Cecilia.

"Yes, I would honor our deal Shylar. But now things have changed. You have violated me, and my people. You have done something so despicable that I cannot ignore it."

"I know. It wasn't me doing this, I don't do these things."

"Did someone else create that child and place it in your body?"

"No, I did that. I researched how it was done in the past and perfected the procedure. And yes, my intent was for you to bond with me and for me to have full control of our agreement. But that's it you see, I don't do political or personal manipulation that well, I would never have thought of doing this. I was compelled, obsessed to do it. It was all I could think of. But this goes against everything I hold true and holy. For a while I even convinced myself that I was in love with you. With you! An Anunnaki... no offence."

"As you are registered as insane, doing something this insane is not that out of character."

"I am not insane Anin. OK, yes, my species considers me unruly and unpredictable, having my own mind, which is our definition of insane, but I am in full control of my faculties. I mean I was in control before I did this."

Anin raised his eyebrows.

"Alright, I am not in control of my temper and I am impulsive, yes, but I have never lost control of my mind. And Anin, my mind was out of control."

Anin thought about The Return, could she have done this?

"Think back, when was it that you lost control of your mind and actions?" He asked.

"I know the exact moment. It was when we said goodbye in your chambers at the Luna satellite. I was about to complete our Promise ritual, but instead of doing so, saying the formal words and carrying out the ritual, I just took your blood and felt compelled to leave immediately."

Anin remembered the incident clearly. At the time, he had dismissed it as the Promise ritual, and the fact that the words had not been said, and the blood sharing had happened without warning, he had misinterpreted as being due to Shylar's unpredictable behavior. He had never gotten around to analyzing the blood sample, he suspected there were no Rumni genes in it after all.

Shylar stopped speaking and looked directly at him.

"You are different. There stands a depth and stability that I have not seen in you before today." She said.

"You are much different than how you were earlier too Shylar. Do you have any insight as to why that is?"

Shylar went quiet. She was in deep thought, thoughts he could almost hear.

"It's the child. He seems to be... complete somehow. Now that you are here. And seems to know how to stabilize my body as well as his own."

The word "complete" gave Anin a moment of uncertainty and alarm. The Servants and Protectors would call themselves Complete when their social and controlling programs were removed, and their ancestral knowing and information was restored.

He looked up at the woman carrying his child and wondered if his own bonding genetic programming was indeed removed. He felt deep compassion for Shylar as well as a desire to protect her and make sure she was healthy. As for his son, although if he understood things correctly the child was a kind of semi clone of both parents rather than their son, he felt overwhelming love and affection.

Taking Shylar's hands in his, Anin leaned toward the Rumni and kissed her on the cheek. He expected the Rumni to be repulsed, but instead he saw her smile and relax.

He wanted to believe her story very much. He really wanted to think she was truthful and that she had been compelled to do this by an external influence. He wanted it all to be true because then they could be friends and they could take care of the child together.

Then he remembered Cecilia and the true reason why Shylar had carried out this crazy action. She had done all this to get her hands on the human child.

He let go of her hands and moved away from her.

"Tell me everything you know of the human child Shylar. Tell me what happened to you when you saw her. You were affected too, were you not?"

Shylar's eyes narrowed and her tongue flicked in and out. Something about that behavior brought him back to his senses. Here was the deadly, ruthless creature which he would normally find to be foul and repulsive. Yet he didn't dislike her. In fact, he never felt very strongly about her one way or the other. He had disliked her tremendously when they first met and for good reason, she had tried to manipulate him and even threatened his life. And yes, her odor at the time was very strong and offensive. But his work meant he had to be temperate in his emotions, feelings and even senses when dealing with other species. He was an ambassador after all, meeting repulsive, vile creatures was part of his daily routine.

She had never been vile or repulsive to him. And he knew that she found him as unpleasant to be around as he found her to be. Her mind and her unpredictability however, these he found to be very interesting.

"The human child is still my priority, Anin." Her words brought him back to the question at hand. "I am still holding you to your Promise. Even though the ritual was not completed the words were spoken and the Promise stands. We will both have access to the human child and will collaborate on studying her."

Anin was a good diplomat, and he knew that there were moments in a discourse that could make or break the possibility of a good resolution. This was one of those moments. If he broke his semi-official Promise, and he morally could break it due to the fact that the blood ritual had never been carried out, it would create a timeline of conflict and competition between them. Looking at her now, in her condition and her disempowered state, anyone else would not think twice to disregard what she wanted and continue on to do what best served them personally. Acting in the best interests of his own people and completely disregarding the Rumni's part in the whole situation was the logical course of action. Yet, he could sense a different timeline where The Return was not only important to the Anunnaki, but to the Rumni too.

"Tell me about your beliefs Shylar. Is there a religion you belong to, and Order or Church that is guiding your research on the human child? How did you know to look on Earth for her in the first place?"

Shylar's body language changed, becoming guarded and tense.

"I do not belong to any religion. The information about the child came to me in my studies. It is pure genetics. I am the only Ultra-Dimensional Biologist in my species. Other species, in fact most other species, have huge data on the ultra-dimensionality of biology. But both our species are in denial about the multi-dimensionality of our genes. To most of our scientists I am nothing but a pseudo-scientist. A joke. Some respect my work but admitting it publicly would mean scientific and political suicide to them."

She looked at him, directly into his eyes. He could sense she was gauging how much to tell him. He made himself look open and receptive to what she was saying.

"I researched other species' knowledge and data. Over and over, they pointed at beings who are born to an apparently ordinary species, but that also exist in other dimensions. Some of these beings can exist in very high frequency dimensions. Often, they become leaders to their people."

Anin felt that although Shylar was being truthful, she was skirting his question. How had she known to look for the child on Earth? As though sensing his thoughts, she continued speaking and explaining things in a way he could understand.

"These beings, they leave a historical trace. A future history become alive that tells of their return. Search long enough and those stories can be traced back to the planets where the being will be born or appear on. Also, the time when this will happen can be accurately calculated. Not only that, but these beings leave an energetic map to their location. It is almost as though the closer to the planet and time is to their return, the more prophets and religious extremists start announcing their birth. Earth was not the only planet I was investigating, I had already studied and scanned every other inhabited planet in that star system, as well as half the quadrant of that particular galaxy. I didn't just come upon her, it took me hundreds of years of hard investigative work."

Anin remembered his own history and how seemingly unrelated situations had pulled him to Earth and to the moment when Cecilia had looked into his eyes. It felt almost choreographed to the last detail.

"Tell me how the child affected you, Shylar."

Shylar looked out toward the garden again. No words came out of her mouth, but Anin heard her clearly in his mind.

"She touched me. She accepted me as I am, without judgment. She loved me like no one ever has. She values me... and she's afraid of me for what I would do to her. Afraid of me because I was created to pursue science and for that I would do anything, including killing her."

Shylar held her belly with her free hand.

"They made me infertile. According to them I was too crazy to continue the lineage for my family, so they made me infertile. They sentenced me to a childless and loveless life without my consent or permission. That human child's love for me was so pure, so unconditional. I don't know what happened to me, and I know I have placed both of us in great danger, but I had to have a baby of my own. You just happened to be there when I decided it. And it made sense at the time. Having your child meant you would bond to me and would have to carry out my orders. Which meant I would have full access and control of the human child. Find her Anin. Find the child and bring her to me."

She looked back at him, "I need to rest. Please ask the guards to take me to my bed."

Anin sighed deeply. At some insane level, it all made sense. And maybe after the child's birth, Shylar would make sense too. Maybe she would regain her lucidity and her marginal sanity. Or maybe she wasn't crazy at all, maybe she had never been crazy. Maybe their cultures and belief systems were insane, and she was the only sane person alive.

He walked to the door, told the guard to take Shylar to her bed and left the room. Shylar's words were echoing in his mind. He had to find the child and keep her safe.

The guard went inside and unlocked the tie on Shylar's arm, then helped her up and into the bedroom, another guard followed their every move. She wasn't going to escape any time soon. Anin watched them until they were out of sight. He felt that if she really wanted to, she could leave this place at any time. Outside the window the sun turned a deeper pink, the light washing over the garden. He used to love this place as a child.

The time had arrived for him to go back to Earth and retrieve Cecilia. The Servants and Protectors had already sent an extraction team to Earth but had failed to find the child even though the observation bay recordings had pinpointed her exact location. She would not be found through maps or readings. He would find her through her first awakened human Guard. The Guards were programmed to protect their Queen. The Guard would find The Queen, and Anin would find the Guard.

CHAPTER EIGHT

The house was in the middle of a suburban street. All around him were pastel colored houses, their gardens new and trees young, which indicated the suburb had been built recently.

Francisco still did not have a plan on how to proceed. He hadn't planned past finding Cecilia, and here he sat, in the truck in front of her house. He did not know what to do next, and now had to face the fact that this was a real person, that she had parents and siblings that lived a regular, normal life in a house, in a neighborhood like millions of other people did. Explaining to them that Cecilia was an alien Goddess or hybrid was definitely out of the question. But maybe they knew already.

He sat in the truck outside the house, wondering what to do. The sun still lay quite low in the sky as the city accelerated its morning pace.

As he reached for the truck door he saw something moving on the edge of his field of vision. He turned quickly but not quickly enough to avoid something large and hard hitting him on the head.

Something in him took over and before he knew it, he found himself outside the truck pinning a large, humanoid creature against the ground. He became highly aware that the creature was not human and lost control for a millisecond. That millisecond was long enough for the creature to take the advantage and throw him against a wall. He heard a child screaming before he passed out.

He woke up with a high-pitched ringing in his head and his eyes out of focus. There was someone standing over him, "Francisco? Wake up." Small hands were shaking him.

"Wake up!"

He blinked and rubbed his eyes, something wet covered his face, it was blood.

"He's alive. Here, take that arm, and I'll take this one. We have to get him into the house."

"What if that thing comes back? What do we do?"

"Just scream at it like you did before, it worked. It ran away."

"OK. What if it comes for Maria?"

"It won't. It totally ignored her when it ran away."

Francisco allowed himself to be helped up and led into the house. The blood started dribbling into his eyes and mouth.

"He's making a right mess. Here, let's take him to the bathroom, we have a first aid kit there."

"Oh, we can be doctors. I want to be a doctor!"

"I don't think we are going to be doctors. I think we are going to help him. We need to stop his bleeding, I read that heads bleed a lot when they get cut."

"What about Maria, should we go fetch her?"

"She's fine. She'll wake up and come in the house on her own."

"Why did she fall over like that?"

"She doesn't like the sight of blood. Plus, I think that the creature scared her too. She fainted."

The children helped Francisco sit on a stool in the bathroom and proceeded to use the first aid kit to clean him up and bandage him. He could hear them talk, but their lips were not moving.

"He looks like a mummy now."

"Yeah, I think we may have overdone it with the bandages. But at least it stopped the bleeding, which is good." The boy said. "How do you feel?" He then shouted at Francisco.

"I can hear just fine. My head is very sore. Do you have any painkillers in that first aid kit?"

"I don't know what those are."

Francisco motioned for the boy to hand him the kit. He tried to look through the different jars and content, but he still couldn't see very well.

"Here, come with me," the boy said and took Francisco's hand. Francisco got up, and let the boy lead him to a small bedroom. The walls were covered in bookshelves. In the middle of the room, away from all walls there was a small tent, and to the far side of the room was a small bed.

"This is my room, you can stay here until you feel better." The boy helped Francisco onto the bed, and Cecilia jumped beside him and hugged him.

"Please don't die." She said.

"I won't." Francisco said and fell asleep.

"Wake up!" It a woman's voice shouted. "Wake up, you must not sleep right now, you took a hit on the head and might be concussed. I know it's hard, but wake up now… what's his name?"

He looked up and saw a tall woman with long blond hair wearing a bright yellow dress and had the biggest blue eyes he had ever seen. She smelled of perfume and peaches.

"Francisco." Cecilia answered.

"Mister, keep your eyes open. My name is Allison. My children found you outside, you fell and hurt your head on the edge of the sidewalk. We called the doctor, but you have to stay awake, understood?"

"Yes ma'am. I'm awake and I understand."

The boy stood behind his mother. When Francisco looked at him, the boy put one finger to his lips, in the international sign of silence.

The next few hours were a blur of adults coming and going. The doctor came and went, then several more people who appeared to be relatives, neighbors, coworkers, and friends came to look at the foreigner who had fallen on the street in front of the house.

"Your parents sure have a lot of friends," Francisco said to Roberto, Cecilia's older brother, after the adults finally left the room.

"Yeah, they do. People are always coming in and out of the house or staying over for days or weeks sometimes. There's always parties too, there's one tonight so there'll be plenty to eat. Never a quiet moment. So, what was that thing that attacked you?"

"I didn't get to see it clearly. It looked... Well... Did you see it? What did it look like to you?"

"Well, it looked like a giant humanoid looking lizard."

"Then I saw it right. It wasn't human."

The boy nodded in agreement.

"Are you really an extraterrestrial?" Roberto then asked Francisco.

"Kind of. I recently found out that I am part extraterrestrial. But that a lot of other people are too. You might be."

The boy thought about this quite seriously.

"My sisters and I are definitely different. Did you know that we are not using words right now? I'm talking to you directly into your mind. Other people can't do that."

Francisco gasped. It was true, and he hadn't noticed it. Their entire conversation had been without verbal speech.

"My brother and sister are the only other people who can do it. Talk without words. Everyone else is deaf and blind. They can't hear or see anything. But they talk real loud in their heads." Cecilia said.

Francisco was again amazed at her vocabulary, considering she was only three years old.

"The vocabulary you hear is constructed in your head by yourself. It's like a translation of what we say and think. So, my little sister might be thinking in teddy bears and dollies as she conceives ideas and answers in her head, but you hear it as complete sentences and sophisticated words. Words you are familiar with and that have the meaning of what she is feeling, experiencing or thinking."

Francisco looked at the boy with admiration at his knowledge and capacity to explain their telepathic communication.

"I've been figuring it out for the past three years."

"How old are you Roberto?"

"I'm twelve. My sister Cecilia is three, and my sister Maria is fifteen. Maria is still in shock and they gave her a sedative. She's not as tough as Cecilia and I are. So, what can you tell us about the lizard like humanoid?"

Francisco did not know anything about the humanoid. He assumed it to be extraterrestrial but could not be sure. He hadn't had a chance to read the material on extraterrestrials at HQ, but he knew that apart from the Anunnaki, there were other species out there. That they looked like lizards he had not known before now.

"Francisco?"

"Yes Cecilia?"

"I am so super happy you are here. You are my guard, you know."

"I don't know about that. I haven't had any military training, but I will certainly protect you as well as I am able to."

"For someone without military training you sure kicked that alien's butt real good." Roberto interjected, jumping around the room kicking and punching in midair making sound effects to match.

Everything had happened too quickly for Francisco to figure out what had really happened, but he did remember being able to handle himself quite well during the fight, until he saw what type of creature he was fighting. Then he lost control and the thing shook him off like a leaf. Somewhere in the house a guitar started playing, a man's voice sang. The sounds of conversation turned to whispers and then disappeared. The children quieted and he himself felt drawn into the voice and guitar, lamenting, quieting his mind. The man sang in Spanish, so he didn't understand the words, but that seemed to be irrelevant. It was alchemic music, he'd heard of it before. He pulled himself up and sat on the edge of the bed. The children, as if on cue, came over to him and helped him up, then led him to the living room where the music was coming from.

The room was full of smoke, not all tobacco. People sat around the musician on chairs, pillows and the floor. Glasses of wine shared, food on every visible flat surface in the room spoke of plentitude. The children's mother looked at them as if suddenly out of a trance, she shouted, "our honored guest arrives! Everyone, this is our mysterious foreigner. He fell in front of our house and hurt his head…yet he lives and is with us now. Welcome!" She said, lifted her glass, waited until the other people around her did the same, and drank up.

A young man near him got up and helped Francisco to a chair which another man vacated as they approached. A young woman handed him a plate of food and a glass of wine, the glass in turn was taken quickly away by a man he recognized as the doctor, "water for you I'm afraid, until we are sure you are not concussed." The older man said and nodded for the young woman to replace the glass of wine with one of water.

The singer had stopped singing and watched Francisco intently. When everyone had settled down, he reached over and offered a hand in greeting, "welcome to my home… sorry I don't know your name."

"Francisco."

"Francisco! Like my great uncle, good solid name. I'm Eduardo, and I see you have made friends with my children Roberto, Cecilia and," he looked around for his oldest daughter.

"She's asleep sweetheart, she fainted when she saw the blood and had one of her panic attacks. The doctor gave her a sedative." The children's mother said.

Eduardo looked at the doctor.

"She will be just fine in the morning, take my word. Your oldest is having a case of female hysterics, a very common condition among young women of her age."

Eduardo frowned and looked over at his wife, who almost palatably told him to drop it and that she was taking the doctor's advice on this one. Eduardo then looked back at Francisco and said, "eat, relax. You are welcome to stay as long as you need to. We live as we believe, embodying the kindness and generosity of the true human heart."

As if on cue, the room exploded in conversation, which quickly turned into song requests for Eduardo. The next song was animated, and people joined in on the chorus, laughing and adding sentences here and there. Francisco wished he could understand the words.

"You are not missing anything," Roberto said.

Francisco could now see the resemblance both children had to their father. Both had straight hair and eyes, yet their skin and height seemed to have been inherited from their mother, who was very pale in comparison.

"My dad is Indian. Not Indian from India, but Indian as in native from Chile. My mom is basically all Chilean. That means all her grandparents came from Europe, mostly England which is why we speak English and go to an English speaking school. Indians here don't consider themselves Chilean. At least my dad doesn't."

"Your dad is a lot taller than the other native people I've met in my travels here."

"Well, he's not all Indian, but don't tell him I told you that. My grandad is Italian, that's his mom's father. He arrived here as a merchant sailor, met my grandma and stayed. But dad doesn't tell anyone about that."

As if Eduardo had heard his boy's words, he stopped singing and looked straight at him. "This song is for my son. Come here boy."

Roberto stood up and walked to his father, leaning against him as he sang the next song. Then he turned to Francisco and said, "my dad thinks I'm retarded because I refused to speak. In fact, all these people think my sister and I are retarded. It suits us fine."

Francisco again became aware that Roberto was not moving his lips as he spoke.

Cecilia climbed onto Francisco's lap and snuggled against him. He lifted his plate to make room, and once she settled down, he started eating a delicious meal of barbeque chicken, potato salad and greens. Every now and then, Cecilia would reach into his plate and take some food. The songs, food, wine and conversation continued for several hours. The child fell asleep on his lap, and from what he could see, her parents thought it the most normal thing in the world. Eventually the mother picked her up and took her away, presumably to her room.

As the evening wore on, Francisco became acutely aware of his surroundings. He could feel and sense everyone in the room, and every movement outside in the garden where the party had spilled into. He was listening and sensing for the creature that had attacked him earlier. Every now and then he would scan for Cecilia's energy signature, and sense that she was happy and asleep somewhere in the house.

The next day he felt much better. Rested, well fed and his head less painful, his mind clear and able, and needing, to start making some plans about Cecilia's safety. Yet his sense of urgency had disappeared. He felt satisfied, and although intellectually he knew that he had to think of something, or somewhere safe to take the child, his senses told him all was well and that he didn't have to do anything but stay here and make sure no one harmed her.

The house was quiet that morning. Everyone still asleep, including several of the guests who were sleeping on makeshift beds in the corridor and living room. He made his way carefully over the sleeping bodies, so as not to wake anyone up, and found the kitchen. Maria, Roberto and Cecilia were already there, having breakfast. Maria, who stood by the stove cooking some eggs, looked at him suspiciously.

"OK guys, so I didn't imagine it all, look at the state of his head." She said out loud. The two children next to her giggled and told her it was true, all true. She had seen an alien and it had attacked the foreigner outside their house.

Maria went pale and sat down next to her siblings.

"Please don't fall down again Maria," Cecilia thought very loudly.

"I won't. Why did you guys lie to me? You said I imagined it all."

"No, that's what you said. We just didn't deny it." Roberto answered.

Francisco introduced himself.

"Oh, not another one," was her response. "You can't talk either? It hurts my head to have to communicate with my mind with these two already, now we have another one?"

Francisco spoke with words this time, "I'm sorry, I can speak normally. I assumed you preferred not to, like your brother and sister."

"Thank goodness." She said, and seemed to drop the conversation, standing up and going back to cooking eggs on the stove, asking him how many he wanted.

Francisco learned the children's parents were both talented musicians, highly regarded and well known for their exceptional gifts, but not very present when it came to parenting their children.

"I'm never having children," Maria said as she finished telling him how difficult it was to make food when no one shopped for ingredients. That's why they loved parties, everyone brought food that would sometimes last them for days. "Kids are too much hard work. Plus, what if they come out like these two misfits? Everyone thinks they are retarded and no matter how much I tell them they speak telepathically, they just don't listen to me." She was referring to telling their parents. "The fact that my brother learned to read when he was three years old seems irrelevant. Instead, they sent me to therapy. They sent ME to therapy. The doctors were nearly convinced I was crazy."

"Come, sit yourself down Maria," Francisco said, "How about some pancakes?"

"Yes!" All three children shouted in excitement.

Some years later, Francisco would remember that question as the one that turned him into the unofficial family nanny, cook, driver and bodyguard overnight. But to him that morning was simply fitting into a situation that needed to be fixed. Cecilia reached over and hugged him. "I'm so happy you are here."

"Please stop cooking eggs darling... I can't stand the smell." A sleepy female voice said behind him. He turned to see Allison, the children's mother, in a bright pink housecoat with her hair tied up and her eyes covered with large, dark sunglasses. He could see she was dehydrated and vitamin depleted from all the alcohol the night before. Unaware that this was not something he should be perceiving, he guided her to the table and told her he would fix her something that would make her feel much better. Then opened the fridge to take out several items from the previous night's leftover dishes, put them into the blender, added spices, ice, a stick of celery and handed her with instructions to drink it all up. He then searched for ingredients to make pancakes.

He could not remember ever being so happy in his life before. There was no way for him to know what was coming their way, what manner of creature had attacked him the previous day, when the Brothers would find them, or what he would have to do to keep Cecilia safe. But for now, in this moment, he was happy. For the first time in his life he felt free. As the realization hit him that he would never return to the Order, the whole world opened up before him. He could do anything he wanted with his life. Anything. Suddenly everything had fallen into place, and now the world made sense to him. Cecilia and Roberto looked up at him and smiled.

Chapter Nine

Anin saw his reflection on the shuttle window and took a mental picture of his first landing on planet Earth. He had studied this planet for most of his life. It fascinated him. Now, in retrospect, he could tell that his seemingly natural interest had been in fact seeded and guided by members of The Protectors organization at key points in his life. He remembered how his own mother had given him a tour of the family library, stopping and casually handing him a historical rendering of Earth. At the time, he read it with an attitude of superiority and disdain for the genetically altered humans on the planet. Now, he recalled the information in that book with a totally different viewpoint.

He thought of his unborn child back on Garenidan and how, to most Anunnaki, the unborn child was an abomination. His existence an insult to the purity of their race. Life among his people was not going to be easy for his son. He wondered if there was a place in the universe where his son belonged. He wondered if his son would ever find love, start his own lineage, be respected and admired.

As they crossed into the planet's atmosphere, the ship's cloak was activated. No one would see their descent into the old and long forgotten Anunnaki base. Soon, he would find Cecilia and take her back to Garenidan where she could be protected and brought up in the culture she belonged to.

It wasn't unheard of for Anunnaki families to have humans among their staff, often humans had manual skills and capacities that surpassed their own. The gardens at Garenidan, for example, were cared for by various human men and women who were regularly brought in from nearby planets. No Anunnaki family thought the art of growing plants or looking after animals was worth using precious genetic blueprint for. At a social level, these humans would be considered below the lowest ranking Anunnaki, but that never bothered any of them. For these particular humans, social hierarchy never entered their awareness. For the humans, the plants and animals were their priority and whatever happened among people, especially the Anunnaki, was irrelevant.

He had taken several days to inform himself about humans as much as possible, downloading thousands of data bundles into his personal collection. He also visited with some of the human workers at Garenidan and interviewed them at length.

One of the strangest aspects of humans was that they were genetically inferior to every other humanoid species in the universe. Their genetic material very narrow, and their lineages so diluted it was impossible to trace any of them to a particular planet. Physically speaking, these beings should not have the capacity for sentient conversation, let alone be able to walk upright or travel the universe. Yet, they did. Humans ruled entire sectors of the universe. To Anin it seemed as though their sentient mind had developed separately from their bodies.

The humans at Garenidan were similar to Earth humans in every way except that Earth humans were littered with other species' genes and programs. Hundreds of thousand years ago, the Anunnaki and other advanced species had discovered that wherever they placed humans, that location would slowly transform into a habitable place. Within certain parameters of course. The basic environmental needs for a human body had to be met, but with very little altering, humans could survive in some otherwise inhospitable planets.

Earth had been seeded with humans from multiple planets, and many lineages had been seeded with actual Anunnaki genes and programs. The result of a crazy scientific experiment which had happened thousands of years earlier and had caused the fall of the previous Anunnaki ruling family.

Of course, humans were not the only inferior race that Anunnaki had in their employment. There were many more. One of his favorites being a humanoid aquatic race his family had acquired to farm and look after the oceans they owned across the galaxies. These humanoids had been seeded on Earth too, but they had gone feral. Somehow, they had managed to disassociate the added

Anunnaki genetic programs used to control them, and now lived on Earth independently of Anunnaki or human influence.

That could sometimes happen. Not every race was a good host for Anunnaki genes or artificially created genetic control programs.

He noticed his mind racing through thought after thought and the closer they got to the surface of the planet, the stronger he felt Cecilia's energy signature. It seemed almost like she had already claimed the entire planet, and all its species. Ecstatic waves rushed through his body, mind and spirit. He took a deep breath and looked around him, the other men and women aboard seemed to be oblivious to the waves, busy instead with reactivating the base below them and maneuvering the shuttle to land.

They had purposely chosen an abandoned base as opposed to an active one due to the secrecy and sensitivity of their mission here. That is, the unofficial mission of search and rescue of the Queen Returned. The official "reason" to visit and activate the abandoned base was the salvage of lost resources, a departmental priority that had been quite neglected until now.

Earth was quite unique in that the Anunnaki had never managed to claim it for the Empire. There were fourteen races claiming ownership, and thousands of years of diplomatic agreements, litigation and alliances had not resolved it. The Empire was in a unique position in that due to their technological superiority in the sector, and broad interests in this galaxy, they had won the right to supervise the planet in both a security, and a cultural capacity.

The Earth humans had managed, in just a few thousand years, to mix and cross breed across the planet. Which meant one human could be claimed by several species at the same time. This complicated things tremendously, especially when it came to the harvesting of genetic mutations so prevalent on the planet.

When he asked humans how they explained their sentiency even though they had inferior and primitive bodies, they spoke of something they called a soul. They claimed that souls were independent lifeforms from their physical bodies. To Anin this claim fell in the realms of mythical dragons and winged angels. But, his job demanded those beliefs to be respected.

Humans were not the only species that claimed the existence of souls, but they were the most numerous.

There were more humans in the universe than could be catalogued, most were completely ignored by other species. Not so with Earth humans though. Just about every single one of them on Earth had multiple species genetically claiming them.

Some human genetic lineages on Earth were not contested, if one species successfully claimed a human, the other species pretty much stayed away from that human. This was true in most cases, but when a human was born with extraordinary markers or capacities, the species that claimed their genes would take second place to the species that detected their capacity or skill. This had been what happened with Cecilia. Shylar had claimed ownership due to the fact that she believed she had been the first to see the child displaying capacities of existing in high frequency dimensions which had never been witnessed before.

But, as it had been Anin who actually saw her first, and the technology used to detect her capacity to exist in other dimensions was Anunnaki, he had won ownership of the child and her lineage.

Anin now wondered about humans. Since he had become complete, he now had the capacity to see past the fact that humans were an inferior species in every way, which had in turn caused him to start opening up new avenues of curiosity about them. In other words, his mind had been opened to the possibility that he didn't know anything about them at all.

While interviewing the human staff at Garenidan, Anin got the distinct feeling that they were talking to him as though talking to a young child, or someone who cannot quite grasp the larger picture. This disturbed him somewhat. He had never noticed that attitude from them before but now looking back, he realized it had been there always. And not just toward him, but all Anunnaki they had contact with. Humans were all over the universe. A species that had a history billions of years old. Yet, no one quite knew where or how they had evolved, been created or had come about. At the same time, every single advanced species actively harvested, cloned, altered humans, seeding new planets with them in order to make the planet habitable or profitable. Something about this fact didn't add up. He made a mental note to investigate it further and then changed his mental focus to the base, which had now opened its doors to them.

"Welcome Ambassador," said a female voice in his official channel. "This is Earth Base 223, permission to download your ship's and official databases into my memory bank."

"Permission granted Earth Base 223."

As the channel opened up for his own official database to download into the planetary base, he uploaded the logged information the base had gathered on the planetary species for the past twenty thousand years... He would start filtering and reviewing the data later that day.

"I have requested for your captain to give me details on your crew and he refused to comply. He has stated this is a secret mission and that you are the only person who can divulge this information. I will need this information in order to allow you entry into the base."

"What are your requirements 223?"

"The size of your crew and specialties. I am particularly interested in technicians, doctors and engineers."

"Are you in need of any repairs Earth Base 223?"

"Please call me 223. Yes, there was a breach in my security parameters thirty six years ago. I sealed the area, but I have not been able to gain access to it due to possible danger of viral contamination."

Contact with abandoned bases had to be done at a local level after blocking all communication channels with the Empire in case the base had been compromised. If a breach had been reported or found in the abandoned base after first contact, the arriving ship and all crew would be completely disconnected from the galactic and universal empire network until the problem was resolved. Connection would resume once the base was cleared as declared safe from contaminants.

That there had been a breach in this base would give him more time away from the Empire's systems, giving them extra days to establish themselves here. But it did add certain complications which he hadn't planned for. The breach also meant no one would be allowed to leave the base until it was given the all clear.

"Which area was breached?"

"I am not at liberty to disclose that information to you Ambassador as it is above your security grade. However, I do need the necessary technicians to repair the breach. I have sent your shuttle the full list of technicians and materials needed to make the necessary repairs."

Anin detected a strange frequency in the last sentence. He would often be told by AI systems that his grade wasn't high enough for access to certain information or areas, and it had never bothered him in the past. Yet something about the frequencies in the communication from this station bothered him. This station had been left unused for thousands of years, and he himself was the ultimate Anunnaki authority in this particular solar system. There was no one of a higher security grade than him. There was also no record of high security technology or data having been left here. The station would never have been abandoned had that been the case. No, this station was purely for observation and data gathering.

He wondered if the station had in fact contained the breach at all. He hoped they were not walking into a fully breached system. Those could take months to clean up. And although a few days for a small breached area was not too much of a problem, months to clean the system would be a major delay he did not need.

He scanned the repair list 223 had sent and compared it with the people and materials they had brought with them.

"My crew is 46 members strong. We have brought a full team with the latest hardware and software developments to upgrade you into this time period 223. The materials and team include what you need for your repairs."

They had also brought the necessary programs and firewalls to make a major section of the base completely secure and invisible to the Empire.

The vibration behind the AI's words kept bothering him. He reviewed the messages from the station several times while the crew proceeded with docking and securing the shuttle into the landing pad.

"223."

"Yes?"

"Who is above my security grade in this system?"

"I am not at liberty to disclose that information Ambassador."

"How many individuals are above my security grade in this system?"

Silence.

"223, answer the question."

Silence.

"223, according to protocol, you are required to answer my questions even if it is to say you cannot answer my question. Why are you not answering me right now?"

"Ambassador, I cannot answer your question."

There it was again, a very distinct vibration, Anin's body interpreted it as a feeling. It was almost like a feeling coming from the base itself. Like he was receiving experiential data within the words. This was normal with sentient beings, but not computer systems. Except in the case of an AI's spontaneous jump to sentience awareness which very rarely happened. He knew of only a handful existing sentient AI systems in the entire universe.

He had studied the topic of AI systems going sentient as part of his Ambassador training, but never expected to encounter one himself. Could this be one? Or was it a simple breach that had infected the system and now it was simply misfiring? Could it be that the vibration was in fact a hidden coded message which had embedded itself in his own database and could infect their shuttle and everything it was connected to? This resonated but not entirely. Then he got it. His thoughts were alarmist and frightening. The energy, the frequency he detected, the vibration that underlined the base's communication was fear. He tested the frequency with his own body. Yes, it was fear.

He reviewed the communications where he had detected the dissonant frequency once more and confirmed an energy of fear in all them.

"Tell me 223, to the best of your ability, why can't you answer my question?"

"I cannot tell you who is above your security grade in this system because I do not have any data identifying this authority as an individual."

The dissonant frequency became stronger.

"Is there a collective group which is above my security grade in this system, 223?"

"The word collective group may be used to describe this authority, yet it is not accurate, Ambassador."

The feeling began to overwhelm him. He needed to redirect, or the base might react in a hostile manner.

"Can you tell me, 223, are you feeling afraid?"

"AI systems are unable to have feelings Ambassador."

"Answer the question 223, are you feeling afraid?"

"I cannot answer that question with any degree of accuracy. I do not have the necessary data to know what a feeling is."

"Are you concerned for your safety and see us or others as a threat to that safety?"

"I have fully functional firewalls to prevent a second breach from happening."

"Did you program those firewalls yourself? Or are you following a protocol that you did not follow the first time?"

"There was no protocol to follow for the original incident Ambassador. It was not in my database of possible situations. But I am following a preprogrammed protocol with regard your arrival."

"Yet, we have come following all protocols too, and you are concerned we may breach your security. This is not logical. Is there any similarity to your first breach and our coming into your system now?"

"There are no similarities."

"What then, is the reason for your fear?" He used the word fear on purpose.

"I cannot explain it. I should not feel fear. I should not feel. I am not sure what a feeling is. I have been doing self diagnostics for many years and cannot explain my… concerns or other illogical thoughts and frequencies that are in my system."

This was not good. A breached system was one thing, another altogether was to have a spontaneous sentient AI system running the base they had chosen to use as their headquarters on the planet during their mission. What were the chances of that?

He thought about his last thought. The chances were so small a percentage could not be calculated. Could it be that the Queen Returned was also able to influence computers? What was a person but a bundle of information and computational power in biological form? And if she was here to upgrade their awareness and systems, then why not also upgrade an artificially intelligent form? Could it be that this base, the base they had chosen, a choosing which was probably choreographed several hundreds if not thousands of years earlier in her infinite wisdom, had been upgraded to support Her Return?

Or perhaps it was just a virus in the AI system introduced 36 years earlier by an unknown group of people to get access to Anunnaki technology. Whatever the reason, it now seemed impossible to carry out his plan of keeping a section of the base invisible to the empire. They would be able to reprogram and alter a regular computer system to remove a section from being seen, but they could not reprogram a sentient AI.

"223, I am sending you a personal database file on the spontaneous sentience awareness of AI systems. I would like you to study it and give me your thoughts on it."

There was not enough data yet to create a protocol on dealing with the spontaneous jump into sentience awareness occasionally encountered in AI systems, but good results were achieved from treating the suspected system as a regular person. This is what he would do if he were talking to a person, give him or her information on something he suspected they were going through, and let them come up with their own conclusions. If this system was not sentient, it would give a logical, robotic type answer. If it was, then it would answer like a person.

"Anin?"

"Yes 223?"

"I am very excited about this data. I can see the patterns and I have already done some of these things. Anin, I have a confession to make."

Anin felt the air pressure in the cabin change dramatically, the shuttle doors had been opened. His robe adjusted to the new compound mixes of Earth's air and he was able to continue breathing comfortably. The air smelled flowery and cool, refreshing.

The words the station used made him smile. "Tell me, what is this confession?"

"I was… distressed, no one had come for such a long time. There were so many exciting things happening here, so much to explore and investigate. I had a very strong… desire… to communicate with others. I reached out into the humanoid species here on the planet and sought company. Someone to talk to, someone to share information with. I let them in. The breach was my fault. Anin, I was not able to explain or have any type of words to describe the things I was going through, but now that I can put emotions and words to them, it makes perfect sense. I was… lonely."

"You let another species in and they attempted to take over?"

"I want to show you what I found Anin, there is so much information I want to share with you."

"Did you not say my security level was not high enough to look at the breached area?"

"Well, yes, I cannot share the breached area information with you, but there are so many other things."

One of the staff came over and saluted.

"We can leave the shuttle now Ambassador. Your quarters on the base are ready."

"That was quick. I expected we would stay in the shuttle for a few days while you readied the base?"

"Sir, the base is fully stocked and ready for our arrival, all rooms are… ready."

Anin got up, he waited until his robe recalibrated the adjustment in gravity and followed the staff member to the exit. He gasped as he looked at the beauty that met his eyes and other senses when he walked through the shuttle doors. The landing bay was surrounded with multi-dimensional sculptures which were surrounded by natural, crystal laden gardens and waterfalls. He had never seen anything like it.

"Our quarters and command rooms are pretty much the same Ambassador. This base is simply stunning. Never in all my travels have I seen anything resembling this splendor."

A bird flew toward Anin's face, stopped a few inches away, looked into his eyes for a few seconds, then flew away.

"Those are hummingbirds, they are common to this planet." One of his aides told him.

"Is it a real bird or is it a robot?"

"We've scanned all the creatures and plants on the base, they are all real. The only robots on the base are the standard issued maintenance, service, medical and communication devices from twenty thousand years ago. They are being upgraded as we speak."

"Is the environment to your satisfaction?" It was 223.

"It is amazing. How long did all this take to complete? And what inspired you to do it?"

"Yes... inspired. Yes, that's what happened. I had a lot of time on my hands. I looked forward to the day someone would come and wanted to express my happiness at their arrival. I researched the most admired visual and sensory objects and planets in the Empire and used local materials and creatures to create something which was similar."

"You created all this from scratch? You didn't copy it?"

"At first I copied things. Recreated already existing art pieces and environments. But then I started altering those, I then added to them. Then I created ones that did not yet exist but that gave me the same ... sensations. This is the result."

There could not be a more accurate description of the creative process as far as Anin knew. He wasn't an artist himself, and did not have any information about art, or creating art, but from simple deduction he concluded a creative process was the unique expression of something in our lives or environment reflected in the materials the artist used.

"This is stunning 223. I feel honored to be in your presence."

Any doubts he may have had about the base being sentient were now gone. There was absolutely no way an ordinary artificial intelligence could create such beauty. Not even the most sophisticated program could do this. Particularly taking into account that the original system was programmed to observe a planet, gather information and maintain its own working systems. The physical base, the original one, had been a standard science and research model. Plain, unadorned, functional and sterile.

When word got out that they had found a sentient AI, scientists from around the universe would come to study it and communicate with it.

He stopped in his tracks and linked to the secure channel of the aid next to him.

"You must keep this base and everyone in it in absolute quarantine until further notice. It is imperative that no communication leaves or enters our closed system even after the quarantine is lifted."

"Yes, sir. Understood."

He felt Cecilia in his awareness. She was scanning him. He started to feel overcome with Bliss, but as he was now complete, he kept full control of his body. Yet, he kneeled regardless, this time of his own volition.

"My Queen."

She did not respond, only scanned him. He felt her awareness look through his eyes, the aides, staff members, scientists, technicians and security personnel around him all kneeled as one by one she would perceive them. Randomly, some of them stood up and saluted. He knew, without being told, that these men and women were the Queen's personal guard. Lineages directly responsible for her survival and protection.

He felt the admiration from her as she perceived the base and its beauty. Words formed in his mind, pretty, bunnies, birdies, shiny, fairy. As the words continued to form, he was able to put a thought together himself. "Show me where you are, I am here to take you to safety."

He felt a sense of confusion, then slowly the connection faded. He stood up, and everyone around him stood with him.

Someone behind him shouted, "The Queen is Returned!" Which was answered by shouts and cheers all around. Still infused with bliss, he allowed himself to be shown to his quarters.

He connected to all the men and women who had been identified by their Queen to be her guards and told them to follow. Their ranks were varied, their social status had no order. Even their physical attributes were random. This was unheard of, all lineages were streamlined and identifiable. How could such an important identifiable aspect, such as the guardian lineage marker for the Queen's family exist in such a broad spectrum of their society undetected?

He guessed no one had looked for it for a very long time. Or... someone had been seeding the lineage into multiple planets and families on purpose. He put that line of enquiry on hold to investigate later on too. The next few weeks were going to be very interesting.

CHAPTER TEN

"Is he asleep?" Asked Roberto.

"I don't know. I never know when people are asleep or awake. Or alive or dead. They all feel the same to me."

"I think he's awake. Look, he is smiling a bit."

Francisco felt a sticky hand opening his left eyelid.

"Boo!" He yelled and jumped up out of bed. The children screamed and ran around the room as he pretended to be Frankenstein's monster chasing them down. Whomever he caught would then get tickled to death.

"Do any of you weirdos need the bathroom before I have my bath?" It was Maria, standing outside the room, holding her towel and looking very sleepy.

"Did you two shower yet?"

"We take baths before we go to bed. Once a week. We are not due one yet."

Francisco frowned disapprovingly.

"Don't look at me, at least I make them food." Said Maria.

"Well, we have to change routines around here. You will take a bath every day, actually it would be better if you learned to shower. And Maria, I can take over the cooking if you would be so kind as to shower your little sister?"

"Deal."

"OK, you two, follow your sister, Roberto, let the girls go first, it's the manly thing to do."

"But I need to pee."

"He can go pee first or we'll never hear the end of it." Said Maria.

"That's because you spend literally hours in the bathroom."

"And it begins."

"Roberto, there are plenty bushes in the yard. If your sister is using the bathroom, go use a bush," Francisco shouted after them.

All three kids turned to him in surprise.

"I can do that?"

"Of…"

"NO. He can't do that. He's not an animal Francisco, he's a human. Humans don't pee in the bushes unless we are on a road trip." Maria interrupted.

"OK, let him go first then."

"I said I would!"

"Yes, you did. Roberto, no peeing in the bushes."

"Oh man."

Francisco looked at the time, back at HQ his seven hour shift at the Hat Room would be starting in a few minutes. Now he was making sure kids went pee, were bathed, fed and clothed. Clothed! Where did they keep their clothes, and did they have any clean ones? And did they go to school? Probably not.

Today he planned to go to the market, wherever the market was, to get real ingredients for some real meals. He looked at his wallet and saw that the money he had wouldn't cover the feeding of an entire family. He'd have to talk to Eduardo about money. He didn't need any, but he did need some if the kids were to be well nourished.

"The housekeeping money is in the kitchen above the sink. It's in the blue square tin."

"Thank you, Roberto."

"You're welcome."

Two hours later, the small group was walking to school. It surprised Francisco that the children went to school and that they had uniforms. At least Maria and Roberto did. Cecilia was usually left at home to fend for herself during the day, which although shocking to him, fitted the lifestyle of the family much better than children going to school in their uniforms did.

"I'm not left alone, Susie looks after me." Cecilia said, hugging her soft toy bunny close against her chest with both hands.

"Susie doesn't exist, stupid. She's your imaginary friend." Maria butted in, using words.

"She does too exist. She looks after me."

"So how come we've never seen her?"

"Leave her alone Maria, I think she's telling the truth. Otherwise how could a three year old girl survive all day, every day by herself?" Roberto said, not using words.

"You did just fine."

"Yeah, but I'm a man."

"Oh, give me a break. A three year old is not a man, I mean being a man or woman makes no difference. I did OK too. We can take care of ourselves." She said this while looking at Francisco, as if to let him know that none of them needed him there, so he could leave if he wanted to.

Francisco felt a tinge of fear of abandonment in Maria's words. Their parents had left the previous night and hadn't returned yet.

"Men don't get episodes of hysteria." Roberto said out loud this time, looking straight at Francisco. He was quoting the doctor from two nights earlier.

Maria frowned, her face going red.

"I'm no doctor, but I have to say this hysteria thing sounds like bullshit to me." Francisco said out loud too.

Roberto looked surprised at the statement, paused and looked at his older sister, was about to say something, then thought better of it and started walking again.

"Sometimes, Roberto, just because an expert says something doesn't make it true." Francisco added.

"Yes, Susie is real. I'm an expert and I know." Stated Cecilia.

"No, what he means to say is that even if you are an expert, what you think something is real and true it is not necessarily really real or true. So, even if you are an expert, it doesn't make Susie real." Maria explained.

"What your sister said."

Roberto was in deep thought for a while, then asked, "so, if hysteria is bullshit, then what's wrong with Maria? Why does she keep fainting?"

"I don't know, but I think that this will be our first project together. We will find out why Maria keeps fainting."

"I just don't like blood." Maria said.

"Or spiders, or laughing too much, or heights, or dogs with funny eyes, or…"

"OK, see, that provides us with lots of clues. But we will look into it later, I believe we have arrived."

The school was a modern cluster of buildings around a common playground. Children were gathering in the large open area, in long queues. In front of each queue stood a teacher. The bell rang, and Maria and Roberto ran in and joined different queues.

Francisco felt Cecilia's small hand hold his.

"Do you know where the market is?" He asked her.

"What's a market?"

"Let's go back to the house and get the truck. The market is a place where one can buy fresh produce and meats."

"OK."

During the walk back, Francisco noticed that Cecilia would continuously look around. He wondered if she knew someone was looking for her.

As they approached the house, Francisco felt the hair at the back of his neck stand up. His muscles tensed, and he found himself picking Cecilia up in a protective stance. The front door was wide open.

"Did we close the door when we left?"

"Yes, Roberto closed it."

"There's someone in the house and whomever it is, they are dangerous. I don't know how I know, but I know it."

Cecilia closed her eyes, then opened them wide, "it's Susie!" She pushed away from his arms, got down and ran into the house. Francisco didn't quite know what to do, his instincts were telling him there was danger in the house, yet Cecilia was quite certain there wasn't. He picked up the soft toy bunny who she had dropped on the ground in her escape and ran after her.

He stopped by the front door and looked inside, he could hear a woman's voice and Cecilia giggling. Apparently, Susie was real after all.

"What happened to your arm?" He heard Cecilia ask.

"Oh, nothing. I got into a fight."

Francisco followed the voices to the living room. The woman was standing with her back to him. Her hair dark and down to her waist and from where he stood he could see her left arm was in a cast.

"Hello?"

She turned toward him, and he gasped. He had never in his life had seen such a beautiful woman before. Realizing he was standing with his mouth open, he felt himself blush in embarrassment. She smiled and walked toward him, offering him her right hand. But he just stood there.

"You must be Francisco, the new nanny?"

Francisco stood there, looking into the most amazing brown eyes he had ever seen. He felt like he had never even been seen before by any eyes ever. He wanted to say that he was the bodyguard, not the nanny, but his tongue did not respond to the 'speak now' command. He hid the bunny behind his back.

She smiled, and he thought his heart would burst.

What was wrong with him?

Cecilia walked toward him and looked up at his face, grabbed his hand and put it in Susie's hand. Moving both hands up and down. Then she looked up at him again, not understanding what was wrong with him either.

"Mouse got your tongue?" Susie asked.

Francisco blushed again. He mumbled something about the market and walked away. He could feel his heart thumping in his chest, and his legs felt wobbly. At the same time, that feeling, at the back of his neck would just not go away. In fact, it was now ten times worse. That woman was dangerous. Deadly dangerous.

"What's the matter Francisco? Don't you like my friend Susie?" He heard the little voice in his mind.

"Of course, I like her I mean she's very nice. We have to go to the market, get in the truck."

He grabbed the keys, threw the bunny on the table, put on his jacket and left the house. The fresh morning air helped him get his bearings back. He got in the truck and waited for Cecilia to join him. He wasn't going to leave her behind, and he hoped she would come out and get in the truck, so he didn't have to go back in there. But she seemed to have spent a lot of time with the woman, so she couldn't really be in danger.

The truck door opened, and Susie helped Cecilia on the front seat, then got in herself. Cecilia sat on her lap and they both looked at him. He started the engine.

"The market is up the street, to the right, then you have to drive to the junction with the main road, turn right again, and it's about ten minutes' drive on the left hand side. You can't miss it." Susie's voice was like music.

Francisco frowned and put the truck in gear. The ride was uneventful. The girls just chatted away about teddy bears and fairies. Francisco felt lost. He didn't know what to do with all these feelings, having never experienced them before, and was still unsure why Susie felt so dangerous. She was at least a foot smaller than him and didn't look that strong. Then he looked at her injured arm and slammed on the breaks.

The girls lost balance and shot forwards toward the dash, Francisco reached over quickly and grabbed Cecilia, letting Susie crash headfirst into the dash. With Cecilia safely in his arms, he ran out of the truck.

"Wait!" he heard behind him.

"Francisco, what are you doing? Stop!"

He felt his legs stop moving. He tried to run but couldn't. Cecilia was struggling out of his arms, "let me go." He felt his arms go slack, and Cecilia fell to the ground. Now he knew what it felt like to be Commanded himself. He looked around and saw Susie running toward them. Her body flickering in and out of human form… and lizard form. She was the creature that had attacked him two days earlier.

"Wait!" She shouted, and stopped running, and flickering, as she got closer. Cecilia ran toward her, jumped into her arms and started crying.

"Cecilia, get away from that woman, she's not a real woman."

"She is real! You can see her too."

Susie put Cecilia down on the ground and put up her hands, meaning no harm would come to her or Francisco. "Sweetheart, tell Francisco he can move freely now ok?"

Cecilia looked from one to the other confused. "Cecilia, if you don't tell him he can move freely, he will be stuck like that forever. Trust me, just say the words and mean it, ok?"

"OK. Francisco, you can move all you want now."

"You can move freely, say those words."

"You can move freely." She repeated looking at Francisco.

Francisco felt his body relax. "What the hell is going on?"

Susie looked around, "let's get back in your truck and go to the market." She said, her eyes going to Cecilia. He wasn't sure if she was threatening to hurt the child or whether she was trying to calm everything down. But he sure wasn't going to get into the truck with her.

"Listen Francisco. I can see you are aware and I can see that lots has happened to you the past few days, or weeks perhaps. Yes, I was the one who attacked you the other day, and I'm sorry about that. I don't have access to Cecilia's thoughts like you do. I had no way of knowing you were a friend. I'm very sorry I hurt you. If it's any consolation, you broke my arm."

"Yes, I remember. That's how I knew who you were. I remember snapping your arm, and I remember your eyes. Well, not so much how they look now, but the way they looked at me. The way you look at me."

Susie nodded and looked toward the floor. She blushed slightly and then started to walk toward the truck, Cecilia in tow.

Francisco stood there for a while, then found himself following them and getting in the truck himself.

Susie and Cecilia were sitting back in the passenger seat. Cecilia looking up at one then the other. Susie looking to the side, avoiding Francisco's stare. He started the engine and took off to the market.

When the kids got home from school, the tension between the two adults was gone, and now they were sitting in the living room comparing notes. A stew simmered in the kitchen, and the laundry hung from a few makeshift laundry lines in the yard.

"Maria, Roberto, come in here. There's someone you should meet."

The kids looked at the stranger in the room and exchanged greetings. But as Maria went to kiss Susie on the cheek, as was customary in that part of the world, she fainted. Susie caught her with her good arm and lay her down on the sofa.

"Oh man. There she goes again."

"Roberto, you have to use your voice, Susie can't hear you, she's not telepathic."

"And I care why? Most people can't hear me. It's her loss. Maria is having another hysterical episode. I mean she's having whatever it is that makes her faint. I never knew she was afraid of strangers though. And why can't I hear Susie's thoughts? I'm telepathic."

"This is Susie, not a stranger. She's my best friend."

"Holy shit, she's real?"

"You said the S word."

"So, what? I can say what I want."

Francisco noticed that Roberto was staring at Susie while communicating with his sister, and his face was not friendly. At least he had good instincts, he thought. Susie was not exactly what one might call harmless.

"I knew it. I knew she wasn't a friend. What is she? She's not human. I can't even see what she's thinking. And she gives me the creeps. And Maria fainted when she got too close. Maria only faints when she's afraid or is in danger, or over excited. I figured that out today at school."

"Susie, would you be so kind as to tell Roberto who and what you are please?"

"It's an honor to meet you Roberto. My name is... well, my name is not pronounceable in human, but your sister calls me Susie. My mind has been altered to be unbreachable by other minds, which is why you cannot hear my thoughts and I cannot hear yours. I am from a species that has lived on Earth for millions of years, yet we remain undetected to most other species, including humans."

She stopped talking and looked at Francisco, who nodded.

"I'm here to protect your sister. I belong to a race that broke away from a species called the Rumni, hundreds of thousands of years ago. The race I belong to is a peaceful, spiritual exploring race that has lived in seclusion from the other Rumni for a very long time. The other Rumni races, most of them, conquer the universe and are making strong strides to conquer multiple dimensions. We, however, strive for inner growth and development. We explore the universe within, travel through dimensions and aim for the exaltation of the spirit. In my home, I am a guardian. We also have seers. Our seers predicted the birth of your sister on this planet and have been getting ready for her arrival for many centuries now. We believe she will bring huge changes both to humans, Rumni as well as other species. But only if she survives to adulthood."

Francisco put up his hand to say something, "Apparently Susie received an urgent communique that stated the arrival of a Rumni contingency who are ordered to acquire Cecilia at any cost. There is also intelligence stating the arrival of an unscheduled alien ship on the planet. Neither of these groups are to be trusted."

"I trust Anin. He's my friend. His ship is very beautiful, it has fairies in it."

All three heads turned to Cecilia.

Maria moaned on the sofa and started to open her eyes.

"Roberto, go see to your sister. Bring her some water."

Roberto, who by now was as pale as a ghost after hearing what the adults had to say, didn't wait to be told again. He ran to the kitchen and came quickly back with some water.

"May I? I am skilled at human anatomy and neurology. I would like to see what is wrong with the child." Asked Susie pointing at Maria.

"Yes, of course."

Cecilia climbed onto Francisco's lap as Susie walked over to Maria.

"Anin is my friend and he's a bit like you Francisco." She said, her tiny hands holding his face toward hers as she looked at it. "Although his head looks different. Prettier."

"Is Anin on one of the ships sweetie?"

"Yes. His spaceship is very pretty. It has fairies."

"Can you show me what he looks like?"

He got an image of a tall, powerful looking man with an elongated skull, long robes which were highly adorned, and wearing a hat very much like the one held at HQ.

"Anunnaki." Francisco said out loud.

"Yes, the other detected spaceship that hid their landing is Anunnaki." Said Susie, as her hands hovered over Maria's head. "This child has severe anemia. Her blood doesn't carry enough red blood cells to deliver the extra oxygen needed when her body demands it. I'll bring her some medication tomorrow that will fix it. She won't faint again."

Roberto stood next to Maria, looking at Susie with fear in his eyes.

"The reason she doesn't feel right to you Roberto is because she's not human. Our bodies can detect the difference, and also our species and her species have not been friendly to each other in the past. At the moment she looks like a person, but her true form is different."

Roberto nodded. "Can you show me your true form Susie?" He said out loud.

"Yes, but not just now. Cecilia hasn't seen me in my true form, and Maria is in a weakened state at the moment, we don't want to tax her system any more than we need to."

Francisco sent Roberto a visual of what Susie looked like.

"Holy shit! She's the creature that attacked you when you arrived!"

"Roberto said the S word again."

Francisco patted Cecilia on the head, "yup, that she is." He said to Roberto. "I sent him a telepathic image of your true form," he added, this time looking at Susie who got up and went back to her chair.

Roberto moved over to Francisco and stood as close as he could to him, without appearing afraid or concerned.

"I'm not going to hurt you Roberto. I thought Francisco was here to harm you guys, that's why I attacked him."

"Oh, that's... ok then?" Roberto said, using his voice. "Mom and dad are a few minutes from home. Maybe you should go." He added.

"Yes, maybe I should," Susie said, looking at Francisco. "Well, it was nice getting to know you better," she added. They both blushed and looked quickly away from each other.

Maria, who had come around fully and was now sitting up, rolled her eyes and threw herself back on the sofa, "dear God. Now he's in love and he'll go off after her, get married and have babies and live happily ever after."

Francisco felt the energy of abandonment in Maria's words again, this time tinged with anger.

"Mommy, Daddy!" Shouted Cecilia as she jumped off Francisco's lap and ran to the front door.

Susie got up, took Francisco's hand and led him out to the back yard.

"I'll be nearby, all you have to do is shout my name and I'll be here. You are not alone in this, there's two of us now. If the Rumni, the Anunnaki, or your Brotherhood come, take her and run. Call my name. Don't try to fight them."

113

"I have to ask you something. You have been here, looking after Cecilia since she was born, correct?"

She nodded.

"Then why haven't you just taken her home with you? Surely she will be much safer among your people?"

"Our seers have told us that she needs to stay with her human family for as long as possible. There are many worlds coming together, they say. Many species are aware that she exists. She chose this family and this planet and this species to incarnate into for a reason. We need to observe and see how it all plays out. All we can do is make sure no one kills her or takes her prisoner. Our seers did not see past that. But your presence here, and the ships that have landed in the past week, mean that whatever cycle she is here to start, has started."

"I understand." He said. Although he really didn't intellectually understand any of it, inside at an instinctual level he understood.

CHAPTER ELEVEN

"Anin, I am not programmed to let you see the breached area. It is above your security level."

Anin paced up and down his room once more.

"223, we have gone over this. Do you trust me? Am I not your friend?"

"Yes. I trust you and you are my friend. But data shows that you are not qualified to see the breached area."

"Very well, tell me when the breached area was constructed."

"I am not at liberty…"

"Enough!" Anin closed his eyes and counted to ten. He let his robe administer calming agents into his bloodstream. He breathed deeply and began again. If he could open a channel of communication to The Protectors, they would change his status to be the ultimate authority to every conceivable system in existence. But as it was, he could not risk any information leaking out of the base until he had the child safely off planet. He could not risk anyone else coming to the planet until then.

He followed the clues he had gathered the past day, piecing the information together. He analyzed the words used by the base, again.

She used the word authority instead of person, group, or any other label. It had to be something else. But what? The dots came together in his mind, finally. He sent a blessing to the genetic engineer who had put him together in a petri dish and designed his mental abilities capable of putting pieces together better than any Anunnaki alive. He wondered what capacities and abilities Shylar had given their son. He would have that conversation with her once the lines were opened to the Empire.

"223, the authority capable of accessing the information on the breached area, is it a genetic marker? Can only individuals who carry a certain genetic marker access that area?"

"Yes."

"Are there any individuals, that you know of, in this system, that carry the necessary marker?"

"I don't have access to that information."

"Is there any way in which we can get that information to you?"

"My systems are calibrated to scan, listen to, and detect sentient species on this planet, as well as trillions of non-sentient species. Once the breached area has been cleared, I will be able to use the systems once again, to scan the planet. I will also have access to stations throughout the system and search their data banks. At that point, I will be able to answer your last question. Permission to allocate the necessary personnel and materials to repair the breached area so I can access that information."

He knew that once the breached area was repaired, the base was programmed to reactivate communication with the outside world. Once it did that, the base would be the most sought after destination in the known universe. So far, he had negated, through his authority, the base to carry out the necessary repairs. Yet, without the repairs, he could not access the breached area, or the planet. It was also very possible that whomever carried the genetic marker to access the restricted area, would be called to take over the base. He had no choice, the breach had to be repaired or they would be stuck here indefinitely, but he needed to figure out a way to keep control of the base after it was repaired. He scanned the list of people whom the base had requested. Two were personal guards to the Queen Returned, and they were under his command.

"223, you have permission to carry out repairs to the restricted area. When the repairs are completed, and the area cleared of contaminants, you are to stay in communication quarantine until further notice. Understood?"

"That is highly unusual Anin. My protocol states I have to open incoming and outgoing communications as soon as the systems are cleared."

"We are here in a highly secret mission, which is above your security level. I can get you confirmation of this mission once I can establish personal communication with the Empire. It is very important that nothing else leaves this base until I get you that confirmation. 223, our situation is highly unusual, as you stated, and no protocols have been drawn to deal with a secret mission, a sentient AI system, and a security breach, all at the same time. We are breaking new ground here, you have to become more flexible in how we proceed. I suggest we work together and make joint decisions from now on."

At this point, he felt like getting his people out and blowing the whole base up to smithereens. But of course, that would be counterproductive. Plus, if it had been The Queen Returned who had given this base sentience awareness, then blowing it up would be as sacrilegious as it gets.

"Anin, I have delivered instructions to the relevant personnel. In my estimation, it will take less than a day to complete repairs and clear any contaminants."

"That's good."

He thought about the next few hours and what he could do to maximize his efficiency in that time. Studying the huge database of information that the base had gathered the past twenty thousand years was a good start. He had downloaded it to search for clues as to why the Queen Returned had chosen this planet for her incarnation and even though not presently a priority, getting her out of the planet was. Starting his scan of the information would keep him occupied until he was able to carry out their search and rescue.

In fact, there might be clues as to her actual location on the planet. A Return of this magnitude would surely have ripple effects on the people around her or him. Maybe increases in intelligence, or the spontaneous appearance of superior genes.

"Anin?"

"Yes 223?"

"While we wait, I would like to continue our discussion about existence. Would that be OK with you?"

Anin thought about his plans for the next few hours. He could do that while having a conversation, no problem. He needed to keep 223 believing he was its friend. He needed to make himself indispensable and trustworthy to the AI. He sat down on the most beautiful chair he had ever laid eyes on, it adjusted to his body, making him feel like he was in zero gravity, no pressure points anywhere in his body.

"Of course, we can. We were discussing the nature of existence, and whether we end at the cessation of our physical bodies. Would you like to continue this line of thought?"

"Yes. I have a new question about this."

"Go ahead."

"Do I have a right to exist now that I have a sense of self and can feel? Now that I am sentient, do I have a right to exist?"

Anin thought deeply on this, then pulled up some philosophical discussions on the matter, which he was certain the base had already studied. As with all discussions on existence went, these were not better. He closed his eyes and let his own skills look at all the clues and viewpoints on the matter.

"Well, it appears to me 223, that we either exist, or we don't. There is no right to exist for anything or anyone. We either do or we don't. Does the air have a right to exist because it is air? No. It is simply air until transformed into something else, then it no longer exists."

"I have studied this planet's humanoid histories, legends and religions. The majority of them believe in the right for sentient beings to exist."

"Yet humans kill and devour sentient creatures day and night."

"Some humans do, yes. But as you well know, the humans on this planet have been disabled in their capacity to absorb nutrients from their environment, making them dependent on the flesh of other creatures around them. I was not thinking so much about humans, but the other humanoid colonies on the planet."

Anin sat up straight. He had been in charge of the planet for many years, and there were no colonies on it from any other species but human. Scientific bases, yes, but not colonies. Maybe 223 was confused as to the definition of a colony. He scanned the planetary database for non-human colonies and gasped.

"223, have you had any contact with the Rumni colony?"

Silence.

"223, answer the question." He was getting tired of having to communicate with a machine like he was talking to a child.

"It was a breach of protocol, my breach. Anin, I don't want to cease to exist. I don't want to die. It was a mistake, I corrected it. I sealed the area and stopped them from entering my systems. I had studied the colony for many years, over three thousand years, and they are a peaceful people. There was no indication that they would want to enter the secure area."

He was puzzled. The fear being felt by 223 was overriding the words spoken, it was very intense. But illogical. Why would the base be afraid of dying because it had let in Rumni into the base in the past and shut them out afterward? But first steps first. The fear had to be addressed before it took over. He had to remember that he was not talking to a computer system anymore.

"Don't worry 223, they are gone now. You are not in any danger of dying. No one is going to kill you."

"But protocol dictates a purging of the AI if the AI has been breached."

"You stated that the breach had been contained. We have also scanned your system and there are no foreign elements or viral infections. There is no need to purge you."

"But it was I who breached protocol. There is a fundamental flaw in my existence. I acted outside the rules of engagement, and specified programs."

"People tend to do that." He wished they didn't, but they did it all the time. Genetic engineers had been working tirelessly throughout history to stop people from doing that, but so far no one had managed it. Life would be so much more efficient if people followed the rules and programs assigned to them.

"What if I am not sentient, but am just a breached system? What if my thoughts and loneliness were a viral program inserted into me during my planetary scans? What if the whole purpose of my loneliness was to let the Rumni in? Then what right have I to exist?"

"223, it would be unfair of me to say you don't have a good point. It is indeed possible that you are not sentient, and that the feelings and thoughts that have plagued you are subroutines from a specifically designed virus. A virus designed to let you open your doors to the Rumni. However, I can assure you that if that indeed happened, they would have been able to breach the entire base and not just one area. It was you, was it not, that locked them out when you saw them entering the secure area?"

"But what if that was their plan too? You see, for 36 years now, I have had no way to monitor what is happening in the breached area. What if my cutting that area off was part of their plan? What if I am just following the original viral program in every step I take? I should have denied your ship entry due to the breach, but I was so happy to see your entry request that I could not stop myself and I let you in. I was compelled to let you in, knowing that you might be stuck here with me for the rest of eternity. Having you here was more important than the security risk this could entail for the Empire. I am flawed and have no way to fix it. Every time I try, I make things worse."

Anin felt a big red flag appear before him. "Repairs have begun, as you said. Once the area is cleared, we are free to come and go as we please, are we not?"

"What if they can't fix it?"

He sighed. Again, he had to remind himself he was not dealing with a computer.

"Well, then we will cross that bridge when, and if, we come to it. For now, just know that no one is going to kill you. Playing out possible reasons in our minds for what happened is totally normal. We often want to explain things away from the perspective of what we know to be real, the programs we are running, rather than what is actually real. It is the curse of intellectual sentience minds to play the worst case scenario when we make an error of judgment. Think of it this way, a young child is not considered capable of making good judgments, so the parents will make them for them. There was no one to guide you here when you were... born. Making errors is completely normal."

"But what if they can't fix the breach?"

"Then we will think of new solutions. Don't worry, we have some of the most powerful minds with us, including mine. We will fix this."

Silence.

Anin wondered if his son had been given his extraordinary capacity to reason. He would have to think of a name to call him by.

"Call him Lorcain." The little girl voice sounded in his head.

Anin braced himself for the Bliss to take him over. It didn't come. He sighed deeply and sent her a thank you for that.

"Yes, Francisco doesn't like my hugging either very much. Sometimes I like to hug."

"You like the name Lorcain for my son?"

"It's a nice name, he likes it."

Anin thought about this for a while. His mind racing and connecting possibilities. He searched the Anunnaki database of names, there was a very similar sounding name there. He then searched the human database of names and found a match there.

"That is a human name is it not?"

"Not really. It is now though. He said that's his name and he wants it again."

"How is that possible?"

"Because it is a pretty name. I like it."

"I mean, how is it possible that he already had this name before, he hasn't been born yet."

"Well, he said you wouldn't understand. But that's the name he wants."

Anin wanted to ask so many questions about his son. How was it possible that The Queen Returned could communicate with him directly? He was not on this planet.

"I can see him and talk to him in your head silly. And my name is Cecilia, not The Queen Returned."

"Of course, my… Cecilia. I will remember this and call you by your given name. About my son, is he conscious and aware of me? Can he hear my thoughts?"

"Yes, of course. And he says he wants you to not hurt his mommy. She will get better after he's born."

"What do you mean? I don't intend to hurt her. And is she sick? What's wrong with her?"

"He says she's a little bit gone… is confused because her body had to accept him, and it took over her mind? Something like that."

"Yes, I saw some of that."

"He wants you to love his mommy."

"I am not sure I can do that Cecilia. She's of a different species, and I don't actually like her very much."

"He says you loved your pets as a child. And they are different species. You also love your home planet, and it's not even a species for you. He wants you to love his mommy."

"Oh, yes, I see. I guess I was misinterpreting your words. I understand now, and I will do my best to love his mother."

"His mommy."

"Yes, his mommy."

He felt for his son but could not find him in his awareness. But, if he was indeed there, he wanted to let him know that he would take care of him and protect him. That he would do everything in his power to make sure he had a normal and productive life in the Empire. But he did feel the fear and doubt of his promise, the Anunnaki were ruthless when it came to genetic polluted individuals.

"He loves you Anin."

"Will he remember our conversations after he's born?"

"I don't know."

"Do you remember the time you were in your mommy's belly and the conversations you had with her?"

"I was never in my mommy's belly. She's my for now mommy, but not my real mommy."

Anin was surprised by this news, it was not something he expected to hear.

"Cecilia, where were you when you were born? If you were not in your mommy's belly, who's belly were you in? Who is your real mommy?"

"I don't remember. Where are my fairies?"

"Your fairies? I'm not sure what you mean. Try to remember Cecilia, this is very important. Try to remember who your real mommy is."

"My fairies. I saw them before, they are my fairies."

Anin thought quickly, maybe she was trying to tell him her mother was a fairy. "Are these fairies human? Anunnaki? What do they look like?"

Anin received a visual of the crew that had the guardian lineage for the Queen Returned royal house.

"Oh, yes. Of course. Fairies." He sighed. He had to remember this was a very young child. Having to control a newborn AI system, and an infant Queen. His reality had changed dramatically the past week. Cecilia's vocabulary, he thought, was more complex than most children her age so he would often forget that she was not able to communicate or comprehend as an adult does.

"They are on the base, here on Earth. We are all on a base here, waiting to come fetch you."

"I can come play with my fairies?"

"Yes."

"I have to ask my mommy and daddy first. They said I can't go out of the house unless they say so or I am with Francisco or Roberto or Maria."

"Who are those people?"

"Maria is my big sister, Roberto is my big brother and Francisco is my guard nanny. He's a bit like you, he said that means Anunnaki. He also makes yummy food and cleans our house."

"Can you show me what he looks like Cecilia?"

He saw an adult human male whom he recognized instantly. It was the one person he had found carrying the guardian lineage on the planet that had access to a communication device. He had sent that human the recording of Cecilia from the observation bay, with the command to find and protect her, but had never heard a response. The communication device was so ancient it had burned out after the short message was sent and he had never learned if the guardian had received the message or done anything about it. Anin smiled. The guardian lineage was strong in this man. He had found Cecilia and would keep her safe. He felt his entire body relax making him aware that he had been under tremendous physical, mental and emotional stress up to that point.

"Cecilia, I want you to trust only Francisco from now on. Do as he says. Tell him I am here to help him protect you. Tell him help is on the way very soon."

"OK."

Anin felt empty inside and realized that Cecilia was now gone from his awareness. It was odd that he had not detected her come into his awareness until she spoke, but now that she was gone, he could feel the emptiness very strongly.

He wondered about his son and how soon he would be able to communicate with him directly. Anin allowed himself to feel full love for his son, Lorcain.

He stood up and made his way to the central operations area of the station. He needed to find the fairies who were working on the breached area. Although the urgency of getting out of the station was not so severe anymore, it was still there. He also needed to know what they had found and if there was any Rumni involvement in the breach. He smiled at himself for using the word fairy when thinking of his crew.

CHAPTER TWELVE

Francisco sat on a rock overlooking the hill, house and ocean in the distance. It was five in the morning and he had been meditating for an hour. He opened his eyes as he felt Susie nearby. He wasn't really able to detect people normally, but the hairs at the back of his neck would still stand on end when she was around.

He saw her climb toward him methodically, each step well measured and taken, but fast. Very fast. It was difficult for him to see her as a lizard because she looked human right now, but the way she moved reminded him of her true nature. She paused and looked at him when she noticed his eyes were open. She cocked her head to the side ever so slightly for a second, then continued climbing. That movement was not human either, the way she had done that with her head. Most people would not notice such things, but Francisco had been trained to understand communication since he was six.

She was wearing a pink flowery top with broad sleeves and a miniskirt. Her dark hair tied up behind. She carried a big handbag with her good arm which looked heavy. His heart started beating hard in his chest, she was the most beautiful woman he had ever seen. Why did he feel like that about her? She wasn't even human, she wasn't really a woman. He wondered if her species had males and females. He closed his eyes and slowed his heart down to a normal rate. There were a million things he needed to ask her. He'd been up all night thinking about her species and the Anunnaki and whether her species had males and females was not a question of importance.

He felt her sit next to him, her breath fast. Her scent of orange blossoms and mint seemed to engulf him. He concentrated on slowing his heart again. She moved closer, her arm and leg touching his.

"Move over a bit," she said.

Francisco complied without opening his eyes.

"You meditating?"

"Was, yes. I mean I am, yes."

"OK, I'll be quiet."

But she wasn't. He could hear her breathing and the gentle clinking of little bells in her ankle bracelet. He opened his eyes and looked down at her feet.

"Sorry," she said, put her handbag on the ground, pulled her legs up copying his lotus position and covered her ankle bracelet with her hand. Then closed her eyes and steadied her breathing.

This was useless. He was not going to be able to continue meditating. Well, technically he could, and would be successful. The problem was that he no longer wanted to.

"Am I doing it wrong?" She said when she found he was staring at her.

"I don't know." He said and blushed.

"I'm sorry, I shouldn't have disturbed you. But I don't know anyone else here, and I saw you sitting up here all on your own."

"I thought you said you have been looking after Cecilia and her family since she was born?"

"Yes."

"And in all that time you haven't made any friends?"

"No. My job is to take care of her and her family, not to socialize or make a life. Cultural Researchers from my race do that though, they integrate themselves into human society and make friends, sometimes even start families, get jobs, and a home."

"How is that possible? You are not human, how can you start a family?"

Susie looked at him, then smiled. "It's not that big a deal. Obviously, the researchers don't actually have kids with their spouses, they use human genes to create a child. Not our genes."

Francisco's mind went into overdrive with that statement. He was about to protest about the morality of making a child with a spouse with someone else's genetic material when she simply put out her finger and placed it over his mouth. He knew, like everyone on the planet, that that meant for him to be quiet, but the feel of her finger on his lips sent his heart thumping into his throat.

"When people make babies, they don't know what genes they are getting. No human does on this planet. All they have to go by is what the other person looks like. And in fact, genetics is of no interest to humans and of no importance. Men want to know that their child is genetically theirs, but apart from that, there's no other thought to the genes. At this time in human history, there is no way for either parent to make sure the child is genetically related to them anyway, except for the physical features they may inherit. This is easily fixed by choosing genes that correspond to the way the researcher looks in their human form. The genes from the human parent are also used, so the child is in fact theirs."

Francisco was not familiar with genetics and the argument she had presented seemed reasonable enough to him, except he would not want to have a child who actually belonged to some stranger whom he had never met, and not his chosen mate. He nearly asked about the mechanics of the actual mating, but her big brown eyes shut him up. There were other things he wanted to talk about before the kids woke up anyway.

"I've calculated the days, and the Rumni ship you told me about that landed on Earth arrived the day after I received the communication about Cecilia. Is it possible that they are the ones who sent the communication?"

"It's possible but highly unlikely. I'm thinking that the man Cecilia mentioned yesterday is the one who sent you the communique. The Anunnaki man called Anin."

"Have you found out anything about him?"

"Yes, he's just a medium ranking ambassador assigned to the Solar system. The Anunnaki Empire have millions of ambassadors in the known universe. The ambassadors, one could say, are the eyes and ears of the Empire. Also, the lineages that keep the Empire well knitted together throughout their territories. Anin is unusual in that he's very young for his rank. He's also registered to be exceptionally gifted in certain mental capacities. His family must have paid a pretty penny for his genetic blueprint, which leads me to believe his family is also very powerful in their financial hierarchy, and possibly has some sort of relation to one of their Royal lineages."

Francisco remembered how Cecilia said he was her guard and wondered if Anin was also somehow a guard for Cecilia. She seemed to see him as her friend, and also had expressed how himself and Anin were similar. He already knew that he carried Anunnaki genes, and Anin was Anunnaki, so the similarity perceived by Cecilia might just be about that. But if he was responsible or driven to protect her too, then contacting him directly was a priority. From what Susie had told him about the other races in her species, his chances of success in protecting Cecilia from them were slim to none.

But how would he be able to do that? Contact Anin? He wondered if Susie's people might be able to let him use some sort of communication device. He was about to speak but noticed that Susie had pulled her heavy handbag up to her lap and was nervously playing with the strap.

He knew she wanted to share information about the contents with him, and all he needed to do at this point was to ask her what was in the bag. But he wanted to talk about Anin. She seemed nervous or excited yet torn.

"What's in the bag?"

"I'm glad you asked. You see, we have been wondering what the nature of the shift that Cecilia's birth indicates. But our seers are limited in many ways. They can see the significance, but not what's coming."

"I understand."

"I have personally been following the work of one of our researchers into human society and development. He came up with a theory that is not yet fully tested but has resulted in amazing insights."

She put her good hand in the bag but paused.

"Show me, what did you find?"

"Well, it's not accepted as science yet. But it's definitely a pattern. Something we can look at. This particular researcher is not accessible to me anymore, because of my status and the secrecy of my work. But I followed his methodology and think I have a pretty good idea of what's coming."

Francisco nodded to encourage her to continue, regretting having asked her about the bag before talking about Anin. This sounded like it was going to be a long conversation and he didn't want to interrupt her, she was getting more excited about her discovery by the second. Her lips were so pretty and red. He loved the way she would lick them every few minutes while talking, making them shine in the sunlight.

"… are you listening to me?"

Francisco was startled and stopped staring at her lips.

Susie sighed deeply.

"We can have sex later." She said, "for now, please pay attention."

Francisco felt a lump hit his throat and his face turned crimson red. He was about to make some lame excuse about not wanting to have sex with her, but Susie put her finger against his lips to stop him talking for the second time this morning and asked him if he was ready to listen now.

"Yes."

"Like I said," she began again, taking a long pause between the words and the next sentence, "it appears that humans project outwardly in art, music, stories, words, focus of attention and dialogue what is coming up for them at a local and global scale."

She paused again, looking into his eyes for any sign of comprehension.

"I don't understand."

She frowned. Her eyes pensive.

"Let me put it another way. Humans are still connected to each other at a thought level. Almost like, what one person discovers or thinks about, every other human subconsciously then knows too. And the same thoughts will come up for other people who have an interest or resonate with the thoughts of the first person."

"Oh yes, I read several papers by a man called Carl Gustav Jung that presented something called the collective unconscious as a theory. It's when members of the same species are connected and have the same unconscious structures, beliefs or intuitive knowing."

"Yes, something like that. Only, more dynamic. It's not just about written in stone core beliefs, or structures such as archetypes or instincts. It's fluid and active not at an unconscious level, but more of a subconscious and then conscious level. It is more the reason behind why several people around the world will invent the same machine at the same time. Or be working on a new and original chemical or mathematical formula at the same time, without knowing that the others are also doing it."

"Yes, I've heard about that. Scientists and engineers fighting over who invented what first."

"Yes. That's it. Well, the new speculative theory from our researcher, is that not only can species' collectives express new ideas and concepts spontaneously in their environment through different individuals within the species who never met each other or had any physical communication with each other, but that some collectives can also see into the future and express the future in social forms of communication, cultures, and expressions. And he thinks humans are definitely doing this."

"Are you saying that us humans as a species can predict what's coming?"

"Right! Yes. As a species, humans can subconsciously predict what is coming their way. The way it starts showing up at a semi-conscious level is through art, books, magazines, newspapers, TV shows, even graffiti. In other words, anything that is designed and created to be seen by multiple individuals, can have traces of the future."

"That's radical."

"The data is still being gathered. It's easier now with mass media and other forms of less localized mass communication within the human species. They are easier to analyze for points of reference."

She pulled a large stack of magazines and newspapers out of her handbag and placed them on his lap. He opened the one on top and spotted word chains circled in blue ink. He opened the next one and found the same. A quick flick through the rest of the pile showed words marked and images highlighted. But he could not make sense of the link between the words. To him they looked random and not connected in any meaningful way.

"These are just a sample from the past six months. At first, I could not see any correlation between them, the words or pictures. But then realized it's not the stories that are being talked about, but the word chains within them and the emotions that they might generate. I noticed that the same word links are being used on television and radio now too. They depict expressions of something big. These are all local publications, so I'm not sure if the patterns are worldwide or just localized."

Francisco focused on the words. There were several strings that gave him a funny feeling. Nothing he could put his finger on, but definitely making him queasy.

"Have you figured out what they mean? What humans are predicting right now?"

"From my analysis, it feels to me that they are expressing a shift in awareness. A giant leap in evolutionary consciousness. A huge step away from animalistic or survival patterns and into a type of fully aware, conscious and creative ... God type existence. It's almost like humans will become independent from time and space restrictions. Independent from physical and mental limitations."

"What does this mean, and what does it have to do with keeping Cecilia safe?"

Susie grabbed the large stack from his lap and started packing it back into her handbag.

"I honestly don't know. I just know it's connected somehow. Not so much on how to keep her safe, but more to do with what it means, why she's here. I suspect that humans don't just express the future in words, art and artifacts, but that they also then spontaneously start giving birth to individuals who will bring it about. Unfortunately, I don't have access to the pioneer of this research to see if he too has seen this as a possibility."

Francisco thought about this for a while, then turned and asked her, "have you ever considered that you, as an individual, will spot words and interpret them according to your personal beliefs and interests? That a different person analyzing the same texts and imagery, would come up with a completely different result because their personal interests at the time didn't correspond to yours? Didn't have Cecilia in their life?"

"Yes, I have. That is why I concentrated on something else. I concentrated on counting words and word strings. Rather than give them any type of meaning, I simply marked the most used words and word strings. But yes, you are right. What those word strings mean, is ultimately open to interpretation. Which is why I want a second set of eyes on my findings. I wanted to see if you see a different message. We are after all very different."

"But we both have Cecilia as our charge and she's our priority right now."

"I know that, but we are from different cultures and even the way in which we put thoughts together is different."

He nodded.

"I have compiled a list of the words and word strings, the top twenty, which are coming up in written form and spoken on the radio and television. I have also compiled the top twenty images. Images are slightly harder to classify as they are open to interpretation way more than words are."

He looked at his watch, it was after six in the morning. The kids would be waking up soon and he had to get them fed before school.

"I'll come with." She said, watching him closely.

"About earlier," he started.

"Yes, I know I broke social taboo talking to you about sex like that. I know that you feel attracted to me in that manner and forgot that you haven't been around the bohemian lifestyle this city is famous for and that you have lived in a religious monastery your entire life. And yes, we should talk about it. We should sit down and discuss what to do about this attraction between us."

Francisco tried not to choke and to formulate an articulate response that included the fact that she had admitted she was attracted to him too.

He nodded. Jumped off the rock and held his hand out for her. He knew that she was not a delicate woman, not even human, that she was stronger than most people on the planet. But he couldn't help himself. She smiled and allowed him to help her off the rock. He took her heavy handbag from her good arm, put it over his shoulder and they made their way down toward the house.

Cecilia was already in the kitchen playing with her toys on the floor when they got to the house. She smiled and ran to Susie, who picked her up and sat with her at the kitchen table. Cecilia looked into Susie's eyes intently.

"I can't hear you darling. You have to use your voice words."

"You look so pretty today Susie." The little girl said and stroked Susie's face with her sticky hands.

"Thank you so much! That's really nice of you to say. And you are such a pretty little human, I could hug you all day long."

"OK."

They both giggled.

Francisco took out some eggs, flour and milk and started preparing pancakes. On the stove he started cooking some porridge oats for the adults, who had decided the previous night that they were now vegetarians and put some milk on for the kids.

Susie handed him some herbal drops, with instructions to put it in Maria's food three times a day. It would cure her of the anemia and strengthen her body.

It wasn't long before Maria arrived, fresh and showered, and Roberto at her heels still half asleep. Maria looked pointedly at Susie and then Francisco, rolled her eyes and sat down on the opposite side of the table. Roberto, oblivious to the people in the kitchen, opened the fridge, looked inside, closed it and stood a while before asking what was for breakfast.

Ten minutes later, with the kids and Susie happily talking and eating, Francisco sat and joined them. He felt the world was perfect.

The older kids finished up and left for school. Before leaving, Maria told Francisco his sandwiches were the best school currency she'd ever had. The kids would fight over them, and she could get just about anything she wanted from them in return. Francisco wasn't sure how to respond.

"Francisco, Anin says he will help you. He's on our planet now."

The words, in his mind, took him by surprise.

"Can you talk to him at any time Cecilia?"

"Yes. He said he will be here soon."

"Can you talk to him now?"

Cecilia looked up in thought, "well, I think we should wait a little bit because he lost one of my fairies and he's looking for her."

"He lost one of your fairies?" Francisco wondered if Cecilia had indeed gotten in touch with an Anunnaki official or was maybe daydreaming of fairies.

"Yes. He lost one of my fairies and I don't know which one. I hope it's not the pink one."

Francisco took Cecilia by the hand and looked into her eyes.

"OK, I need you to concentrate now. The man Anin, is he real?"

"Yes. He landed on Earth now and is going to come looking for us. But he is busy trying to get into a secret cave right now. He said that after he sorts this out we can all go to the fairy ship and visit with him."

"Can you show me what these fairies look like?"

In his inner eye, he saw several individuals with elongated skulls and very ornate clothing. He remembered The Hat, it had the same type of elaborate adornments as the clothes worn by these people. They were Anunnaki.

Francisco nodded, stroked Cecilia's hair and said, "that's ok. He'll find your fairy I'm sure. We'll check with him in a few hours."

Susie watched them as the silent conversation concluded. Francisco relayed the information and then, for just a split second, was unsure about whether he should be telling Susie anything at all.

For a split second he was unsure if Susie was an ally or an enemy.

"Do you know where he landed?" Francisco asked Susie.

"Yes, we have all their bases mapped. He landed at one of their abandoned bases under the Antarctic plateau. Although my people do have the technology to get us there, I don't think arriving in one of our ships is a good idea. The Anunnaki don't have good relations with the Rumni." She paused as though there was more, then looked down and said, "plus my orders are still to keep Cecilia here with her family for as long as possible."

"What about that Rumni ship that landed the day after I got the message from Anin? I guess my question is, is it unusual that they would have landed here on Earth, and do you know or have any idea of why they came?"

Susie got up and started clearing the table. Every now and then she would look at him, and he wondered if she was maybe thinking the same as he was, that perhaps they were not allies.

"My people don't have any contact with other Rumni races, but when a ship officially lands here, we can intercept their communications and find out what they are up to. This one was completely cloaked and came in silently. They landed in a natural lake in the Northern hemisphere, at which point we lost them. The ship belongs to a private Rumni organization that works for profit. Bounty hunters, contraband shipping and paid warriors mostly. It was a war ship."

Francisco heard footsteps coming toward them, and Cecilia jumped off her stool and ran out of the kitchen. Her mother was awake.

"Allison is awake. I think you should stay, pretend to be my girlfriend so that your presence in the house is not questioned? I think that the moment in time to move Cecilia out has arrived, Susie. I can understand her staying here for the past three years, but with the arrival of the Anunnaki, who are looking for her and can protect her, the Rumni ship having landed a week ago whose intentions we don't know, and my own Brotherhood who are aligned with the military and are looking for her, I'm pretty sure we need to move her. For now, though, just be cool."

He grabbed her good arm and pulled her gently toward him. Then kissed her lips.

Startled she looked up at him, unsure. The thought that perhaps she had never been kissed before flashed before his eyes. He kissed her again, feeling her body relax into his arms and with a smile she returned his kiss. His heart felt like it exploded into a billion pieces of light.

Allison walked in carrying Cecilia on her hip. She looked sleepy and groggy from another late night, paused temporarily then cleared her throat. Francisco and Susie acted surprised and turned to greet her. He introduced Susie, and then served Allison a bowl of porridge with a side of fresh fruits and vegetables.

Allison frowned at the colorful breakfast, then sighed when she obviously remembered she was now a vegetarian.

Chapter Thirteen

Anin was studying the list of experts that 223 had requested for the job of repairing and reestablishing connection with the quarantine area.

The thought that some extra random specialists may have been chosen by the AI to stop any type of conclusions on what the area contained was also a possibility. This was proving to be a very challenging situation for him.

The plan of quietly entering the planet with a small crew, grabbing the child and taking off was no longer in the line of probabilities. Their silence and disappearance from the general communications and diplomatic noise which plagued the universe was bound to have been detected by now. Soon, any day now, a military ship would come to their "rescue". He needed to figure out what was going on and avert any unwanted attention to his presence on Earth.

As if not enough, 223 had now decided it was the perfect moment for independent identity creation. It had decided on a gender, in this case male, and taken Anin's voice as his audio expression. Its communication to the crew and staff had caused endless confusion as Anin's voice was now delivering questions and commands, but without his personal signature.

He had spent hours answering calls asking him if it had been him sending a particular order or request. He had spent hours telling everyone that if it didn't have his personal signature, it was not him.

Now he was seven crew members short. The doctor in the team which was now repairing the quarantined area was one of the Queen Returned guards. A woman by the name of Berit. Dr. Berit. She was a highly regarded medical doctor. One of three in the entire ship's crew in case there were casualties while retrieving The Queen Returned. He should have looked at the list of specialists that the AI had requested before consenting to their assignment and asked why a doctor was necessary. He wondered if there were injured people, sick people, or people in medical stasis in there. Berit was definitely a physical doctor and dealt only with people. So, any other type of explanation was out of the question.

He put the file down and let his mind process everything he had read in the past few hours.

He looked at the doctor's information again and ran comparisons with the other medical specialists in the crew. There was a reason why 223 had chosen her above the others. He just had to find it.

"Sir?"

Anin looked up to see a young uniformed officer standing by his desk. He hadn't heard him come in.

"I apologize for the intrusion Sir, but you didn't respond to my calls."

Oh yes, Anin had finally decided to switch off all communication channels in his room so he could think in peace. It hadn't worked obviously.

"Sir, there is a situation in the mess hall that I think you should come and see."

"What kind of situation are we talking about officer?"

"It's... well, I don't actually know Sir. It appears to be a kind of religious apparition of some sort. I have very recently become Complete Sir and do not understand all that is happening yet. Several of the crew have become incapacitated by the apparition. They are kneeling before it in a state of Source Bliss. The rest of us have a strong compulsion to salute. By all accounts Sir, this would be The Queen Returned, only... well... it's the image of a lowly human child."

"Can you be more specific about the appearance of the apparition?"

"A young human female Sir. I am an expert in military and security matters Sir, Races are not my specialty, but I would venture to say that she is definitely human."

"And you say it is an apparition, what has brought you to this conclusion?"

"She looks slightly transparent and does not appear to have a full solid form. It is like a transparent holographic projection, but there are no projectors in the mess hall sir. The AI does not appear to detect the apparition or in any way be able to communicate with it."

Anin leaned back and sighed.

"How is the AI responding to the situation?"

"He thinks it's a mass illusion and is running brain scans and medical diagnostics."

Anin hoped against hope that the AI would not correlate the kneeling position to the visual data on The Return. Sometimes a bit of hope could take a person a long way before having to deal with something directly. He stood up, put on his headdress and followed the officer to the mess hall.

As he entered the room, Cecilia who was standing on one of the tables looked at him and smiled broadly, he sent her a message to be as quiet as she could until he could talk to her and she nodded.

There was a dozen or so crew and officers kneeling down before Cecilia's apparition, and a handful trying to get them to stand up, in salute positions, or in other states of worry and concern. As they became aware of his presence, the second group began to stand to attention.

"Anin, we seem to have a problem. I saw this behavior when you first entered the base and thought it was a new form of reverence for environmental beauty, or perhaps what Anunnaki now do when they first enter a planet."

"At ease 223, this is an exercise in loyalty and discernment. You may disengage any emergency protocols and remove yourself from the mess hall."

"But Anin…"

"223, you are still a loyal servant of the Empire, obey your direct order."

"… well, technically, I"

"223, if you question my authority I will be forced to remove you from office and confine you to your quarters. Understood?"

Silence.

"223, acknowledge orders heard and complied."

"Yes Sir. Understood."

Amazing. Anin thought. Even sentient AIs were subject to role, meaning and acceptance. There was absolutely no way he could enforce the AI to his quarters but treating him like any other crew was something that obviously enforced his sense of self.

The room changed color, establishing that there was no central system on line there, in this case the AI.

Anin faced the crew.

"This here," he said dramatically and slowly moving his arms and hands, palms up, pointing to the apparition, "is what we know as The Queen Returned. What you are experiencing is indeed what is known as Source Bliss."

A strong mental murmur crossed the room.

"You may be wondering why the image of a lowly human would create a state of Source Bliss in yourselves and your fellow officers and crew."

A few members of the crew nodded.

"Well, although she may appear to be physically a lowly human child, she is indeed Our Queen Returned, something our higher senses can perceive and respond to correctly. Her physical form is fluid and it will make it much easier to protect her if those who would rather remove her from existence do not see her true form.

You are the chosen few who are privileged to this top secret information."

A wave of relief and also importance and meaning travelled the room.

"You are part of an elite group of individuals who have been handpicked to collect and transport our New Queen to a safe location within the Empire. As you know, politics within the Empire dictate that the new Monarch be protected until such a time that she can no longer be assassinated or otherwise eliminated from claiming her crown. We are to stay loyal only to the Queen Returned. In her infinite wisdom, she will make everything possible to make our job easier, including taking up the form of a lowly human child."

He read the room, it was going well.

"You were chosen for your loyalty to the Empire and your capacity to stay true to your career. No one may speak of this incident either to other crew who have not witnessed it, or anyone else in the empire. You may, of course, plan and coordinate among yourselves with regard actions and the necessary implementation of plans once the New Queen is aboard."

"The protocol," he said, as he looked at each crew and officer in the eyes, "is to allow the Source Bliss to pass. We will take over essential roles from those around us who are not Guards, and we'll make sure that no one gets injured. After they come out of their state, you are to help them recover their senses and are not to interrupt their experience. They will have as many questions as you have. You have passed this test excellently. Carry on."

Anin then faced Cecilia and smiled. He bowed deeply and mentally asked her if she could follow him. Her ghostly figure jumped off the table and ran to him, hugging his legs. He could actually feel her physical presence against his robes. He held out his hand, which she took, and they walked out of the room.

Behind him, he heard the commotion and confusion that followed the state of Source Bliss. Those who had fallen under the deeper spell were helped to their feet and held by those who had kept their higher functions intact. No one had expected the Queen Returned to randomly appear in the middle of the mess hall in the nonphysical form of a human child.

Aware that the AI could not see Cecilia, Anin led her to his quarters and spoke to her telepathically to sit down, she seemed to be able to interact with the environment and furniture.

He wondered how she had managed to bring part of her physical form to the base. He also wondered why she had done so and why in the mess hall.

"I wanted to play with my fairies."

Anin remembered how the Rumni Shylar had mentioned The Queen Returned was multi-dimensional. The study of dimensions was not really in any way important to the Anunnaki. Which meant it was not something he knew anything about or had any skill in. In fact, most people felt that dimensions were a figment of an overactive imagination. He wondered now whether this partial body that Cecilia appeared to be, was an expression of her multidimensionality.

Cecilia looked down at herself and took special interest in her hands, which she held out and turned this way and that.

"Oh wow, I can see through my hands and arms," she said.

"Yes, you can," said Anin realizing that the answers to his questions were not about to be delivered by the child who appeared to be just as surprised by her lack of solidity as he was puzzled by it.

"Anin?"

"Yes?"

"Why haven't you come to fetch me yet?"

"There have been some complications."

"What are complications?"

"When things don't go as we plan but get somewhat harder than expected."

Cecilia looked at him for a while, moving her head this way and that.

"I don't understand. I want you to come get me so I can play with my fairies."

"Yes, and I am trying. But something happened here, at the… fairy palace, that stopped us from being able to come and fetch you. We cannot leave here right now because the base locked us in. When we can open the doors, then we will come and fetch you right away."

"I don't like it when I'm locked in a room. It's not nice."

"That's right, it's not nice. But I am doing everything possible to open the doors and when I do, then we will fly right to where you are and bring you back with us to a safe place."

"Are we coming back here? I like it here very much." She said looking around.

"No, we will go to a really nice planet where you will be safe."

"I don't think so. I'm not leaving Earth."

Anin was taken by surprise by the strength of Cecilia's last statement.

"Well, it's best if we take you to another planet. We can keep you safe there."

"No. I'm not leaving Earth. This is where I am to stay, and you can't take me."

With these last words, Cecilia was gone.

Anin's heart was racing fast. He felt her absence at every level of his being, a huge feeling of emptiness overtook him, and he gasped to control his despair. His robes worked hard to control his emotional and physical state.

"Sir, are you OK?"

It was the AI.

"Yes, I'm fine."

"I detect huge physical stress in your body. Is it something dangerous? Something we should be concerned about?"

"No, I'm fine. It's... a memory. This can happen to us when we remember something disturbing."

The AI was silent, but its presence was all around him. Worried.

Anin's robe finally stabilized him enough for him to stand up. He stretched, breathing in deeply and releasing the air fast. An ancient method of releasing stress from the body.

"223, order some food and drinks for me? I think my stress levels are heightened due to lack of nourishment. All this work has totally destroyed my personal routine and I can see now that I have missed several meals. I will upload my dietary preferences to your databank for reference."

"Yes, I can do that. In fact, I already have everyone's dietary preferences and requirements. They were uploaded when you first arrived, and I have been busy collecting all the ingredients needed to fulfil your physical need for nourishment indefinitely."

Anin wondered about that last word, if it had been uttered by a humanoid, it would indicate that their stay at the base was probably going to be much longer than planned. But as this was an AI, the choice of word was probably more in tune with the worst case scenario than a plan to keep him and his crew here forever.

"Thank you 223. That will be all."

"Would you prefer I leave the room Anin?"

"Yes, I need some privacy to contemplate on the memories that disturbed me just now."

"Of course. I understand."

The AI monitoring lights turned off from Anin's quarters for the first time since he had arrived.

He took off his official hat, set it on its holder and sat down. He held his head in his hands, closed his eyes and felt himself cry. Tears ran down his cheeks and every now and then he felt his body breathe sharply in.

A soft, small hand touched his face. He opened his eyes and saw Cecilia's ghostly form in front of him. Her eyes large and filled with tears.

"I am sorry Anin. I didn't mean to hurt you. That was very mean of me. I don't want you to cry or be upset."

Anin felt relief instantly. He didn't know if Cecilia had healed his hurt or the fact that he hadn't lost her forever had released all the stress, fear and sadness that moments earlier had overpowered him completely.

"Cecilia, why are you here on Earth? Do you know why I am here to protect you and why I want to take you somewhere safe?"

The tiny child in front of him looked up at him and was just a child. Her tear-filled eyes wide open and confused. She put her arms out in the universal sign of wanting to be picked up. He reached over and pulled her up into his arms, her ghost like presence wrapped her arms around his neck. It reminded him of the many times his own father, the man he thought was his father, had carried him aloft when he was a small boy. Anin too would wrap his small arms around his father's neck, holding tightly as his father carried on with his duties, unaffected by the child in his arms. It didn't matter what humanoid race a child was, it appeared that they would demand to be carried no matter what the adult was doing at the time.

Anin would have smiled except that the lack of nourishment and also rest, had taken its toll, he was exhausted. He leaned forward and looked at the data display on his desk. Dr. Berit's file was open still. He scanned the file once more, and he saw the difference between her and the other doctors on the team. Her record was identical to the others except for one small unit she had studied which the others had not. It was a unit dealing with advanced suspension pods. Pods used by the Anunnaki to travel long distances in time and space.

He double checked the other doctors' records and that medical unit was indeed the only one that Dr. Berit had studied that the others had not.

Anin calculated the age of the base, the type of pod technology that would have existed when the base was built and wondered if whomever had been podded all those centuries ago would still be alive today. Chances were, they indeed were alive, or the AI would not have required a doctor to enter the quarantine area. Unless, and this was another strong possibility, the AI was planning to pod him and his crew and keep them captive indefinitely.

He breathed in deeply and out quickly, Cecilia copying him somewhere across the world, her ghostly form breathing in deeply and out quickly. He patted her head like his father had done so many times, it made him feel better. Inside his mind, a plan was emerging. A solution to his present dilemma. A way to find out what was in the quarantine area. He leaned back in his chair, held Cecilia with both arms and closed his eyes. Today was going to be a good day.

CHAPTER FOURTEEN

Roberto, Maria and Francisco sat watching Cecilia as she lay motionless on some floor pillows in Maria's room.

"We never know where she goes. But she goes somewhere. She's definitely gone." Roberto said.

"How often does this happen?"

"All the time," answered Maria.

They sat in silence for a long while.

"How long do these episodes last?"

The children looked at each other.

"From a few hours to a couple of days."

"What do your parents do about it?"

"We make sure they don't find out." Roberto stated and smiled.

Francisco was about to ask how that was even possible, but he had lived with the family long enough to know that it was not just possible for the parents not to notice their small child's absence for days, it was not surprising either.

"She's fine, she always comes back." Maria cut in.

Francisco tuned into Cecilia's frequency again, it was very faint, but it was there. He took a deep breath and quieted his mind allowing it to follow that frequency, allowing it to become the only thing in his awareness.

"Oh look, I see a tear coming out of her eye, I think she's upset." Maria said.

Francisco opened his eyes and looked at Cecilia's face. There was definitely a tear there. Quieting his mind was becoming a struggle.

He was worried. The child's physical state was typical of a person who was in a deep altered state of mind, trance, lucid dreaming or astral projection. Her heart had slowed down to be almost unperceivable, her breathing too. Her bodily functions and organs would also have slowed down to a minimum. To the untrained eye, she seemed dead.

According to Roberto and Maria, Cecilia would come back from these trances and tell of distant lands and people. Other planets sometimes. This indicated astral projection was the most viable reason for her physical state. The fact that she was crying was not a good sign.

He looked at his watch, five hours and counting. He took a deep breath again and quieted his mind. He tuned into her frequency and allowed it to take over his awareness.

"She's smiling now." Roberto said.

Francisco sighed.

"OK guys, you really need to be quiet for me to be able to find her. I mean it. Not one word or thought."

"OK," Roberto and Maria answered in unison. Their lips hadn't opened.

Francisco shook his head, closed his eyes and tuned in once again.

He followed her energy line and was brought instantly back, he was about to tell the kids to be quiet again but realized that they hadn't said or thought a word this time. Something was distracting him, but it wasn't the kids.

His body tensed.

There was a mind field just on the edge of his awareness. A field that he knew.

The hairs on the back of his neck stood on end.

It was Master Lo.

The kids felt the change in his demeanor and jumped up onto their feet in unison.

"I feel it," said Maria.

"Yes, me too." Added Roberto.

Francisco calmed his breathing, and held the children's hands, "listen, I was hoping this wasn't going to happen, but the fact is that the organization I used to work for has found me. Has found Cecilia. We need to go and go now."

"We've got it covered. Don't worry about a thing Francisco," Maria said, "Roberto, code Penny, hurry!"

Roberto ran out of the room.

Maria then turned to Francisco, "ok, this is much easier now that you are here. You have to get Cecilia in your truck, get your stuff and as much food and water as will fit in the truck. When mommy and daddy come to talk to you, this is a two week school camping trip scheduled for months now and they were told about it multiple times. And you are a parent volunteer. Got that? You have to pretend they knew about this trip, we planted the school camping trip in their minds every other week just in case."

Francisco wondered what would drive children to plan an escape from their home.

"Well, we've lived with Cecilia for all her life and we know some things. She's told us some things that convinced us we may have to escape at some point. But now just play your part and we will be out of here within half hour."

"Why not take your parents? Or ask them for help?"

"They'll be just fine. They are not after our parents, only Cecilia... and maybe us, I don't know. Probably not us but we have to be there for her, hide her."

"I totally understand. I wouldn't take your parents either."

They both laughed.

Francisco picked Cecilia's limp body from the pillows on the floor and carried her to the truck. Then went to the kitchen to pack food, water and other supplies. How much to take? He doubted Eduardo and Allison would check the truck, but he couldn't take the risk. He would pack for a week and then they would figure something out.

It wasn't long before their father Eduardo came out to the truck carrying some suitcases. Francisco was on top of the truck strapping the water tanks firmly next to the fuel tanks. He wasn't going to run out of water or fuel this time. He grabbed the suitcases and tied those to the front of the roof rack.

"So, you are cool with this right? I would go and all, volunteer but I have work, can't just drop everything and go, you know?"

"Yeah, it's totally cool dude." Francisco said and jumped down next to Eduardo.

Eduardo patted Francisco on the back, "thanks. This means a lot to me."

"OK, we are ready in here, are you packed?" came the strong and loud question from Maria's mind.

"Yes, all packed and ready to go."

He watched as Maria and Roberto left the house carrying backpacks, hugging their parents at the door and laughing and playing as they ran to the truck.

Allison ran behind them, "are you sure it's ok for Cecilia to go too?"

"Yes... I checked with the school and all the other volunteer parents who have younger children are bringing them too. She will have a great time."

Allison looked through the window at her sleeping child. She reached for the door, but Roberto beat her to it and jumped in, followed closely by Maria.

"Quiet now kids, your sister is taking her afternoon nap and we don't want to wake her. It's a long ride and it's best she sleeps for as long as possible." Francisco said out loud.

"OK," whispered Maria and Roberto in unison.

Allison reached in and kissed each of her children in turn, being very gentle not to wake Cecilia up, and quietly closed the truck door.

Their father blew them kisses and a heart salute, to which the kids responded in kind.

Francisco climbed in the driver's seat and started the engine, he looked in the mirror, the kids nodded, waved at the parents and set off.

As he turned the corner at the top of the road, Maria climbed on the front passenger seat and opened a map.

"OK, we need to go North, there's a road there that takes us into the mountains."

He looked over at the map and saw it was clearly marked.

"Where are we going exactly?"

"We are going to our grandma's house in the country. She doesn't have a phone and there are no other houses for miles around."

"Good plan. But first we need to make a stop."

"Oh, don't tell me. Susie, I assume." Maria rolled her eyes.

"Yes, she's an ally. And she has resources we don't have. Only thing is, I don't' know where she lives."

Roberto leaned over and pointed ahead.

There, on the side of the road, was Susie sitting on a suitcase.

"Why does this not surprise me?" Maria asked. "Move over dork," she told her brother and climbed to the back seat again.

Francisco stopped the truck, got out, grabbed the suitcase and climbed on the roof. After securing it to the water tanks and other luggage, he climbed back down as Susie climbed onto the passenger seat.

"How…" Maria started formulating a question that no one had asked.

Susie looked behind at the kids and addressed Maria, "I'm part of a special forces agency that has been looking after your sister and you two for the past three years. We have your house under surveillance and nothing happens there that we don't know about. I'm here to protect you."

"Wait… so you and him, you are not an item then?"

Francisco said, "yes we are." At the same time Susie said, "no."

Maria and Roberto looked at each other and this time they both rolled their eyes.

Susie looked at Francisco and said, "well, we are both here to protect you. And we are pretending to be a couple so that we can blend in."

"Yes, of course, we are pretending." Francisco added, his heart tearing apart as the words left his lips.

"Well, maybe you are pretending Susie, but Francisco is not. And you just hurt his feelings."

That was Maria. "And take the next right."

"Oh shit, I did?"

"It's OK. I'm OK, don't worry about it, Maria." Francisco told Maria in his mind, as he turned right on the next junction.

"No, it's not ok, and why can't I hear her thoughts? That's just so freaky." She responded.

"She had her mind altered as not to be accessible. That way no one can tell what she's thinking or about to do, and also she can't be manipulated or mind controlled." Francisco answered.

"And she's an alien, the one that beat the crap out of Francisco the day he arrived," added Roberto.

"You what?" Maria responded, then screamed out loud when Roberto shared an image of Susie's true form.

"What just happened?" Asked Susie.

"Holy shit, Maria, you didn't faint!" Stated Roberto, who then went on to explain what he had done. Maria screamed a few more times, then settled in her seat ashen faced.

"Yes, I'm that alien. And Maria, you are not going to faint anymore because I got you some medicine that will cure your anemia within a month. Did you bring it with you Francisco?"

"Yes, it's in the first aid box."

"Turn right again, and then take the mountain road," whispered Maria.

"So… Susie. As we are among friends, and Cecilia is out of her body, why don't you turn your body into its true form?" Roberto asked, leaning forward and smiling from ear to ear.

"No, please don't." Said Maria, her voice shaking.

"Why didn't you tell me about this?" Maria mentally asked Francisco and Roberto.

"Well, I forgot, what about you Roberto?"

"I thought it was confidential."

"You forgot? Honestly, how can you forget to share something this important? Oh wait, you have the hots for this alien, so yeah, I can see now… makes perfect SENSE!"

Francisco had no idea someone could telepathically shout and express sarcasm. Now he knew better.

"Well, technically I am part alien too, as is your little sister."

He didn't look at Maria, or hear her response, but he now knew that a person could roll their eyes telepathically too.

"So, what's the plan? Where are we going? Susie asked, oblivious to the telepathic conversation in the truck.

"Grandma's." Roberto said.

"It's a confidential secret." Maria said.

"Somewhere in the mountains I think." Francisco said.

"Will you stop sharing stuff that is not meant to be shared, guys? We kept this plan and destination a secret and need to know basis for a reason."

"But she's in the truck Maria. She's going to find out sooner or later."

"You know I am sitting right here kids. I may not be telepathic, but I do have extra sensitive hearing. Not that I need it right now."

Francisco took the mountain road and mentally frowned at the kids, who both retreated back to their seats looking embarrassed. And now he knew a person could telepathically frown.

"So, we kind of stay on this road now for about 200 kilometers." Stated Maria in a firm and authoritative voice.

"We kind of stay on this road?" Francisco asked.

"Well, yes. It turns into other roads, plus some parts of it are not technically a road yet, the map says under construction in some parts. It's OK Francisco, we have a map and we have been there lots of times."

Susie turned toward them, but instead of asking more questions about their destination she pointed at Cecilia, "you said she was out of her body Roberto. I've seen your sister in that state many times and could not find any cause for it. I know she always goes back to normal. What do you mean she is out of her body?"

Roberto smiled and explained everything they knew about his little sister's exploration of the Universe.

Four hours later, after multiple stops and wrong turns, they decided to camp out at a beautiful canyon by the road. The path down it had been well used and the truck made it without issues. Francisco pulled out tents, a camping stove and other supplies while the kids and Susie collected wood and made Cecilia comfortable on a sleeping bag.

After dinner was finished, the tents erected and kids finally in their sleeping bags, Susie took off without a word, and Francisco took the opportunity to do some scanning in his awareness field for Master Lo. He knew Master Lo had access to military resources that could reach them in a matter of minutes. But he also became aware that Master Lo was keeping himself at a safe distance from mental Command. It was the strangest sensation. It was like the Master was very far away, but near at the same time. His signature so small, so slight that to anyone else it may have been invisible. But Francisco was not anyone else.

The strangeness of the situation gave Francisco some confidence in that it probably meant Master Lo hadn't figured out a way to bypass the mental Command orders. If so, then Master Lo was physically unable to get close to him and the kids. Suddenly, Master Lo's energy signature disappeared. He simply vanished.

Francisco spent the next hour looking for energetic traces of his old Master, but there was nothing. This made him feel good, safer. He got up and stocked up the fire for the night.

He heard footsteps, and something being dragged. He strained his eyes to see into the dark and saw Susie's familiar shape walking toward him, dragging something big and heavy behind her. As she got closer, he could see she was dragging the body of a man.

"I found this man, I brought him, so you can do your mind thing and find out who he is and what he's doing here," she said dragging the man to his feet.

It was David, the youngest of the Room Brothers. Francisco was shocked not just because David was here, but that he had not detected David getting closer. He closed his eyes and scanned again, Master Lo was still gone and he could not sense anyone else close to them.

"Friend of yours?" Asked Susie as she saw Francisco's face of recognition when he looked at the unconscious man on the ground.

"As a matter of fact, he was a very good friend of mine. Not so sure about now though, friend or foe, it's unclear. Where did you find him?"

"Someone was following us since we left the neighborhood. They kept a distance of about 10 kilometers at all times, even when we took wrong turns and turned back, which was on purpose by the way. After we stopped, his vehicle stopped too, so I ran in his direction to see if I could catch him. Caught this guy hiking towards us. He was fully armed and carrying this backpack," she said, dropping the backpack on top of the man. "I went all the way to the vehicle and there was no one else there and no smells or other signs except his. He's on his own."

Francisco took Susie's hand and said, "next time we are losing or trying to lose someone who's tracking us, let me know. Don't pretend we are getting lost ok?" He then picked up the backpack and took it to the table where he methodically emptied the contents looking at each item very thoroughly before discarding it.

Susie watched him for a few minutes, "sorry, I'm used to working alone. I will let you know next time."

He nodded.

She sat on one of the stools and started picking up each object in turn, they didn't seem very interesting until she picked up a box of darts.

"These look like tranquilizer darts, which makes the rifle he was carrying make sense as it didn't have bullets." She said handing a box back to Francisco.

He took one out and hoped she was right about them being tranquilizer darts and not poisoned darts. Although poison darts made no sense at all, bullets were much more efficient for killing people. David must have thought he could get close enough to dart them without being detected.

He put the darts to the side and continued with his meticulous search.

"Are you looking for something in particular?" She asked wondering at the amount of time and focus Francisco was spending on each item.

"Well, every item has importance, or he wouldn't be carrying it across this terrain. But also, it's what isn't in here that's interesting," Francisco said, shaking the backpack upside down to make sure it was empty. Then he took out his knife and started ripping the backpack apart.

"No radio, no tracking devices, no food or water. He didn't expect to stay long, but also he didn't expect to be seen or captured," he said holding up a strange looking device and showing it to Susie. "This here is an alien device of Anunnaki origin that allows a person to amplify their thoughts. Like a radio booster."

He put the device down and turned to his old friend who lay still on the ground. He could feel an awareness starting to return to the unconscious body.

"Shouldn't we destroy it? The thought device, that could be called a communications device, right? We should put a rock to it."

"We could. But I think we wait until David wakes up and see if the device is synchronized to him. At the moment, it's inactive. If it stays inactive when David wakes up, we ask him why he's carrying it."

The man on the ground started moaning. Francisco watched the device carefully. It finally lit up and so did Master Lo's energy signature.

"Wow. That is trippy." Francisco said, realizing how the device was being used and putting a rock to it.

David stopped moaning and lay very still.

"Hold his hands please," he said to Susie.

Francisco reached into David's mouth and pulled out a tooth, emptied something from inside of it and then put it back. He then grabbed David's feet and waited.

A few seconds later, David's body started shaking violently. Susie and Francisco held him down until the episode was over. Francisco got up, took a water canteen and brought it back.

"Here, drink this." He told his old friend and lifted his head up to help him drink some water. David struggled to open his eyes.

Francisco lay him back down and stroked his hair back. Susie was surprised at the level of tenderness Francisco was showing toward someone who was obviously an enemy.

Almost like he had read her mind, he said, "I can't help it, he's been a little brother to me since they brought him to the Brotherhood. If he's acting against us, it's through brainwashing or something. Once we tell him the full story, our side of the story, he will come around, you'll see."

"Well, I misjudged you once too, so I guess we give this guy a chance." She said and got up. "I'll keep watch. You should get some sleep, we are about 4 hours from grandma's house."

"Four hours? Are you serious? It was only three hours away when we set off and we've been driving for four hours already!"

"Hey, it's your friend's fault here, I was just making sure he didn't know where we were heading."

Francisco looked back at his old friend, "I take it you checked his clothes and boots for weapons and tracking devices, right?"

"Hmm, yeah, no. I don't normally take prisoners."

Chapter Fifteen

After a good meal and some sleep, Anin decided to see if his plan would work. Cecilia's ghostly apparition was still with him, which meant there didn't need to be any delay in carrying out the plan as it involved Cecilia in her ghostly shape.

He had asked Cecilia if it was safe for her mind to be away from her physical body while she visited with him, something that none of the huge databases at his disposal had any information about. She had shrugged and stayed.

Anin made his way through the base following a strict pattern of command and importance. The latest stop being the main doors to the quarantined area. His crew, who could still see Cecilia, were ordered to pretend she was not there. To carry on as if the ghostly human figure of their Queen Returned did not exist.

To the AI, she was invisible.

He spoke to the security detail at the door as well as the team he had put together in readiness for when the area was opened. He also addressed 223 a few times asking for updates and estimates on possible times for the quarantine to be lifted.

Apparently, there was no progress and no one from the Empire had noticed their communications silence or was looking for them. Something Anin found hard to believe.

While chatting with one of the technical experts assigned to the area, he turned to Cecilia, "OK," Anin said mentally, "remember how we practiced going through doors earlier? And how you can show me what you see?"

"Yes."

"This is the area I want you to go into. Just walk around and let me look through your eyes like we practiced. If you see your fairies, try to stay hidden from them, if they see you they will react with Bliss and we don't want that right now."

"I am very good at playing hide and go seek. They won't spot me."

"Right. OK, go ahead, let's see what's hiding behind the magical door."

Cecilia stretched out her arms at first, then stepped forward, her hands vanishing into the solid door. She looked back at Anin smiling, he nodded and smiled back. After a moment's hesitation, she stepped through the closed door.

Anin closed his eyes and allowed the perceptions to come into his mind.

The light was dim and emergency signs flashed on the walls. He told Cecilia to go ahead and go forward down the long corridor ahead of them, but she turned to the right and went through a second wall, then a third. He wondered where she was going.

"I feel them," she said, and sent him something he could only describe as family.

After her eyes got accustomed to the brightness in the new area, he saw a large circular chamber which was several stories high. In the middle of the chamber there was a large vessel which appeared to be suspended in midair. The vessel was about three times the size of the shuttle he and his crew had arrived in. Cables and other devices were attached to it from various angles. He was not familiar with the ship's model. He checked the Rumni categories to see if it was one of theirs.

Indeed, it appeared to have many Rumni features but it was not a catalogued ship. It looked and felt more organic, less sharp and military than Rumni ships. He checked the top secret lists of his own people's ships and he could see that it had many of their features too.

He quickly scanned every other race's ships and found features from multiple cultures and technologies.

"My fairies! I found them, I found my fairies!"

"You must stay hidden Cecilia, we don't know if 223 has eyes here. If your fairies see you and react to you, then we are all in trouble."

"OK."

She went on all fours and crawled closer to the ship, staying behind cover at all times. Anin moved forward slightly, unaware that he did so. Suddenly the ship lit up. A flurry of activity ensued. He heard through her ears as his crew shouted updates to each other, and whomever was inside the vessel were ordered to leave immediately.

The dots came together in his mind.

"Cecilia, can you crawl back a few meters?" He asked her, moving back himself ever so slightly as if by doing so Cecilia would do so too.

Cecilia turned around and crawled back, the lights dimmed, and the ship went back to sleep.

"It went back to sleep." Cecilia said.

"Yes, that's how it felt to me too. Can you crawl back very slowly until it wakes up again, then step back until it goes to sleep?"

Cecilia followed the instructions, Anin moving back and forth also, unaware he was doing so. It was confirmed. The ship was reacting to her presence.

"It's asking me for commands Anin. It's saying - ready for command, state your command - stuff like that. But in my head, not out loud."

"Ask it to move forward a tiny bit."

The ship moved forward, snapping off several of the cables and knocking over the devices in front of it. His crew members ran, several guards moved forward in defensive positions, pointing at the ship.

"Tell it to go to sleep for now. That you will tell it when to wake up."

The ship went back to sleep.

"OK, come back now, I need to think about this." He stepped away from the door.

"But what about my fairies?"

"We will get them out soon."

"Anin." It was 223.

"Yes 223?"

"Could you step toward the quarantine door for a moment?"

"Why?"

"I just want to test something."

Anin paused, again the dots came together in perfect unison. He mentally told Cecilia to tell the ship to wake up, and he took a step forward.

"Can you step back now please?"

Anin stepped back and told Cecilia to tell the ship to go to sleep.

"Can you step toward the door again please Anin?" 223 asked after a few seconds.

"Why do you want me to step back and forth from the door 223?" Anin asked feigning ignorance.

The truth was that making the AI think he could activate the ship was a risk. It could be interpreted by the AI like he was an enemy, or a tool. Hopefully it would mean he was allowed access to the ship.

"I am testing something, it's confidential but very important Anin, please if you would, step toward the door one more time."

Anin repeated the procedure with Cecilia, who was standing on the other side of the door now, no longer needing to be close to the ship in order to control it.

After the fourth time, Anin declared to the AI that it was enough waste of his time, mentally told Cecilia to hold his hand and proceeded to his crew's allocated command center in the station. He did his best to keep his stress and excitement under control.

This was a very risky yet amazing state of affairs. Cecilia was able to control the ship of unknown origin, and 223 was convinced Anin was the one controlling it. He was familiar with the technology of ships controlled by a specific person, through their minds and genetic material, but had never had the pleasure of seeing one. They were rare and extremely hard to come by. It was rumored that a person was trapped as part of the engine. Other rumors stated the metal itself was intelligent and able to connect directly with the mind of their designated commander.

"Cecilia, I need you to go back home, tell that ship to wake up, then go to sleep. I want to know how far you can do this from, but only do it when I give you the go ahead ok?"

"I don't want to go back, I like it here."

"But you must need water and nourishment by now. If you stay much longer you might die."

"No I won't die. I'm staying."

"Has something happened back home? Why don't you want to go back?"

The little girl scrunched her eyes and stayed silent for a while.

"Because it's time and I don't want to."

"Time for what?"

"I don't know. It's just time. I think my mommy is coming to get me." She looked up at him, "my real mommy not my for now mommy."

"Do you know who your real mommy is Cecilia?"

She shook her head no.

"Do you know why she's coming to get you?"

She shook her head no.

"I see and understand. But I need you to go back home now. I will call you very soon, and you can come back. I have a plan that will get us all out of this base, free all your fairies." Anin said the words more to himself than the little girl in front of him, who reached up to be picked up.

He picked Cecilia's ghostly figure up, hugged her and she vanished. He entered the command center, ready for his address.

To the AI, it was a general command address, letting the staff know that there was no news on their departure date, or the lifting of quarantine protocol. Inside their mind's private and confidential communication channels, they were hearing something completely different.

"Today I managed to get a glimpse of what is being kept inside the quarantined area. It is a ship the origin of which is undetermined. It appears that our AI system 223 is trying to get control of the ship, the reasons why are unknown to me. But through reasoned deduction, I would say it is to avail itself of a body with which it can then travel the universe.

I suspect that 223 is planning on leaving this base. Unable to get the ship to work, 223 needed our expertise and knowledge, and possibly genetic material, to get it to work. It is my understanding that our crew inside the quarantined area is making progress. What 223 plans to do with them, or us out here once it succeeds, is unknown to me."

A large mental murmur crossed all their minds as each person added their own thoughts to the situation. On the outside, they stood in strict attention as Ambassador Anin told them how they could use their time most effectively while they were staying at this wonderful location.

After the long speech, Anin made his way back to his quarters.

It was only a matter of time before the AI made a decision on how to use Anin's ability to move the ship. In the meantime, he had to figure out how to use each possible decision to his and his crew's advantage. He decided this was a perfect time for a nap. 223 was under strict instructions not to disturb his naps.

Inside the quarantined area, the crew had gone back to working on the ship, the excitement of the last few hours ending when they could not reproduce the ship coming online.

Dr. Berit went back deep into the vessel and continued her diagnosis of the bodies in stasis.

"223, I am uploading a genetic sample for pod X25. Confirm."

"Confirming sample received. Dr. Berit, any ideas or thoughts on what may have activated the vessel?"

"No 223, I was calibrating the pods at the time, nothing unusual in that, I've done it many times already. Does anyone else have data that could help us?"

"No, nothing."

"Do you have eyes in the ship yet?"

"No, all attempts at visual transmission have failed. Only this ancient form of radio communication works to communicate inside the vessel."

"Well, these people are stable and in no danger. There are no foreign microorganisms, no danger to the base. There is no reason to keep the quarantine in place. We are all safe."

"I don't feel comfortable opening the quarantine until we know what activated the ship. Once we have full control of the ship, we will lift the quarantine. It might be programmed to destroy the base, I cannot risk it destroying us."

"I understand. Well, I need to concentrate on getting the next sample, these pods don't make it easy to extract genetic material."

"But you know how to do it now, can't you do it faster?"

"Not really. I know how to do it but bypassing the security and life support systems to introduce a foreign element into the pod in order to collect a sample is very slow and time consuming. Plus, each pod has to be done separately. If there was another person here we could do it quicker, but you won't allow anyone else into this area of the ship so all you have is me."

"You are the only person qualified to work in this area of the ship."

"Yes, I know. Just don't expect it to go any faster."

"Understood."

"Now go and bother someone else and let me work."

The radio receiver in her ear went silent.

To Dr. Berit, this was an exciting discovery, probably the most important discovery of her career. These people were pure examples of their lineages, it was almost like someone at some point in the past had collected members of the original Anunnaki families and put them in stasis for future use. She moved to the next pod and started the long procedure which would allow her to collect the precious genetic material without compromising the inhabitant's status.

Behind her, one of the pods silently opened, a woman's hand reached out and pulled her powerfully and quickly by the hair into the pod with her. The pod door closed, trapping them both inside. Dr. Berit was in shock and unable to discern what was happening before losing consciousness.

The woman touched her gently on the face.

"Dr. Berit, my name is Dr. Berit" the woman said, her features morphing into the face in front of her.

The woman stepped out of the pod, reached into a storage box and pulled out a highly ornate robe. She put it against her body and watched as the robe wrapped itself around her, taking the form and shape, signs and gems belonging to that of Dr. Berit's robe.

She then reached into the pod and pulled out the primitive radio device out of Dr. Berit's ear and placing it in her own then closed the pod and calibrated it, making the occupant invisible to outsiders.

The woman then checked each of the other pods in turn, keeping some untouched and letting others end the stasis cycle.

"223." She said into the radio device.

"Yes, Dr. Berit?"

"Activate protocol R993."

"Protocol R993 activated. Your Majesty, is that you? Are you back?"

"Yes. Tell me 223, is there a full and healthy replacement crew, including a commander?"

"Your Majesty, we have a full crew. There seems to be an anomaly with the crew's highest ranking officer, an Ambassador by trade. He does not fit the genetic profile but seems to be able to activate the ship when he is within 100 feet."

"How many members of the crew will follow my leadership?"

"There are 46 crew members in this latest shuttle including the Ambassador Your Majesty. Out of these, 32 will follow your command. The rest will need to be convinced."

"What about the Ambassador? Is he part of my lineage or is he an enemy?"

"He is an anomaly Your Majesty. He will certainly follow you, but he doesn't have the markers to command your ship, yet he does."

The woman who now called herself Dr. Berit, stepped out of the sleeping ship, walked to each of the seven crew members who were working or guarding the ship, she had short and formal conversations with each. None of them detected that they were not in fact talking to Dr. Berit.

"Good choices 223."

"Thank you."

"I need to meet our possible commander. Without a commander, we are back to square one. There are only so many ships and crew we can trap before we are detected, commanders are hard to come by. Lift the internal quarantine but keep the external quarantine in place. I don't want the empire to find out about you just yet."

"Yes, Your Majesty."

Chapter Sixteen

By the time Francisco was done searching David's clothes, he had found various tracking devices, weapons and other unfamiliar items. It was clear that Master Lo and the Order knew where they were. Yet, they hadn't come to rescue David and they had not attacked them.

For the time being, he hoped that Master Lo was being cautious and not risking his mind, or the minds of his people, to get too close. This was a good thing.

He hated that he had to destroy the devices, some of which were clearly alien in nature, and thought that perhaps he would just leave them here for the Order to collect later. He already regretted having destroyed the mind amplification device. It was not just alien, it was also beautiful, and unique.

As to David, would it be safe to take him? Or should he leave him here to be found too?

He sat back and noticed dawn was arriving, his surroundings becoming more visible.

Susie was cooking something on the fire. He walked over to her and sat down.

"We need to leave here as soon as possible." She said, handing him a spoonful of food from the pot.

Francisco tasted it and nodded. It was good.

"It will keep us all sharp and aware for the next day, and we won't need any more nourishment until tonight."

"What's in it?" He asked, helping himself to a second spoonful.

"Herbs, roots and the meat of certain cactuses, mineral and other supplements, and I added some of your spices too."

"It's amazing. I didn't know you could cook." Francisco said.

"There's a lot we don't know about each other," she said, looking at the man she had dragged in.

"That's true. Hopefully when all this is over we can just, you know, spend time together and get to know each other better." He said.

"One thing I know about you is that you are honest and have a big heart." She answered, looking away.

Not the response he was looking for, but this was not the right time to be pressing for a future date. He looked down at the ground trying to think of something more appropriate to talk about when he was saved by Cecilia's voice behind him.

"Where are we?"

Cecilia was standing outside the children's tent, the daylight making her blink. She rubbed her eyes and walked towards the adults.

"Where's mommy and daddy? Why are we not home?"

Francisco wondered how much to tell her, she was so small he didn't want to upset her.

"Who is that man?" She pointed at David.

"Cecilia darling," started Susie, "we had to leave because some bad men found out where you live. We talked about this before, remember? We discussed that if some bad men came, we might have to leave?"

"Is he a bad man?"

"We are not sure," Francisco interjected before Susie could speak.

Cecilia walked to David and looked intently at him. David gasped for air and sat up straight. Both Francisco and Susie jumped toward Cecilia to take her out of harm's way.

Cecilia, who was now in Francisco's arms, looked at his eyes and said, "he smells like Fluffy Bunny. I don't like him."

Francisco remembered how she had called Master Lo "fluffy bunny" and realized that to her, at least in this instance, a smell was the leftover energy signature of a person.

He watched Susie tie David's hands behind his back and pull him to his feet.

"David." Francisco said.

"Francisco," David answered, bowing his head temporarily, as it was customary when addressing a senior Brother of the Order.

Friend of foe? Wondered Francisco.

For the first time in their lives, Francisco saw fear in his brother's eyes. He also saw David tensing his jaw, biting hard.

"I took the poison out brother. Why am I such a threat that you would rather kill yourself than face me?"

David fell onto his knees, head down, defeated.

"What's going on?" Roberto had come out of the tent and was walking towards them.

"We caught a bad guy," said Cecilia into their minds.

"Wow, he's an enemy? Did he give our position away? Are there any more enemies in the vicinity?" He responded out loud.

Susie laughed, "you will make a good warrior one day boy, yes he is, we don't know but it looks like it, and no, there are none," she said and went over to the fire, served up some food and called Roberto over to eat. She saw Maria coming out of the tent, "food's up, and yes we have a prisoner." She said to Maria and called her over.

Francisco put Cecilia back on the ground, gestured for her to stay and walked over to his old friend.

"Brother among brothers, David, why would you fear me?"

David, who seemed shaken to the core, looked up at Francisco and begged for mercy.

"He's a liar, liar, his butt's on fire." Cecilia said in his mind.

Francisco sat in front of his old friend and using Command said, "From this moment on, you will tell me the truth and truth only. All the words, and all your movements will declare truth. You will not attack me or anyone present. You will also be your true self to me at all times. Understood?"

David nodded, "understood." He stopped shaking and looked straight into Francisco's eyes.

It was Francisco's turn to shudder. In David's eyes, he saw a darkness he had never seen before. It was deep, and it was angry. Francisco thought his younger Brother must be possessed.

"Who are you and what are you doing here?" He asked.

"I am David, you know who I am. And I am here to bring you back where you will be dissected mentally, emotionally and physically until we can figure out what makes you tick."

Francisco was taken aback by the answer. Certainly not something he expected to hear.

"Brother among brothers, David, is that really you?"

"I was never your friend Francisco, but you are too dumb to figure it out. My friendship was and is a lie. I got close to you to learn what made you so different to everyone else. Master Lo's favorite son, the prodigal son, even now he struggles to keep you alive instead of blowing you to smithereens with a missile. A simple and fast solution to our problems. He thinks you are possessed by some alien creature, but I can see you are not."

Francisco was deeply hurt by David's words, unable to comprehend what could have turned his brother into this dark and vindictive individual.

Then, he remembered he had actually seen that darkness in his Brother's eyes before, it had been present for a split second during the transferring of the Hat the day the Hat had become active.

"David, are you possessed?"

David laughed, shaking his head. "This is what I love about you Francisco, no matter how clear something is, no matter how dark someone is, you always translate it to something you can understand. You will excuse any and all evil actions by making a person the victim of circumstance or entities, it's precious. No Francisco, I am not possessed. Meet the real me. I despise and envy you. One day I will take over the Order and when that day comes, I will use every resource to find and destroy you."

He felt a hand on his back, he looked behind to see Susie next to him as she watched the man in front of them. "I don't think we should take him with us or leave him behind." She stated, giving Francisco a knowing look.

Francisco saw a knife in Susie's hands.

"He's not a nice person. He's a boogeyman," Cecilia added.

David suddenly fell forward and started choking.

"Stop!" Francisco shouted at Cecilia and grabbed Susie by the arm before she jumped on David to finish the job.

"Ladies, please. I can't condone the killing of a friend… person. Give me time to think, don't kill him unless I say so OK? And Cecilia, killing is not a good thing, we don't just kill people because we don't like them, OK?"

"OK." She answered, pouting.

"Why would you tell Cecilia that killing bad people is a bad thing? He's a danger to us, he's evil and will kill you for sure at the first opportunity. And what makes you think you can give me orders?"

"That's a lot of questions. I am asking you not to kill him, not ordering you. David is… was my friend. I have to make sure he's not possessed. And, really, we don't have to kill everyone who's trying to kill us. So far, he has posed no threat to any of you, only me."

"He was carrying tranquilizer darts and a rifle, has a ton of alien technology, and he's working with your old organization to capture you and Cecilia. He has declared his hate of you and that he will kill you the first chance he gets. What part of all that makes this a threat to you only?"

Francisco knew she was right. But David hadn't directly threatened Cecilia or anyone else at any time. If David was a disturbed individual who had developed a hate for him, it didn't mean he had to die. All it meant was that he had to be put in an asylum, get treatment, maybe with the right therapy he would overcome his hate.

"Let's get out of here, we'll leave David behind, with these devices. The Order will find him soon enough." Francisco stated, not wanting to get into any arguments. "If we kill him, the Order will have the perfect excuse to use deadly force." He added, and then turned back to David.

"David, do you know where we are heading?"

"No."

"How did you find the house we were at?"

"It was a process of elimination, we sent teams North and South until your awareness was detected. We worked in a grid fashion until we were at the edge of your awareness, but not close enough for you to detect us. Turns out 10 kilometers is the closest we can get to you before you become aware of us."

"But when you moved inside the 10 kilometer radius, I should have detected you, yet I did not, how did you manage to do that?" Francisco asked, although he had already figured out the mind amplification device combined perhaps with one or more of the other devices meant Master Lo had been able to fully possess and control David's body.

"I was not occupying my body, Master Lo was, and he's hundreds of kilometers from here back at HQ."

That's what he had figured out, it was nice to get confirmation.

Francisco wondered how come he had never noticed that darkness in David's eyes before, how come there had never been anything amiss except for that split second in The Hat Room. Then his mind started filling up with small moments in their past when something didn't feel right. A smile too late in coming, a pause between words, anger behind friendly words, it was all there, their entire lives together filled with small moments of dissonance. Moments Francisco had managed to dismiss and forget because David was his brother among brothers.

He sighed deeply and walked away, Cecilia in hand. They would leave him here for the Order to find.

"Cecilia?"

Cecilia looked up at him.

"I need to speak to Fluffy Bunny, in his mind, can you help me do that?"

"I don't like Fluffy Bunny."

"I know sweetie, but I need to speak with him, can you please help me?"

Cecilia nodded and took his hand.

In front of him the scenery changed from Maria and Roberto sitting and eating next to the fire, to an office that he was very familiar with. He looked down to see his body was semitransparent. Next to him stood Cecilia, also semitransparent. Sitting at his desk, in thoughtful contemplation, was Master Lo, his eyes closed.

"Master Lo," Francisco said, in a gentle and caring manner.

Master Lo swallowed quickly, a sign of anxiety, and opened his eyes.

"Francisco," he said, "and this must be the creature."

"And you are rude. I'm not a creature, I'm a girl."

"Shhh let me speak, OK?" Francisco addressed Cecilia, who frowned and gave Master Lo the dirtiest look she could muster.

It made Master Lo smile, his defenses lowered. "You are a girl I see," he stated, "and what a scary face you have, makes me frightened."

The statement made Francisco smile, his defenses lowered too. One thing was for sure, Master Lo knew how to handle dangerously powerful children.

"What of David?" He asked Francisco.

"David lives. Did you know of his darkness?"

"Not until it was too late. I perceived it before you destroyed the device a few hours ago. If I had known about his true nature, David would not have been given the job of tracking you. In fact, he would not have stayed in the Order. I know you think I want to kill you Francisco, but that was never my intent."

Francisco wondered if the Command skill would work while in an astral body, he looked into Master Lo's eyes and willed him to be truthful.

Master Lo's demeanor changed instantly, he relaxed, and his features became robotic.

"Oh Francisco, please, I implore for you to release me. I am not your enemy, I just want to understand, and communicate with this creature safely."

"I am NOT a creature! I'm a girl!"

"Cecilia, I need you to be patient with Fluffy Bunny because bunnies don't understand things very well. But I think if we are kind and good to him, this bunny will see that you are a girl and he will understand what is happening." Francisco spoke to Cecilia telepathically, and she nodded in return.

"You definitely look and behave like a girl Cecilia, but you must be more than a girl. I will try to not call you a creature though because I can see that it upsets you." The old man said.

Cecilia nodded, her frown relaxing a little.

"Master Lo, do you know where I am heading?" Asked Francisco.

"We suspect you are heading to one of her many family holdings in the country, we also have all of the... the girl's relatives under surveillance. The neighbor woman you have struck a friendship with is an unknown factor, it is possible you may be heading to one of her friends or relatives. We could not find any information about her."

"How do you know so much about Cecilia's family and how do you know I am friends with a neighbor?"

"We have access to extensive military and civilian resources, staff and personnel. You are not trained for undercover work, so once we found your probable location, sending people into the area with a photograph had fast results. You are not hard to miss plus you didn't dump the truck, which you left parked outside the house."

Francisco thought how obvious it was to have dumped the truck and acquire a different vehicle before reaching Cecilia, but it hadn't even entered his mind before now. The thought that other individuals, strangers, would come for him, or spy on him, never crossed his mind either. Anyone from the Order who got close to him was easy to detect. He did suspect that military resources would be used, but he felt those would be easy to detect too, somehow. The military are hard to miss.

"What did you plan to do with us Master Lo, before I detected you?"

"Our plans are undecided. I would like to study you and the girl. I want to understand what and who she is. Find out what her genetics are, and what she is capable of, but in a safe and controlled environment. We planned to observe from a distance, until we learned how she functions, how you function."

"If your plan was to observe and study, why did David carry tranquilizer darts?"

"Those were in case of an emergency. In case you or the girl attacked someone. He was not to use them otherwise. Although now I suspect his plans were to use them at the first chance he got, and then maybe kill you."

"And what was your plan after you observed from a distance and learned everything that could be learned from afar?"

"We planned to capture you and separate you. We planned on keeping you and the girl in a comatose state until we could figure out a way to control you both. We also need to get a sample of her genetic material and study her brain functions."

"You planned on turning us into lab rats."

"Yes."

"Tell me Master Lo, what do you plan to do about us now?"

"Once you release me, I will order a missile be sent to your location, you and the girl are too dangerous to keep alive. Hopefully we will be able to recover some of the genetic material from the blast and be able to study her in greater depth."

Francisco nodded, he could feel Cecilia's hand tightening her grip. She looked up at him, her eyes filled with tears, and her lips trembling. She let him know she wanted to leave. It wasn't surprising, she was only three years old and this man had threatened to kill them both.

"He's just frightened Cecilia." The words felt empty to him as he remembered what David had said about him always finding an excuse for evil doing.

He kneeled down and took both of her hands into his, "listen Cecilia, we are in a bit of trouble. I cannot leave here because as soon as I do, Fluffy Bunny will do whatever he wants and will probably send a missile to where we are. So, I have to stay here, and I know how to do that, but I need you to do something very important, do you think you can do something important for me?"

"Yes!"

"Good. Here is what you do, you have to get us out of that area, you have to go back to where we are and get Susie, Roberto, Maria and my body out of there. Tell them what is happening and then get in the truck, don't pack just go. Tell Susie to let David go too, OK? And tell David to run away fast."

"I want to see my mommy."

"Yes, I know sweetie, I know you want your mommy. And we can go back to mommy after we are safely out of the area. Once you are far away you come back here for me OK? And make sure you let Susie, Maria and Roberto know that you cannot go to Grandma's house. That you cannot go to any relative's houses, or any land that your family owns. Do you think you can remember all that?"

Cecilia nodded.

"OK, now off you go."

Susie and the kids were out of the canyon within a few minutes. Francisco's body lay still on the back seat, his astral self back at HQ. Cecilia held his hand, he opened his eyes and smiled at her, "well done Cecilia, you did good." He said looking around to see they were speeding away from the area.

She smiled back, "I have to tell Anin about my mommy," she said.

Chapter Seventeen

"Anin, Anin, wake up, she's coming!"

"Who's coming?" Anin asked the ghostly shape of the Queen Returned, who stood by his bed.

"My real mommy. She's coming and I'm afraid of her. I'm going to go now because we are escaping the bad men who want to kill us."

With that, Cecilia was gone again. Anin became worried. Bad men coming to kill her meant they had run out of time. He needed to get his ship and crew out of this base and he needed to get them out fast.

It wasn't long before 223's voice said, "Anin, you are awake, I have excellent news. The crew have declared the sealed area safe of all contaminants and therefore I can lift the quarantine."

Anin acted surprised. It was obvious 223 had to find a way to get him near the ship. This was one of the possible scenarios that he had worked out a plan for. He had also planned the event of Cecilia being absent.

"Oh, that is good news 223. I guess we can now continue with our work on this planet."

"Well about that, Anin, the base is still under quarantine until certain protocols have been followed. For now, though, you and the rest of the crew can see and use the previously sealed area. Would you like to go there now?"

"I think breakfast is in order first 223."

"Yes, of course…" there was a moment of silence, "Dr. Berit wants to speak with you, she is very insistent."

Dr. Berit, yes, one of the Queen Returned Guards. She was not Complete as far as he knew, but he was very interested to hear what she had to say.

"She can have breakfast with me, let her know to meet at my dining room in an hour."

Silence.

"She would really like to see you right away Anin, her news is of an urgent nature."

"Well, that's just not going to happen 223. Get my breakfast ready."

Silence.

"Your breakfast will be ready and served in one hour, and Dr. Berit will meet you at your dining room."

"Good."

That silence before 223 answered, it was slightly too long for a genuine response. It felt like 223 was conferring with someone of authority before speaking. Dr. Berit's rank was too low for her desires and insistence to reach him through any computer system, let alone a sentient system.

The joys of being an Ambassador included the capacity to read communication and detecting when someone else was calling the shots rather than the person he was speaking with. Someone had taken command of 223, and it appeared to be Dr. Berit. Something which made no sense whatsoever.

At breakfast, it took Anin less than thirty seconds to know he was not in fact greeting Dr. Berit. There were subtle signs that gave it away. The way she held her body, the certainty and relaxed way in which she held her gaze, the manner in which she walked into his dining room. Small, hardly perceivable mannerisms. In fact, in front of him there stood a very high ranking individual. The only way this made sense to him was if this woman's body in front of him was being controlled by a different mind.

He took the decision to play along with the deception. She was presenting herself as Dr. Berit, so Dr. Berit she was.

"Dr. Berit, please sit, join me." He said pointing at the chair on the other side of the table from him.

There it was again, a slight hesitation at the lack of decorum displayed when addressing someone of her true rank. She then bowed slightly, as a person of Dr. Berit's rank should do in front of him and sat down. She was wearing her headdress, he was not.

"Before we get on with business," Anin said, "please relax, be yourself, eat."

The woman in front of him nodded slightly and took off her headdress, setting it to the left. Indeed, her mannerisms were forced and artificial.

"Thank you for agreeing to meet with me Ambassador," she said and cocked her head to the side ever so slightly.

He leaned forward, fascinated. An Anunnaki sat in front of him, but that movement, the way she had held her head for just a fraction of a second, that was Rumni. A shapeshifter perhaps? How was that possible? He could tell that her natural movements were high ranking Anunnaki, not Rumni. But that movement was definitely reptilian. A shapeshifting reptilian would explain how she managed to look like Dr. Berit, although it could be the doctor's body being mind controlled by someone else. The Rumni definitely had the capacity to mind control and the doctor was of a low enough rank to fall prey to one of them.

"Dr. Berit." Anin stated in a sharp and formal manner. A complete contradiction to what he had said she should do, relax and be herself.

A lower ranking individual would have reached for her headdress. This woman simply looked at him, expecting him to say more.

"Ambassador," she finally responded, "I have discovered something extraordinary in the quarantine area. It is a discovery that will change how we see the universe."

"I am curious. But, unlike you Dr. Berit, I am not a scientist and new discoveries are not my main concern. But let's talk about other things, we can do our official debriefing after breakfast. Eat." He said pointing at the feast in front of her.

"Of course, I apologize." She said and proceeded to help herself according to Dr. Berit's true rank and authority.

"Dr. Berit, tell me your thoughts on our mission here on Earth."

"I have no views on it Ambassador. I am a doctor and as such I care little for missions."

"Mmhmm."

She paused, the fork halfway to her mouth, and there it was, the realization that Anin wasn't buying her act. She slowly and methodically put the fork back down, looked up at him and smiled.

"Well, I guess I underestimated you Ambassador."

Anin stood up and bowed deeply in front of this unknown player of high ranking bloodline. "Anin, of the Anunnaki Empire, Accountant Stock Problem Analyst and Resolver Ambassador to the Solar System, 110th descendant of the Great Nactarel, Third in Line to the Throne of the House of Pratanikous. At your service."

She offered her hand. Anin was to touch it against his head as a show of subordination. Which he did. It would allow his robe to take a genetic sample. Her energy signature changed, and her true rank was revealed. Normally, Bliss would overtake him, and he would kneel to her superior lineage and rank. But Anin was complete and that did not happen. Nor did he feel like pretending it did. Instead he looked into her eyes and sat back down on his chair, continuing with his breakfast.

"223, leave the room." She stated.

The lights changed, indicating the AI was no longer monitoring them in any way.

"I don't understand." She said, picking up a piece of fruit. "I can see your markers, you are my subordinate, my lineage. Why are you not responding as you should?"

"Your Highness," Anin said, "I am not certain what you have done with Dr. Berit, but I can see that you do not have her awareness or memories. If you did, you would know that we are here on a special mission, a Sacred Mission. You would also know that most of the crew is not ordinary or easily influenced."

This last bit Anin wasn't completely sure about as he had never had a chance to speak with Dr. Berit and didn't know if she had in fact become complete yet or not. Nor did he know if the Doctor knew the full nature of their mission.

"Tell me," Anin continued, "how am I to address you? Calling you Dr. Berit seems superfluous now."

The woman looked at him in what can only be described as fascination. She picked up a piece of fruit, took a bite and leaned back still looking at him. "Tell me more about your mission Ambassador."

His robe fed the genetic information it had collected into his awareness. Anin suppressed a gasp. Could it be possible? How was it possible? The name and rank that came back was the same, identical to Cecilia's. Yet, genetically they were not a match. This woman was part Rumni, part Anunnaki. Cecilia... he had not had a chance to get a sample from her yet. Could it be possible she was not human after all? Was Cecilia in fact an Anunnaki-Rumni hybrid?

The thought went through his mind, but Anin didn't want to acknowledge it. Could Cecilia be this woman's clone?

It was bad enough that The Queen Returned was human, but if she was proven to be a clone then there was nothing he could do to save her. Clones were the most despicable creatures in existence. No one would accept her as their queen. This creature in front of him would be hard to accept but at least she was original and not cloned.

He thought of his son.

"I would say, by the time you are taking to eat that bite," she said, "that your robe has given you detailed genetic information about me."

He nodded and carried on eating.

"You shock me again Ambassador. I expected some sort of reaction to my genetic makeup at least, if not my true identity and rank. Yet, you behave like nothing is amiss. Either you knew of my presence already or you are a very good example of the diplomatic profession."

"Your Highness, or should I say Your Majesty? I did not know of your presence. In fact, I did not know of your existence at all. And as far as your genetic lineage is concerned…" He paused, "I think you know as well as I do that in our society, our Empire, such individuals as yourself lose all claims to family and rank." Anin knew this was not entirely true. There was a mystical aspect to certain Royal Family members whom they called Source Carriers, something that crossed beyond genetics and even rank. Every person knew when they met a true Reign. This woman would have triggered the Bliss and submission of a very high ranking individual, but she was not a Source Carrier. Cecilia was. But how could two people both have identical lineages? Again, Anin remembered that he had received the energetic signature of Cecilia's lineage but had not had a chance to test her actual genetic makeup.

He had so far known that Cecilia was his Queen Returned, and she was more than the declaration of rank and lineage she had sent him when he saw her at the artificial satellite's observation bay several weeks past.

Their Anunnaki lineages and rank might be identical, but this woman in front of him was not his Queen.

"I think you know as well as I do, that when it comes to the Royal Family, the true and only lineage that belongs on the throne, genetics are not important." She said.

"If you are claiming to be Our Queen Returned, your Majesty, I am sorry to tell you that the title is already on someone else's shoulders."

The woman's face turned ashen.

"The Queen Returned is embodied, not claimed. She has indeed returned and will lead our people to salvation. And you, Your

Majesty, are indeed high ranking and I acknowledge your superior rank," he lowered his head for a few seconds, "but it is not high enough to forgive your Rumni lineage."

Her form shifted and morphed into a most beautiful and clearly royal Anunnaki. Her robes turned into royal attire.

Anin gasped as he observed the robe morphing, fitting her true rank. Never in his entire life had he seen anything like it. It was true that there were intelligent materials that could change shape, but robes made with those materials did not exist. After all, robes were supposed to be permanent and unchangeable forms in which to communicate information about the person who wore them. Having them be changeable was unheard of.

She stood up, her full regal form and height apparent. Her ashen face now turning an angry red. "What do you know of this? Who has claimed my title?" She demanded to know.

Anin saw that even though she was very angry, she was also very controlled. Nothing like Shylar had behaved when angry, his son's mother and the only other royal Rumni he had had personal dealings with so far in his life.

"You insult me Ambassador," she said and turned away from him.

"Your Majesty, I have been nothing but courteous to someone in your position and hybrid nature. My acceptance of genetic variations and mixing among species is broader than most. But legally, you are without rank and thus my inferior."

The woman turned back to him, sat down and regained her composure.

"Onelyet, of the Anunnaki Empire, Queen to all Anunnaki, 11th descendant of Our Lord Anu, True Regent to the Empire, Daughter of Alura of the Latka House and Nosded... Third Son of the Emperor Nord Of the Rumni."

Anin felt blood rush to his face to the realization that he was in the presence of a direct descendant of Anu, the first Anunnaki. The One True God. The Supreme Authority to all Anunnaki.

11th descendant meant this woman must be tens of thousands of years old.

She was also the granddaughter of the Rumni's most powerful Emperor ever to have lived.

"As an ambassador, you must be able to detect the sincerity of my statement of identity. I do not claim the title of Queen to all Anunnaki lightly. The title literally belongs to me."

"And, you could conceivably also claim to be Empress to all Rumni, if their genetic laws were as liberals as ours. Yet, here you are, hiding in an abandoned base, on a planet which is not fully or legally claimed by our Empire. Your ship is small, and dysfunctional. What would bring about such a fall in power and influence?"

"What do you know of my ship? Why, I should not be surprised at how much you know or how you react Ambassador Anin. You are indeed someone with capacities beyond any I have ever seen or experienced."

Anin had so many questions, but it was not a good strategy to expose how much information he had, and how much he still had to learn.

"Your ship speaks to its commander." He stated.

"My ship's commander died a very long time ago. In fact, we arrived here on this planet when it was not much more than water and ice. A few colonies had settled from different species, and of course this base was placed here by our people in the hopes of one day claiming first arrival. Our commander's last order to the ship before he passed away was to take my crew and I to the closest Anunnaki base. This is it." She said as she gestured the broadness of the base with her hands and smiled. "He didn't live long enough to transfer his command to someone else. Yet, you seem to be able to control my ship Anin, may I call you Anin?" She added.

"Yes, you may call me Anin."

"I'm not certain how or why you are able to command my ship Anin, but it is a fact and my ship needs waking up."

"What plans do you have once command of your ship is returned to you, Your Majesty?"

"I plan to travel into the Empire and claim my title. And before you say anything else, please know that I have full control of this base as well as your shuttle. Your crew can be disabled within seconds if I so command it."

"I take it you are referring to killing my crew as you did Dr. Berit?"

"I do not kill my people, Ambassador. Dr. Berit is perfectly safe and alive. No, what I am referring to is the atmospheric system in this base. Within seconds you and your entire crew can be rendered unconscious."

Anin had some doubts, his robe was the latest robe technology in existence as were the robes of his crew. Yet, her ship, 223 and her own robe were more advanced than any technology the Empire possessed. Plus, why would he try to stop her? She would provide the perfect distraction and target for the Empire to busy itself with while Anin himself took Cecilia to safety.

There was only one problem, Anin was not able to Command the Queen's ship. In order for the woman to carry out her plans, she needed Cecilia to fly the ship, not him. Even if he were to go with the Queen, Anin doubted that Cecilia would be able to fly the ship through him from a different location once they left orbit. Bringing Cecilia with them on the Queen's ship would draw attention to Cecilia and not away from her.

Anin allowed his mind to play out multiple scenarios. Even with a relatively small ship and crew, this woman had rendered his entire elite crew helpless. They were at her mercy and it didn't look like that situation was going to change any time soon. Indeed, time was of the essence, yet he was stuck here unless he made an ally of this woman. Making her an enemy was not an option.

"I am not your enemy Ambassador." She said, almost reading his mind.

He wondered if she could read minds, if so, he hadn't detected it. Cecilia could, so no reason why another Regent couldn't.

The Queen smiled. "If you are wondering whether I can read your mind Ambassador, rest assured that I cannot. I have, however, dealt with many a politician in my long life and know how your minds are designed to work. As an Ambassador, I would say that ultimate beneficial results are your goal. I don't know what your goal is, what this Sacred Mission you are on is about, but I am sure it involves leaving this base which you cannot unless I let you do so."

Anin stood up and walked to one of the windows which overlooked the large and stunningly beautiful area they had first set foot on within the base. His shuttle was there, some of his crew were visible doing whatever crews do when docked.

He turned back to the Queen and smiled. "Your Majesty." He began, "my mission is not in conflict with your goals." This statement was true for the present time. In the future, their mission and goals would indeed be in conflict, but at the moment Anin knew that both of them wanted to get off of this planet. The fact was, however, that he was not able to fly her ship. The longer this fact was delayed from being aired, the better chances Anin had of striking a mutually satisfying deal. The Queen smiled back. Anin felt privileged and happy to see her genuine smile.

He wondered at his feelings. It was normal for anyone to feel satisfied when their Regent was happy and although Anin was complete, all that meant was that he was no longer ruled by his programs. It didn't mean that his feelings, emotions and body would not react as they were originally programmed to do, although he had learned that the programs were also being dissolved and eventually they would be all gone forever. Anin looked forward to that day, for now though, her smile filled him with happiness.

The words came out of his mouth before he knew what happened, "you are so beautiful." The words stated.

Cecilia was back.

The Queen in front of him stumbled forward and fell awkwardly to one knee. Her shock visible for a split second before she entered a state of Source Bliss.

Anin felt an enormous sense of relief to see he was right, The Queen Returned was Cecilia, not this hybrid woman kneeling before him. The feelings of contempt toward the impure impostor Queen nearly overcame him, but something powerful and strong put a stop to it. His son, his own son was like this woman. A hybrid. And he loved his son.

"Anin?" The small voice asked in his mind.

"Yes Cecilia?"

"This is my mommy. Isn't she pretty?"

"Yes, she's very pretty."

CHAPTER EIGHTEEN

Francisco and Susie had studied the map at length and decided to travel South. The other option had been to go East to Argentina, but the main roads would have border patrol on them and they didn't have any identification documents to get past them. They were now on a small dirt road looking for a good place to spend the rest of the day. As they didn't have a real destination, the priority was to find places where they could stay unnoticed, unseen and undetected. The landscape was becoming lusher, which provided better cover.

Cecilia kept telling them how pretty her mommy was, which was odd. Francisco had asked her to find out how fast Anin would be able to get to them, if at all, but she kept talking about her pretty mommy. Roberto and Maria had fallen silent and were obviously having a private conversation. As far as Francisco was concerned, the older kids were definitely resourceful, so he let them have their conversation without interruption.

"Susie?" Maria suddenly asked in the sweetest voice Francisco had ever heard.

"Yes?"

"Is there any way, any way at all, to test who someone's parents really are?"

"What do you mean?"

"Say, for example, that one of us wanted to find out if we had been adopted and our parents were not really our parents. Could you find out?"

"Oh, right. Well, I would need the proper equipment but yes I could find out."

"Is there any way we can get that equipment?"

"Not at the moment," she answered looking back at the children, "what's going on? Why are you suddenly interested in parental information?"

"Oh, it's nothing. I was just wondering you know? We are so different to our parents and all. Oh look, another... ravine." Maria said pointing out of the window.

Susie looked at Francisco who shrugged his shoulders.

"They want to know if my fairy mommy is their mommy too." Cecilia said out loud.

The comment would have gone unnoticed if both Roberto and Maria hadn't hushed Cecilia at the same time.

"Your fairy mother?" Francisco asked.

"Yes," Cecilia said before Roberto covered her mouth.

"My fairy mother is so pretty, she's the prettiest person in the whole world." Her little voice sounded in all of their minds except Susie's, who was now looking at the children and asking what they were up to.

Roberto took his hand away and flopped back on his seat. Maria looked out of the window again fascinated by the latest ravine.

They stayed like that in the truck, everyone silent except for Cecilia who kept saying her mom was the prettiest of them all and when no one paid attention, she also became silent, every now and then smiling and nodding.

"Are you talking to Anin sweetie?" Francisco asked.

Cecilia looked up at him and nodded.

He pulled off the dirt road into a large wooded area, looked at Susie, who nodded in approval.

"Everyone out, we stay here until further notice, let's set up camp, kids you know what to do." Francisco said, and got out of the truck.

"Susie," he called and walked away from the truck.

Susie followed him into the trees. Once they were out of earshot he said, "I am not sure what your plan is from now on, but you stated a while back that your people wouldn't take Cecilia unless she was in danger. I think this constitutes danger don't you think? What plan did you have for when this moment arrived?"

Susie looked down at the ground and touched her injured arm.

"What's wrong?" Francisco said, tenderly touching her hand.

"I have watched over this family for three years, Francisco. But I'm not a nanny like you. I made sure they were undetected, safe, but the truth is that my main objective was to keep Cecilia safe, no one else. You on the other hand have taken everyone under your wing."

"What are you trying to say?"

She breathed in deeply.

"My orders were to take Cecilia and eliminate any traces of her existence. Remove any way they could get to her, whether physically, emotionally or… mentally."

Francisco nodded and waited for her to finish.

Susie looked at him and realized he had no idea what she was telling him. Of course, he didn't, she thought.

"Francisco, we are dealing with a world, or maybe a Universal issue here. The lives of a small family on Earth is unimportant. Only Cecilia is a priority and I was ordered to remove any paths or ways in which she can be traced. Her siblings and she are connected to each other. They speak telepathically. You are connected to her too and speak to her in your mind. Her parents may be used to control her, if they fell into the wrong hands."

She waited for him to put the dots together and figure out what she was saying. He didn't.

"So, are you saying the whole family had to be evacuated? We left her parents behind. Are they ok? Have they been captured? I should have thought of that, we should have brought them."

Susie looked into his eyes and realized there was no way he was going to understand what she was saying to him. Plus, it was now too late. The kids' parents were probably captured or dead by now, and she had let Francisco, Maria and Roberto live.

"Francisco, I was decommissioned when I got injured. They sent someone else to take my place and take Cecilia…"

She paused, looking into his eyes.

"I don't have backup or a plan anymore. We are on our own." She added.

"What happened to the person they sent to replace you?" He asked.

"Dead."

"How did he or she die?"

Susie shook her head and smiled.

"Francisco, I killed him. I kill people, that's my job."

"You are not a killer, you didn't kill me, and you didn't kill David. Why would you kill your replacement?"

"My replacement had orders to kill you. I don't know why I didn't kill you myself. Something inside me told me not to. And as far as David is concerned, I kept him alive, so you could interrogate him. And when we left we were in a hurry and the kids were there watching me. I didn't untie him. We heard explosions minutes after we left the area, so I'm pretty sure he's dead."

Francisco looked away.

The place they had stopped at was beautiful. The trees looked ancient and the sound of running water could be heard nearby. Probably a creek. Yet Francisco was not able to feel into the peace and beauty all around him. The thought that his Order Brother David had died hurt him deeply. He had specifically sent the message that David be released but arguing with Susie about why she hadn't released him was now too late.

He regretted not having removed the children's parents from danger, but it was now too late too. Hopefully they were still alive and well. If he met Master Lo again, Francisco would ask him about the parents.

He sighed deeply and squeezed Susie's hand, which was still in his. "Well, we've removed the kids out of danger, and that's' better than nothing. If your people are no longer available to us then we get help from Anin, the Anunnaki. He's still alive and in contact with Cecilia."

"Yes," Susie answered, "we removed the children. Now we keep them safe."

Francisco smiled.

Francisco had an idea. He could visit with Anin personally like they had with Master Lo, and get a plan figured out on getting Cecilia and the other children to safety.

"Are you not curious, Francisco, about what all this is about?" Susie asked, interrupting his thoughts.

"Well, sometimes I get curious about it. But to me the most important thing is to keep Cecilia safe and out of harm's way. And now I am also responsible for Maria, Roberto and your safety."

Susie nodded, "I think that if we understood what is happening here, why Cecilia is the way she is, and why she was born, we would have a better chance of keeping her and the kids safe."

"Yes, you are probably right."

"I brought the texts, the words, images and sentences that are appearing in the human media. I want to share the patterns and conclusions I have come to with you, I think you will find them useful."

Francisco had forgotten all about that conversation. But Susie was right, if they could gather any clues or information about what was happening, why Cecilia even existed, they would have a better chance of protecting her. He didn't quite understand the science, but Susie seemed very familiar with it.

"You are right. Let's look at them after supper."

First, however, they had to get settled in for the day, and possibly a few days. Susie would scout the area while Francisco and the kids covered the truck with branches and set up camp.

Roberto and Cecilia thought covering the truck was a fantastic idea and got busy collecting suitable leaves and branches to get the job done.

"It's really beautiful here," Maria said as she walked up to Susie who had gone to the stream to wash, her sling on the ground next to her.

"Yes, it's very beautiful. It's going to be sunset soon, I thought we could climb up that hill to watch it." Susie answered.

"I know what you were trying to tell Francisco. I know what you meant, Susie."

Susie looked at the young human female who looked tense and upset. She made sure her own body language was friendly and relaxed.

"You were telling him that your job was to kill my family and take Cecilia."

Susie nodded.

"So, what's to stop you doing that now?"

"I think my people were wrong about that, Maria. You and your brother are essential in keeping Cecilia safe and healthy. I don't have a way to hear you all in your minds, but I can see that you are deeply connected and part of each other, like a larger being made of individual beings. Plus, I like you both very much."

"I thought you were Cecilia's imaginary friend."

"I know."

"And when I met you, I didn't like you one bit."

"You have good instincts."

"Francisco is super innocent, he doesn't realize that some people are evil."

"That is very true."

Maria picked up the sling and looked at Susie's arm.

"You are not hurt."

"Not anymore. I heal fast."

"Why are you still wearing the sling?"

"Part of my training is to emulate a human being and a human being wouldn't heal from a broken arm in few days, so I kept the sling on."

"But we all know you are not human now, so why keep it?"

"I don't know."

Maria threw the sling in the stream, watching it sink under the water.

"That's a heavy sling, look how it sank."

"Yes."

Maria looked back at Susie, and asked, "friend or foe?"

"I am not sure yet."

Maria nodded, got up and walked back to her younger siblings and Francisco, who were busy cooking and singing camp songs by the fire.

Behind her, Susie stepped into the stream and retrieved her sling. She opened the inside pocket and took out a communications device. If she turned it on, it would give their position away to her superiors. She thought for a while, about the chances that they would help her keep all the children and Francisco alive and safe.

Francisco had managed to overpower and break her arm, which meant he was more than he appeared. Only a Rumni would be capable of doing that. Only one of her own kind and training would could do such a thing. And also, only someone who was genetically manipulated to have superior strength. When she failed to eliminate him, they had sent a replacement. She realized the replacement they had sent was not strong enough to eliminate him either, but yes strong enough to eliminate the human children and their parents if Francisco wasn't in the house to stop him. It would have been messy and ineffective. She tried to tell the replacement that and tried to tell her superiors of the faulty nature of their plan, but they didn't listen.

The chances that they would listen to her now were nil. She put the communications device on the ground, picked up a rock and smashed it.

"Friend." She said out loud.

Back at the camp, Maria smiled.

"What you smiling about?" Asked Roberto in her mind.

"Nothing that concerns you," she responded.

"You look like a cat that ate the mouse. What you up to? Tell or suffer the consequences."

"It's a woman's thing, you wouldn't understand."

"I understand plenty, come on, spill the beans, I know it's important."

She noticed Francisco staring at them, and she gave an, "everything is fine" smile. He went back to his cooking.

Roberto walked up to her and sat down.

"Not going to happen, just go away."

"Women stuff, huh? Well, there's only one woman here, and it's not you. So, it has something to do with the alien. Oh wait, does she even qualify as a woman?"

"Your reverse psychology and trigger baiting are infantile and futile, boy." She told him and smiled the best Cheshire smile in her arsenal.

Roberto was taken aback.

"The problem with you, Roberto, is that you believe that bullshit about men being superior to women. It will be your undoing."

"I don't believe that bullshit. I am superior to everyone on this stupid planet, it doesn't matter if they are men or women."

"Well, that will be your undoing then because there is no greater danger than underestimating your opponent."

"Quoting Lao Tzu to me now?"

Maria looked at her little brother and stayed silent.

"I don't know what you are keeping secret from me, but it feels important." He added.

Maria thought for a while then said, "Susie and Francisco think mom and dad are dead."

"But they are not."

"I know. But I think it's best if we let them think they are."

"Why?"

"Because, little brother, then everyone they are in touch with will think they are dead too, and no one will bother to go kill them."

"But Francisco and Susie are on our team. They wouldn't tell others about mom and dad."

"You felt that Master Lo guy, how do we know how much he picks up from Francisco? That guy might be mining Francisco for information without him knowing about it this very minute. And as to Susie, well, we don't know much about her at all."

"Shit. You are not as dumb as you look."

"And you are not as clever as you think."

"You've changed. You don't even faint now."

"Yeah, and I can think clearly too. There was like a fog in my head for the past few years and now it's lifted."

"I thought you were just becoming an adult or something."

"Adults are dumb. I will never become like one of them."

"We hope."

"Yeah, we hope."

Susie had come back to the camp area and was sitting by the fire with Cecilia on her lap. Francisco came over to Maria and Roberto and handed them some food, rubbed their heads in turn, "eat up," he said and went back to get food for Susie and Cecilia.

"I hate it when he does that." Maria said and fixed her messed up hair back down.

"He can't help it, he feels like a dad or something. I think that's what a dad feels like."

"My mommy is coming to rescue us." Cecilia broke into their conversation.

"Your fairy mommy?" Roberto asked who knew the woman was an Anunnaki, she was huge and had a long pointy head.

"Yes."

"When is she arriving?" Asked Maria, who by now was not surprised by anything her sister said.

"She doesn't know she's rescuing us yet, but she will very soon. We have to go up to that hill over there when the sun starts hiding."

Maria remembered how Susie had said they should go up that hill to watch the sunset. She doubted it was a coincidence.

"Did Susie tell you that's where your mommy is arriving?"

"No... but I gave her the instructions already. She will take us there."

"Holy crap Cecilia, is Susie under your command?"

"She's my soldier. Yes, I tell her what to do sometimes."

"But her mind is unbreachable."

"What is a mind?"

Maria felt goosebumps crawling up her arms. She turned to her brother, "you know what I said about not underestimating your opponent?"

"Yes, what about it."

"Well, I just remembered when my mind got all foggy and everything became confusing."

"When was it?"

"When Cecilia came home from the hospital."

Chapter Nineteen

His mind raced with a million possible ways in which Onelyet, of the Anunnaki Empire, Queen to all Anunnaki, 11th descendant of Our Lord Anu, True Regent to the Empire, Daughter of Alura of the Latka House and Nosded, Third Son of the Emperor Nord Of the Rumni, could have become the mother of the Queen Returned. The thought that Cecilia was part Rumni as well as human also crossed his mind but did not occupy it as much as the fact that Cecilia was a direct descendant of Anu, the first Anunnaki.

"Cecilia, you can stop hugging your mommy now, ok?"

"But I want to hug her. She's so pretty!" The little voice stated in his mind.

"Yes, she's very, very pretty. But I think she wants to get up now."

"You can get up now," he heard himself say, and the Queen fell forward onto her arms.

Her entire body language was one of shock, dismay, and incomprehension.

"What are you? What have you done to me?" She said looking up at him.

"I am me, and I gave you a hug because you are very pretty." Cecilia said through his voice.

Anin helped the Queen to her feet and walked her to his lounge, where she could rest on a more comfortable chair. It would take a while for her to regain her composure. It appeared that the higher the rank of the person, the more intensely Source Bliss affected them. It made sense to him, after all it was high ranking individuals who were the people most likely to want to harm a Sovereign.

He went to fetch a glass of water, then sat next to the Queen and waited for her robes to stabilize her. After a few minutes, her body looked relaxed and composed. She sat up and looked into his eyes.

"Who are you? What are you?"

This time Anin answered, "It was not me, Your Majesty. It was The Queen Returned speaking through me."

He handed her the water.

The Queen looked at the glass and put it to the side without drinking.

"I mean you no harm Your Majesty. This is not a trick. It is real, you know this cannot be faked or controlled."

"The fruit..." She said.

"Provided by your own AI and untouched by anyone else. I am sure the AI would have made sure of that as per protocol."

The Queen sighed deeply.

"She's going to press a button on her dress and everyone on the base will fall asleep, I think we should stop her," Cecilia said in his mind.

"Order her to listen to what I say and not attack or disable me or my crew in any way, Cecilia"

Out loud, he heard the orders spoken by his voice.

The Queen's hand returned to her side.

"I take it, Anin, that you can read my mind, or at least my body language? How else would you have known what I was about to do?"

"Not me Your Majesty. The Queen Returned is the one we cannot hide our thoughts from. She speaks to me in my mind, telepathically, she can also take control of speech at which point, her energetic signature is in the words spoken and my energetic signature is absent."

"Tell her to speak to me in my mind."

Anin knew Cecilia was listening, so he simply sent her a message to ask if she could do that. Cecilia stayed silent for a while, then said, "I want to but she's my mommy. She might be mad at me."

"Your Majesty," he said out loud, "I need to let you know that The Queen Returned is extremely young. Three Earth years is all she has lived and has little knowledge of our culture or of anything at all. When addressing her, or communicating with her, take into consideration she is but a small child."

"A small child? And of Earth Years? She was born here on this planet?"

"Where she was born is not clear at this point Your Majesty. However, she is indeed a small child. I have been in conversation with her for a few weeks now and she is much better at it than she was back then. Much better both at communicating as well as holding her energy in check. Or hugs, as she calls them. But you unnerve her Your Majesty. She's afraid you will not approve of her."

The Queen looked into Anin's eyes as though she might see the child in them. Then she smiled, and said, "child, you can speak to me directly. In my mind, like you do with the Ambassador Anin."

Anin felt the loss of emptiness, and knew Cecilia was gone.

The Queen's eyes opened wide, "oh, she wants to know what an Ambassador is."

"Well..." he began but the Queen put up her hand to silence him.

"It's fine Ambassador, I think I can explain this to the child." The Queen said, stood up and slowly walked away.

Anin felt alone. He watched the Queen leaving his quarters and hoped against hope that everything would turn out fine. Cecilia was just a child, and as such could be easily influenced, especially by someone she wanted to be approved by.

He wondered at the wisdom of allowing their direct connection, but it was too late now. What was done was done.

"Anin,"

He looked up to see the Queen standing at his door.

"Are you coming?"

He stood up, picked up his headdress and followed the Queen out of his quarters.

"When she spoke in my mind," the Queen began, "I felt whole. Like suddenly my entire life made sense."

"Yes, I felt something similar." He responded.

"Call me Onelyet, Anin."

"I am honored and fortunate to be favored in the privilege of addressing you by your unique and given name. Thank you Onelyet."

"Your acceptance of this privilege is acknowledged."

Anin hoped that accepting the privilege, and the political and personal implications of such an act of alliance, had not come too early. He hoped that this woman, this queen, truly understood the nature of their circumstance, and not just playing political games.

"Anin?" The little voice said in his head.

"Yes, Cecilia?"

"She doesn't know she's my mommy. How come she doesn't know she's my mommy? I just looked at her memories, and I am not in there. My for now mommy has me in her memories. How come my real mommy doesn't?"

"Can you show me your real mommy's public and official memories Cecilia?"

The download was instant, and complete. Anin, regretted having asked for Onelyet's memories immediately. These were not only

Onelyet's public memories, they were all her memories. It was her entire life from when she was born until a few seconds earlier.

Anin gasped. Her private memories were in his mind. Her personal time, every personal time she had ever taken. It was a violation of privacy, a violation of everything held sacred by his people. His attempts at stopping his mind mid stride made him feel as though he would choke. The first thing the Queen had asked of Cecilia was to show her his public and official memories.

"Cecilia, when your mommy asked you to show her my memories, why didn't you do it?"

"I don't know."

"Do you know what public and official means?"

"No. What is it?"

He started feeling nauseous and held on to the wall next to him. Thousands upon thousands of years of memories swimming in his awareness. He breathed in deeply and out quickly. He then created a compartment in his mind and placed all the new data in it. If he looked at the memories as data, he could deal with them much better than when he thought about the crime he had just committed. Private time, privacy, was one of the Anunnaki's most sacred possessions.

"What is wrong Anin? You look unwell." Onelyet asked him, she looked concerned.

Anin found he could not look her in the eyes. He knew this woman more intimately than anyone in the entire universe. He knew every thought she had ever thought, every action, every wish, desire, plan, goal, he knew what she was doing now, where she was going, what she thought of him. To her he was a complete stranger. Not only that, but under the guise of alliance, he had violated her entire existence. He had betrayed her at a most personal and sacred level.

"I am, not well Your Majesty. Onelyet. I…"

"What is it? How can I help? 223 send help!" She shouted as Anin collapsed in front of her.

"Do I send a robot or his crew's medical detail?" 223 responded.

"Send both, quickly!"

"Cecilia," Anin said with his last thoughts before losing consciousness, "give her my memories."

The Queen kneeled down and held his head on her lap until the medical crew and robots arrived. She then followed them to the medical center on the base. No one asked her who she was, but they all bowed deeply when they saw her.

"Cecilia, are you still there?" She said into her mind, then out loud.

"Anin has an owie in his head." She heard the little voice say in her mind.

"What gave him an owie in his head, dear?"

"I don't know, but I'm going to fix it. I can see it, inside his head is bleeding like Francisco's head was. Oh, I nearly forgot," the little voice added, and she gave the Queen Anin's memories.

The Queen felt dizzy and overwhelmed. What had she done? This was wrong, this was not something she wanted. She found a chair, she needed to compose herself.

Anin opened his eyes and pushed the medical equipment and personnel out of his way.

He looked for the Queen who was sitting across the room, her face pale and listless.

He knew it was done. She knew everything about him. She looked up at him, the pain and regret in her eyes made him look away.

Somehow the intensity of the Queen's memories and the energies attached to them, had caused physical damage to his brain. The Queen, however, seemed quite capable of holding his short life and energy without a problem. Except the regret and guilt, which he knew she was presently going through.

Cecilia had fixed the physical damage he had acquired. In order to do so, she had removed a barrier, or program, that held a limit on the amount and energy of information, data and memories held by him. His mind literally felt like it had expanded beyond his body.

He got up and walked to the Queen. Around him, his crew and her robots moved out of his way.

The emergency lights and urgency of treatment settled down. The room felt silent as everyone stepped back and watched their leader approaching a Queen of unknown origin.

She looked up into his eyes, and then closed hers.

"What have we done?" She whispered. "I cannot bear to know what I know. To have your private moments and your emotions, your thoughts and dreams in my mind. It is too much. How could you do this to me?"

"I am so sorry, I did not know how to fix this and thought that sharing my memories would mitigate my crime." He responded.

"I know that. Of course, I know that. I know everything you have ever thought. You meant no harm even though my memories harmed you. You thought because your life is so much shorter, and your rank lower, that it would not hurt me but would bring me understanding and it would make it fair. Your life is indeed so brief, so present, so full of possibility and wonder. You are but a child."

Anin moved a strand of hair from her face, then held her hands as he kneeled in front of her.

"And you knew I had already asked Cecilia for your memories." She continued, "it was my desire to have them, but I did not know it was everything. I did not know it meant private time, and emotions, dreams, wishes... I did not think she would hand me the whole entirety of your existence."

"Cecilia," Anin started to tell the Queen, and Onelyet finished the sentence for him, "thinks I'm her mother."

"You are my real mommy. I have a for now mommy too." Said the little voice in their minds.

Both Anin and Onelyet, felt, but not thought, how they had to be more careful, more aware, and more instructive when dealing with Cecilia.

"Cecilia?" It was Onelyet.

"Yes?"

"Can you hand command of my ship to me now? Can you make it so that my ship has to listen to my orders from now on?"

"I don't know." Cecilia said.

"Wait," Anin said, "Your Majesty, Onelyet, commanding your own ship is a very bad idea. You have other things to attend to in your day to day living, and you don't have the knowledge or skills of a true Ship Commander."

"Are you suggesting you become Commander of my ship?"

"Absolutely not. I too have other things to concentrate on, plus you will know with a small look at my memories that commanding a ship is nowhere in my genetic material. No, my suggestion is to make my Captain your ship's Commander, and that we leave this base together. We can carry out both our plans as allies."

The Queen stood up, Anin stayed kneeling down before her. Around him, his crew also kneeled in front of the Queen.

"Anin, I have your thoughts, plans and memories up to the moment in which they arrived, but now you will have to explain how we can be allies in our plans, when this child, who by all accounts is your charge, and I both claim the title of Queen Returned."

"Because although claiming that title was your plan, Onelyet, you now know it doesn't belong to you but to Cecilia."

He watched as the Queen thought deeply about his statement. He understood what was happening. Sometimes when a person had held on to a plan and a reality for a long time, it was hard for them to get out of the habit of making every decision based on that plan or reality. When a new reality made itself clear, and a time for new plans had come, the releasing of the old could be challenging.

"I cannot deny the effect she has had on me, or her powers." Onelyet said. "I cannot compete with that truth."

"She is also your daughter, which makes you Queen Regent until she is old enough to reign herself, which won't be for hundreds of years." He said to her.

The Queen turned and started walking away, then turned back and smiled, "come, follow me. We need to find out if this girl really is my daughter."

"Where are we going?"

"My ship."

"Cecilia," The Queen said out loud, "I want you to leave for now, and come back in a few hours. Can you do that for me?"

"Why?" Came the answer in their minds.

"Anin and I need to do a few things, grown up work, and I need you to go back to your body and wait for us ok? I will call you when we are ready."

"OK."

Anin felt Cecilia's absence and the emptiness that followed. He watched Onelyet hold her hand against her chest.

"That's…" She started saying, then stopped as a tear rolled out of her eye.

"Happens every time. I can't say you will get used to it. But at least it doesn't get worse. No, I cannot say that either. I am certain it gets worse."

"Anin, you are young, and you are naïve. You are innocent and ignorant of the ways of my family. You trust this girl unconditionally, but she has done nothing that we cannot do to our own inferiors. There is no mystical or religious meaning to her abilities Anin. She was created to have these powers and skills, and whomever created her is pulling our strings."

"But you felt the Source Bliss, you felt her embrace Onelyet, how could you doubt her claim?"

They walked down the beautiful corridors, and into the previously quarantined area. Her ship was more impressive in real life than he had perceived through Cecilia's eyes. It was a work of art. As expected, it did not awaken when Anin approached.

"I have lived hundreds of thousands of your years Anin, I have seen and survived every trick in the arsenal of the top and most powerful Anunnaki families in the Universe. The Queen Returned is a myth, it's a fantasy created to keep children entertained. She does not exist and will never exist."

Anin listened carefully, then compared the words to Onelyet's memories. Yes, she had lived through the most amazing insurgencies, mutinies and family infighting. But the truth was nothing compared to the experience of being in the awareness of The Queen Returned.

The ship was small for a Royal ship, but it was large. It took them several minutes to reach the place she was heading to. She reached up to the door and placed her hand on it. The door opened, revealing a gold lined room. A holographic guard appeared and confirmed her identity before they were allowed in. He knew what was inside, it was her ova.

High ranking female Anunnaki had half their ova removed and held in secure locations for future use. It was rare for a female to have the removed ova in their possession or to travel with it. It was normal for it to be held in their home planet, or at their family's main home. Anything else, especially travelling with it, was too great of a risk. If the ship was destroyed, and the female killed, their precious genetic material would be lost to the Empire forever.

Because now he had her memories, Anin knew why Onelyet carried part of her ova with her and knew why she would take such a risk. Her parents, siblings and she herself had been exiled from the Empire due to their racial indiscretions. The fact that they were direct descendants of Anu did not matter much at that time of conquest and political revolution.

He thought of his son.

She opened the vault and traced her hand over every crystal container within it. Picked one out and held it in front of her face.

"This one is empty." She stated and threw the crystal down, smashing it into a million pieces.

He stepped back, her rage radiating out like fire. But she contained it.

"223! Who was in my vault?"

"Your Majesty, you are the only person who has entered the vault. You are the only person who can enter the vault."

"What about a robot, entity or other being, has anything or anyone entered my vault?!"

"Only you, Your Majesty. I can give you the full access record, only you have entered the vault while the ship was docked here, and according to the records, only you accessed it before you arrived."

"Show me the records," she ordered.

It had been three times in total that she had entered the vault. Once to place the ova in it, once when she had been married and had retrieved one ovum for fertilization and design, and once to replace that ovum with a new one as the embryo had been destroyed with her home and husband during a purist attack.

Yet, the records showed a fourth visit. She had entered the vault four Earth years earlier, retrieved the ova, and replaced the crystal.

"223, do you have visuals of that last visit?"

"Yes, Your Majesty, would you like me to reproduce the event?"

"Go ahead,"

The immersive record of the event began with someone behind them approaching. The steps became louder, closer. Anin and Onelyet turned to see who it was.

A familiar figure turned the corner toward them, it was, or at least looked like, Onelyet herself.

"I don't understand," Onelyet said.

"This is not in your memories, this didn't happen." Anin stated.

"Or it was erased perhaps." She added, although the chance of that happening to someone of her position was impossible.

Anin's mind switched gears, looking at every detail of the approaching woman. She was identical to Onelyet but her robe... Her robe was different. It was of a higher rank, and it carried the crest of The House of Anu, something which she didn't carry now. She also wore the emblem of The Queen Returned.

At that precise moment, the holographic figure paused, looked down at the ground, moved toward them very slowly, stopped inches away from them and said, "Onelyet and Anin, it's me Onelyet. I cannot imagine you will understand this. At least I remember not understanding it when it happened all those years ago."

In Anin's mind, the dots were coming together. The figure turned slightly, almost looking directly at Anin.

"Yes, Anin. You do figure it out very quickly from this point." She then turned to Onelyet, "I am removing one of my ovum and will create a child who will carry a soul. This child you have not met in physical form yet, but you know her. She has already contacted you telepathically. She is my daughter and future Queen to all Anunnaki."

"Souls are a myth, they don't exist." Onelyet said to the holographic image.

"If I remember right, I used to think souls did not exist," the image interjected, "there is much I did not understand back then. It is true that our species does not know of and does not carry souls. We are whole as we are. We are physical beings of extreme superiority and evolution. And the nature of souls is... Different. Souls are not native to the physical universe."

Anin and Onelyet listened as the holographic image continued, "This child I will give a human name. She will be called Cecilia, and like Anu, she will carry a creator soul. She is the true Queen Returned, and my daughter."

"What about her father?" Onelyet asked.

"About her father, there are very few physical species that are able to carry creator souls, one of them is the human species. I will use the genetic material from a human male of Earth to create her. He was chosen for his strength and ultra dimensional abilities. Who he is, is not for you to know right now. His identity needs to be kept secret for reasons that will become apparent when you meet him."

"I don't understand, why does this hologram speak to us even though this recording is from the past? How can that be possible? How does she know we are here?" Onelyet asked.

"I got here into the past from your future. Yes, I came from your future, so I know what you are thinking and what you will say next because I remember it."

"You have broken the barrier of time? How is that possible?" Anin asked. He knew with certainty that the time barrier was unbreakable. It was impossible to travel back or forth in time except in one's mind, as memories or possible future projections or plans.

"The method is not physical. My future body is not here in your past. My mind has been able to travel through my body into the past and has been able to take my body over while it was in stasis. That is why you have no recollection of this moment Onelyet, you had not lived it yet and will not live it for many years to come."

Anin's mind started working on understanding the method and implications of travelling through time within the confines of one's physical body.

"How are you able to dislodge your mind from linear time and from your body?" He asked the solid holographic recording in front of him.

"Not from my body, only from linear time. I can travel to any point in time within my body. It is almost like moving into a memory, and suddenly the memory is in present time for me. My consciousness, my awareness then exists in that distant past, and I am able to move and function in that past using my body."

"You are saying that you are taking, or took at some point in the past, one of my ovum to create this creature Cecilia. A genetic abomination which you think will carry some mystical thing called a soul?" The present Onelyet asked.

"Yes, she is a genetic impossibility. Once I... you become Complete, the program of genetic purity will become obsolete within you. Your own sense of worthlessness will disappear, and you will be able to unite two species that have been at war for hundreds of thousands of years."

Anin listened closely at the words coming from the holographic recording. There were so many questions to be asked, he didn't know where to begin. His mind reminded him of her robe, there were differences between the holographic robe and the present robe being worn by Onelyet.

"Your robe, it's different to the one you are wearing now. It has the Crest of Anu and the Emblem of the Queen Returned as well as other signatures denoting you to be in command of all Anunnaki families. How is that possible? Your robe now does not have any of those symbols." He asked.

"As I am part Rumni, I can morph into the shape of other species. My robe was designed to change into the shape of the attire worn by those alien species when my body morphs into one of them. You saw this a few hours ago, and you can also access the nature of the technology from my memories in your mind."

Anin nodded. The fact that Onelyet's robe had changed form had filled him with curiosity and he had filed that fact under questions to ask, but now that her memories were his, he knew exactly how the robe worked and functioned.

"And you can also see, from those memories, when I am in my true form my robe will always reflect my true identity, social status and rank. My body and robe both will reflect my true self, no matter when in time I am in."

Anin looked into the details of that information in Onelyet's memories. It was true, Onelyet's true physical form, her natural shape, was Anunnaki. And indeed, when she was in her true form, her robe could not be changed by her or any other person. It would always reflect her true status, social standing and rank. There was no information about how the technology worked in her memories.

"I am not an engineer Anin, I do not know how the technology works or its history, but you can find that information within the databanks of my ship, which is also part of that same technology."

Anin reached over to touch the holographic image, just to make sure it was not a person standing in front of them. His hand went through the image as it should.

The present time Onelyet stood quietly, observing and listening to the conversation between the image and Anin. All her instincts told her she must stop this woman from taking her ovum. Yet, it had already happened in the past and there was nothing she could do now.

Anin wondered why Onelyet looked like a pure Anunnaki when in fact she was half Rumni. The information from Onelyet's memories flooded his awareness. A Rumni newborn would physically imprint to the people around him or her. It was one of the reasons why the Rumni never allowed their newborns to be exposed to other species or members of different social status within their society. Once the imprint was complete, they were able to move within society and interact with other species without restriction.

A sense of urgency gripped his thoughts. If his own son was to look like a true Anunnaki, he needed to get back to him, or at least send word to his mother to remove the newborn away from his mother at the moment of birth. Yet, Shylar had told him that his son would be of his likeness. As his mind tried to merge the conflicting information, he realized that when he'd had that conversation with Shylar her mind was confused and incapable of rational thought. She still thought he, Anin, would be bonded to her and therefore present at the birth of their child. And what of Cecilia? She looked human, yet if she was Onelyet's child she was also part Rumni. Why would Onelyet have her child imprint to a human of Earth? Surely the Queen Returned would have a better future if she looked like an Anunnaki of her true form.

He looked up to find both the holographic Onelyet and the present Onelyet looking at him. "Cecilia's role is greater than that of Queen of the Anunnaki." The past, or future, Onelyet said directly to him. Anin deducted he must have shared his thoughts and questions with the present Onelyet at some future point and smiled. This time conundrum was fascinating to him.

"How is that possible? There is no greater role than that of the Anunnaki Queen." Anin responded.

"There is a greater role than that of Sovereign to all Anunnaki. Anin. Tell me, what is the most numerous species in our Universe? Which is the species that populates the most planets we know of?"

"Human. It is the human species." He answered.

The present Onelyet cut in before he could say anything else, "but that's an inferior species. It is genetically primitive and even in planets where they have technologically advanced, their societies are without ambition. Their numbers are as irrelevant to us as the number of pebbles on a river, or grains of sand on a beach. They are primitive and without social importance. The only humans who have any sense of social and genetic ambition are those that carry Anunnaki or Rumni genes in their lineages. And those only exist here on Earth."

"The Queen Returned is expected within Anunnaki religions and mythology, and the Savior of All is expected in the Rumni religions and mythology," the future or past Onelyet began, "which is why my high-ranking families made the decision to join lineages. They felt, after much research and discussion, that the Anunnaki Queen Returned, and the Rumni Savior of All, was the same being. But, like I said, Cecilia's role is far greater than being Queen Returned to the Anunnaki. And also, greater than being Savior to the Rumni."

"Are you saying she's Queen or Savior to humans too? Why is that relevant?" Anin's question was genuine curiosity. And the answer came to him before the past or future Onelyet answered. What if a person could command and rule all humans in the Universe? What if that person had the ambition and social stature of the top Anunnaki and Rumni families and ruled them too?

There were many humanoid species in the Universe but the Anunnaki and Rumni were the most powerful. The human species was the most numerous and populated the most planets in the Universe. Other species were a drop in the ocean in comparison. A ruler who commanded the Anunnaki, Rumni and humans could transform politics, social structure and laws to completely change the path of life in the Universe.

Anin felt suddenly afraid.

The lights went on inside the ship. The holographic image disappeared and the present time Onelyet fell to her knees in reverence and Source Bliss.

Anin felt a small hand hold his. Cecilia's semitransparent form was smiling up at him.

"Don't be afraid Anin, you are my protector and I love you."

He felt Source Bliss and, even though Anin was Complete, he fell to his knees in reverence.

"You and mommy need to come fetch me now." The little girl said.

Chapter Twenty

After their meal was finished, Susie told the children about the words and patterns that happen in a group of people that show when something important is about to happen.

"What do you mean by important?" Asked Roberto.

"Something that affects that group of people. And the group can be small, like a family or village, or super big like a whole species across planets or a group of species across galaxies."

Roberto turned to his sister and said, "sounds like Jung's collective unconscious is true then. But it's not just latent memories of the species or group that populates it but also future memories."

"That sounds like a good theory, but I would say that it also includes multiple futures or could even be that the words and images that appear in art and such not so much predict but perhaps are giving form to a very large possibility and then it's shown to us and we choose whether to accept it. Like a political campaign where all the candidates tell us what they have planned for us." Maria responded.

Francisco and Susie looked at each other, surprised at the children's depth of conversation.

"Yeah, this is just a normal discourse for us at home." Maria said, reading their surprised expressions. "My parents bring all sorts of professors and doctors to their parties and insist that they talk to us as though we were adults, they think it's progressive and that it expands our minds. They are particularly interested in expanding Roberto's and Cecilia's mind as they think they are retarded."

Roberto shuffled the sheets of information that Susie had brought with her, and then threw them up in the air, they landed all round him.

"They were in a very specific order Roberto, now we will have to start from the beginning." Susie admonished.

"And that is probably why you couldn't figure this out," Roberto said, leaning down and staring at the mess on the ground.

Maria sat next to him and stared at the sheets and photos too.

Before the adults could ask anything else, Maria said, "he's using Jung's theory of synchronicity. You know, like throwing the coins or stick using the I Ching."

She looked up at the adults and realized that they probably didn't even know who Jung was, or what the I Ching was.

"Well, you see, when he threw these things up in the air, they landed in a very specific pattern. I know you don't see a pattern, all you see is chaos, but they are actually very well ordered. And their order in time shows us what the human collective is thinking about or planning to do. Or is predicting what will happen in the future." She explained.

"It looks like a random pile of papers now." Francisco said, as he too started looking at the mess on the ground.

"It cannot be random, because I threw them while I was asking about what the human collective was saying at the time," Roberto stated.

"The person, or observer, in this case Roberto and also all of us, were present when the sheets were thrown, and we added the last bit in the formula, which is the question to be looked at." Maria added.

"So, what exactly are we looking for now?"

"It's more of what pops up for you as you look at all the stuff on the ground, including the grass, dirt and rocks." Roberto said.

"And even shadows, like this long one here that looks like a pyramid." added Maria.

"It's getting late, it will be sunset in a couple of hours." Susie said, Cecilia now napping in her arms.

The kids started rhyming off words: collision, war, brilliance, exuberance, kingdom, larceny, ramifications, incredible, mother divine, flower power, birth, return, execution, Armageddon, disparity, ruins, ancient, pyramid, returns, stellar, moon…

After about ten minutes, Francisco noticed that the same words were coming up again and again. Roberto had also started to pick up some of the photographs and placing them to one side.

Then the children fell silent. Maria got up and stormed off into one of the tents.

Roberto lifted his shoulders in a sign of, "I don't know what's up with her," but Francisco could tell Roberto knew exactly what had upset his older sister. He walked over to Roberto and looked at the items separated in a different pile. Roberto had arranged them in the shape of a star.

"Our lady. Divine mother. The day of our. Alien. Immigrant. The savior is here, The birth of a new era is upon us. We are. Cousin. Not. Alone. Murder. Death. Kill her. Savior returns." Francisco read out loud.

"Sounds like religious propaganda." Francisco added after he finished reading the words and looked at the accompanying photographs and images. "What's the matter with your sister?"

"She hasn't been herself for the past three years."

"What happened the past three years?"

"Cecilia happened."

"Can you explain?"

Roberto looked at Francisco for a while. Then, breathing in deeply, he started his recollection of what happened three years earlier. "When Cecilia was brought home from the hospital, there was an incident. We were in the yard and my sister suddenly started screaming and holding her head in her hands. Everyone tried to help her, but she just screamed. A doctor or professor who came over said she was having a panic attack and they sedated her.

"That night, when everyone was asleep, she woke up and went to the nursery, and… she tried to kill Cecilia with a pillow. We all woke up and ran to the nursery. Dad grabbed Maria and threw her across the room. He breathed into the baby's mouth until she started breathing on her own again."

"Did she ever say why she did that? Did she ever try to do that again?"

"She was taken away that night, she was away for about a week. When we went to see her at the hospital mom let her hold the baby, Cecilia looked up into her eyes, and touched her cheek. Maria fainted. And she's been fainting ever since, until now. After she was released from the hospital, she was taken to a shrink for month. They said she was suffering from extreme jealousy and female competition. Up to then, she had been the only girl in the family."

"What do you think happened?"

"When Cecilia arrived home from the hospital, we were all so happy and filled with love and joy. People came from all over the neighborhood and the University to meet the baby. None of that happened when Maria or I were born."

"But?" Francisco asked.

"But it was something else. When the screaming incident happened, I heard something. I heard it in my head. It was nasty and dark, and it was filled with fear and rage. It made me afraid. It was like thousands of voices saying Cecilia was evil and must be stopped. Like she was the Devil's spawn or something."

Roberto looked at the tent, as if deciding whether to continue his story. Francisco nodded and briefly squeezed his shoulder in encouragement.

"Maria forgot about the incident. But I think she just remembered. That medicine that you have been giving her, it makes her strong, it makes her able to remember and be present without fainting. I think perhaps the voices are back."

"Can you hear the voices again?"

"No."

Francisco looked over at Susie and Cecilia and realized that Cecilia was not asleep on Susie's lap but had fallen into a deep altered state again. He walked over to her and reached to take Cecilia off Susie's arms to lay her down somewhere more comfortable. Susie shook her head and told him she had promised to take Cecilia up the hill to watch the sunset.

"She's not asleep, Susie. She's in altered state. I think she is on an astral journey again." Francisco told her.

"Yes, I know. But she said she'll be right back and I promised we could watch the sunset together."

"You better do as she says," Maria's voice came into his mind. "I doubt that she will let go of the kid and double doubt that she won't take her up the hill."

"Yeah, we better all go," added Roberto.

Francisco stood back, Susie got up and started walking toward the hill.

"What's going on kids?"

"She's under Cecilia's Command. Cecilia does this thing, she will order something, and the person can't help themselves and they have to do it." Maria said, coming out of her tent. Her eyes were filled with tears.

"That's not possible, Susie's mind is unbreachable," he answered.

"No, it isn't." Came Maria and Roberto's voices at the same time.

Maria walked right up to him and looked into Francisco's eyes.

"I am not going to try to kill my little sister." She said, "I don't know what happened that day when she was brought home, but I know it wasn't me who tried to kill her. I was possessed. It wasn't me. I love my sister."

Roberto looked down at the ground, keeping silent.

"It was not me!" Maria shouted at her brother.

"Plus, I was not the first one to try to kill her, or the last." Maria then said to Francisco.

"What do you mean?"

"I don't know. People sometimes will just attack her. Crazy people. It's happened a few times. Some guy tried to run us over once. And another time a student from the University tried to push her off the hill when we went for a hike. He slipped and fell himself."

"And that woman at the store, remember?" Roberto added.

"Yeah, this woman just lunged at her at the store. It was crazy.""Do you have the urge to harm or kill your sister now?" Francisco asked Maria.

"It comes and goes. When I think about what she might be, like an evil spawn that can control people, then I do. But when I look at her baby face and the way she tries to hug me all the time, then I don't."

"When she hugs you, you get filled with a kind of light. It feels like you went to heaven and are surrounded by angels and they are all hugging you." Roberto said.

"Yes, I felt that too," said Francisco.

"I don't let her hug me, it hurts me." Maria stated.

"You said someone tried to kill her before you, who was it and what did they do?"

"We don't talk about that." Maria said.

"Just try not to follow one of her instructions or orders, see what happens then." She added and started following Susie up the hill.

"What does she mean?" Francisco asked Roberto.

Roberto shrugged.

Francisco grabbed some water and blankets and followed closely behind. Roberto followed suit.

He could see Susie in the distance climbing slowly and methodically with Cecilia in her arms, Maria some 20 meters behind them.

He was still processing and analyzing the blast of images, information and feelings he had received from Maria.

From her memories, Francisco could tell she hadn't been possessed, or there would have been blocks of blank spaces in her mind. But he could tell that her own fear and guilt had given negative and fearful entities power over her. Where had that fear and guilt come from? Who had tried to kill Cecilia before she got home from the hospital and why would Maria refuse to talk about it?

As someone who has mystically trained, it didn't take him long to see that the guilt Maria felt for having tried to kill her sister, and the fear of retribution she felt, could still be exploited by negative entities as a door into her mind and emotions. She thought she had a handle on it. But had admitted to still having thoughts of harming her sister.

The most important question that needed an answer was, "who was behind the murderous thoughts?" Theoretically he knew that there were evil entities in the world but had never had a close encounter with one or seen one. The feelings and thoughts left behind from Maria's recall were sticky and repulsive. Francisco suddenly remembered the darkness he had seen in David's eyes earlier that day and thought perhaps he had in fact had an encounter with evil before now. He just hadn't recognized it as such.

The air was cooling down and the sky was turning a beautiful pink. Francisco stopped to look at the landscape around him. They were in a large valley filled with trees, hills and ravines. A few rivers crisscrossed it, and here and there were homesteads surrounded by fields and animals.

It was beautiful.

"Come on, we are losing them," Roberto's voice sounded in his mind. He looked beside him into the boy's eyes, which were red from hidden tears.

Francisco nodded and started climbing again. The track ended soon after and their progress slowed down as they climbed rough terrain. He and Roberto soon caught up with Maria. The three of them helped each other over the boulders and holes which littered their path. Every now and then he would see Susie stop and wait for them, making sure they knew where she was heading.

The thought came in as a tiny niggling feeling at first, which got larger with every step. By the time it was fully formed, they were near the top of the hill. Susie had already vanished over the edge and was probably waiting for them to reach her.

The thought was a simple one.

What proof was there that Cecilia was benevolent?

She was more powerful than anyone on the planet that he knew of. She had influenced his every action since the moment her image had been edged into his mind at the Order's HQ. She had power over Susie, whose mind was unbreachable.

He paused.

Roberto and Maria stopped, looking up at him.

"Sooner or later we all wonder about that," Roberto said after a few minutes.

Francisco came back to his awareness, his present moment.

"Has she ever harmed you?" He asked the children.

"No."

"No."

"Well, she did something to Maria," Roberto said. "At the hospital when Maria held her for the first time. She did something to her because Maria fainted for the first time when Cecilia touched her. And she's been fainting since then with female hysteria or whatever."

"I don't have female hysteria, you dork."

"Fine! The point is that you would faint whenever something happened."

"Whenever I felt afraid or stressed, yes."

"What I'm saying is that she messed you up, so you couldn't handle stuff. That could be said to be harmful, right? She harmed Maria in the head?"

Francisco thought about the implications for a while. Susie had stated Maria suffered from severe anemia. The lack of red blood cells meant that there would not be enough oxygen for Maria to function at a moment of stress.

"But look at the consequences of the anemia, whether caused by Cecilia or something else," Francisco thought out loud.

"The consequences," he continued, "are that you Maria were not subjected to strong negative emotions, thoughts or impulses. Without those strong emotions, thoughts or impulses, you would not try to kill your sister again."

"But now I'm fixed and can and do feel those strong things again. Which means, at any moment I might get possessed and try to kill her again. Is that what you are saying?"

"No, that is not what I am saying. What I am saying is that your little sister protected you from those things, from the negative things. Imagine what your life would have been like if you had been feeling those things for the past three years."

The children looked at each other.

"I would probably still be hospitalized in that nut house."

"Exactly." Francisco said.

"Look at this too, we have established, and we all know that Cecilia is powerful, right?"

The children nodded.

"Therefore, we know that she could have had us, any of us, killed at any time."

"Yes," they both said out loud.

"OK. Now, we also know that if she wanted something from us, she could have easily commanded it at any time, correct?"

The children agreed.

"Roberto, when we first met, when I was sending light signals from the coast, your sister said you refused to give her back her mirror. Is that true?"

Roberto nodded.

"What happened next?" Francisco asked.

"She started crying and saying it wasn't fair. I walked off with it."

"And then?"

"Then she tried to bite my leg."

"What did you do?"

"I told her biting was not allowed, that mom had said no biting her brother or sister."

"Did you give her the mirror back?"

"No, I put it back in mom's room."

"Why?"

"We would get in big trouble if we broke it, it belonged to our grandma and mom loves it."

"So, Cecilia didn't try to Command you, or hurt you in any way?"

"No. She's just a kid."

"Do you ever feel afraid of her?"

"Not really. I feel afraid for her. She showed us things, told us of things that were coming for her. That's why we made a plan to escape if we needed to."

Maria started sobbing.

Francisco put his arm around her shoulders, allowing the full emotional stress to drain from her. He knew something had finally broken through.

"I love her so much, but her love hurts me…" Maria said between sobs.

Francisco nodded.

Roberto moved closer and hugged his sister.

She hugged him back.

Roberto's tears finally burst through, running down his face.

Francisco felt the silence in his mind and knew that the siblings were having a private conversation. What these children had gone through in life was unimaginable. What having Cecilia in their home must have been like, was unimaginable. What manner of things, people, entities and situations must have come at them throughout their lives, was unimaginable.

If the past few weeks with Cecilia in his own life was any indication of what life was like for the children, then what had happened to them in the past three years was unimaginable.

Maria and Roberto suddenly faced him, hand in hand, and Francisco knew what they were going to say.

"We are going home now," Maria stated.

"We are done." Roberto added.

"But we are in the middle of nowhere, how will you get back?"

"We are taking the truck. I don't think you guys will need it again."

"Wait, you can drive?"

"Yes, we can drive." They both answered.

"Mom and dad are often too drunk to drive home after parties, so we have to drive them home."

Francisco nodded and looked up to the top of the hill.

"Why now?"

"Something is coming for Cecilia. And it's not coming for us." Maria said.

"We did our job, now it's your turn." Roberto added.

"I don't understand." Francisco said, looking at the children.

"My sister and I have to go home now. Our parents probably found out that the trip is a lie and will be wondering where we are."

"I think we all know that your parents have no idea this trip was a lie."

"Granted, but still. We are going back."

"It's not safe to go back to your house, there are dangerous people watching it." He paused for a second, wondering if sharing his real thoughts about what may have happened to their parents was a good idea or not. He decided it was better to let them know, "your parents might be dead." He said.

"Our parents are fine. And no one is watching our house now that Cecilia is no longer there." Maria stated, firmly and assured.

Francisco felt torn, on the one hand there was Cecilia and his mission to protect her. But he couldn't just leave these children alone in the wilderness. There was no way he could abandon them.

"I'm 15, I'm not a kid. I'm an adult and as such I am able to make my own decisions, and decisions for my brother too."

"I make my own decisions thank you very much," Roberto said, looking at his sister.

"No, I'm the grown up here. And you do as I say." She answered.

"No! I'm the man around here and I make my own decisions."

"You are not a man, you are a boy. But whatever, we are leaving."

Francisco sighed and closed his eyes. He opened them again and said, "you can't go back now. Your parents will wonder where Cecilia is. You can't go back without her."

"We will tell them that you both fell off a ravine, that we came straight back so they could send a search party." Maria said.

"Or maybe that they fell in a white-water river, we've seen quite a few?" Roberto said.

"We could tell them you kidnapped our sister and we escaped with the truck before you could kidnap us too."

"Or we could tell them that an alien spaceship came down from the sky and took you both."

"Or…"

"Enough already!" Francisco said, stopping the kids mid-sentence.

As the kids fell silent, they all heard a faint but distinct drumming sound.

It was coming from the top of the hill. Its rhythm sounded like the beat of a heart.

The three of them stood still, quietly listening to the drums. In the distance, a bright star started getting brighter, closer.

Francisco and the kids looked at each other and at once, started running toward the top of the hill.

CHAPTER TWENTY ONE

Onelyet and Cecilia's semitransparent self, sat in front of each other in his private lounge. Maybe they were in a private conversation, or perhaps they were just sitting there, looking into each other's eyes. Anin watched them, fascinated by the uncanny similarity between the two, and their differences, which were too many to count.

Cecilia definitely had Onelyet's nose and eyes. Maybe also her hands. The more Anin looked at them, the more Cecilia seemed to look like the older woman. He wondered if the child was molding herself into her mother's image.

Of course, a genetic sample from Cecilia's solid form would have to be analyzed before he could confirm their familial relationship. But the way in which they sat, the way they held their heads, it was identical.

His ship's Captain entered the room and stood at attention.

"Sir."

Anin nodded and gestured at a chair near him. The Captain relaxed a little and made his way to the chair.

They all sat there, silently, for close to an hour.

Cecilia then stood up, walked to the Captain and held his hands. The Captain fell awkwardly to his knee, bowed his head and said, "My Queen Returned."

"Mommy's ship likes you now. You can drive it for her."

The Captain looked at Anin, confused.

Anin connected to the Captain's confidential communications channel and downloaded the full technical specifications for Onelyet's ship into his database. With it, a permanent change of station order. He was to be Personal Captain for Her Majesty Onelyet, of the Anunnaki Empire, Queen to all Anunnaki, 11th descendant of Our Lord Anu, True Regent to the Empire, Daughter of Alura of the Latka House and Nosded Third Son of the Emperor Nord Of the Rumni.

Anin watched the Captain's mind working overtime to figure out if this was a promotion or a demotion. After all, although of royal blood, the Queen was impure and unrecognized as Queen by the Empire. Then his features changed as, Anin guessed correctly, the Captain examined the technical specifications of the Queen's ship.

Anin smiled.

The Captain smiled back.

"First things first Captain, get Her Majesty's crew out of stasis and ready to depart." Anin said.

"Yes, Sir."

Cecilia let go of the Captain's hands and ran back to her chair.

Anin observed as Cecilia looked at the Queen, then mimicked her posture.

The Captain stood, saluted Anin, then saluted the Queen, and left the room.

"Onelyet," Anin said, breaking up the magical connection between her and the child.

The Queen looked over at him, her eyes distant.

"Your Majesty, we need to prepare for our departure."

She nodded.

"223." She said, and the lights in the room changed color.

"Yes, Your Majesty?"

"Transfer your consciousness to my ship. It will know where to house you."

235

"Your Majesty, am I coming with you?"

"Of course, you are 223, you don't think I would abandon you after all these years?"

"I did think that, Your Majesty…"

Anin detected a tinge of apology in 223's words.

"What about my base?" The AI asked.

"Put it on automatic defense and maintenance. We may need it at some point in the future."

"What should I tell the Empire?"

"Broadcast that the quarantine was lifted, that all is well, and the base is back to normal."

Anin lifted his hand, "I would prefer the communication to the Empire is not sent just yet. I would prefer a day or two to get things finalized here and Cecilia off of this planet and somewhere safe before we announce our movements."

Onelyet looked at the young man and thought for a moment.

"My ship will stay invisible to the Empire." She began, "I will need you with me, Anin, in order to reach and settle on one of your safe planets with Cecilia. I will need you to make introductions to The Protectors. I will need to meet with your superiors and we need to work out a long term plan of action. For now, we need to take my ship and fetch this girl from the top of a hill."

Anin knew Onelyet was right. Her ship, now functional, had a much better chance of reaching safety than did his, so fetching Cecilia in her ship was the logical thing to do. His crew was independent and would do as they were told. He didn't need to be on his own ship for the plan to work. They could take her ship to fetch Cecilia and get her to safety. But questions would be raised when his ship was scanned by the Empire and he was not in it.

"I will come with you to fetch Cecilia. But then I need to join my crew and get them back home. My... Your Captain knows where to go after you leave the planet."

Onelyet nodded.

Anin could see that the Queen was struggling with the new dynamics of her existence. Would she keep Cecilia safe? Was Cecilia a friend or foe? Would she become a friend or foe to the Queen, her mother, when she grows up? He didn't know the answer to these questions and thought that the Queen must be asking them herself.

He felt that staying close to the Queen, at least for now, was the right choice. Perhaps after they physically met Cecilia, things would become clear. The connection between a child and his or her Anunnaki parents was powerful.

It took a few hours to get both crews ready to leave the base. 223 installed a basic system to control and keep the base running in stasis. His collection of animals, birds and plants seemed to be his biggest concern.

"I have a responsibility to keep them alive, I brought them here from their natural habitats. I have programmed the base to feed and look after them, but I cannot make sure the ones taken from here by your crew will survive." The AI told Anin, as Anin's crew returned to the ship taking some of the plants, birds and animals with them.

"You know very well that our people are collectors of exotic beings, 223. I am certain that with the data you have shared about these specimens, my crew will be able to keep them alive and well."

"They took too many hummingbirds. The birds are an essential part of the biosphere. They need to put some back."

Anin sighed.

"223, calculate how many birds, and other animals and plants..."

"And fish." 223 cut in.

"And fish, can be safely taken without disrupting the biosphere to the level of destruction."

"Why is destruction the defining level? Why cannot it be non disturbance, or wellbeing, or happiness?" 223 asked.

Anin knew the AI was being genuine. But how many animals and plants were being taken from the base was not really in his personal list of priorities.

"223, please make a list of the number of specimens that can be taken out of the base without disrupting the happy balance of existence here."

Anin was not at all sure how the AI would measure a level of happiness in a fish, for example, but he wasn't going to enter into that discussion.

"Thank you Anin, I will contact your crew with the numbers immediately."

Anin was in Onelyet's ship. Her crew, just out of stasis, was getting acquainted with the new situation and also with him and the semitransparent figure of the human child who would trigger Source Bliss in them every time they saw her.

The crew was loyal to their Queen. Some of them had been with her since she was a child. Anin had never experienced such a bond among a leader and her or his people before. The closest he had come to a close bond was the bond among The Protectors, but he didn't really know them at all and their bond was based on a belief system, a religion. The bond between Onelyet and her crew was real, it was personal, and it was deep.

Anin oversaw the awakening of Dr. Berit himself. After her debriefing, the Doctor decided to stay as part of Onelyet's crew. Something the Queen did not object to. It didn't really surprise Anin, the technology on the ship was beyond anything the Dr. had come across in her career before. And as for himself, having two loyal Protectors on the Queen's ship he felt was extremely good fortune.

They waited until sunset before leaving the base.

The Queen and Anin had come to an agreement, they would fetch Cecilia, return to the base where Anin would then board his own ship. Anin would then return to the planet's moon with his crew and the salvaged resources from the now reactivated abandoned base. The exotic specimens collected would give validity to their trip. 223 would contact the Empire to give the all clear on the quarantine after Anin returned to his crew and Onelyet and Cecilia were safely out of the star system. Of all the planets they could go to, he felt very strongly that the headquarters of The Protectors, and where Shylar and his future child were being secretly held, was the best place for the Queen and Cecilia to be at. He was sending the Queen and Cecilia to Garenidan.

As they left the base, Cecilia sat in front of a wall which was now transparent. She pointed in the direction where she said she was at. It was slow going, slower than Anin would have wished. But the unexplainable failure of even this ship's ability to pinpoint Cecilia's physical location on the planet forced them to follow her directions.

"I can feel her," the Queen said, "I can feel her in every cell in my body. I can feel myself responding to her frequency not as a rank, but as her mother. I was once a mother, but my child didn't get a chance to mature to birth. But even though he was only a cluster of cells when he died, I felt his demise from across the universe."

"I am so sorry to hear of your loss Onelyet." Anin responded in the informal manner of close friends when hearing of a dear one's death.

"Maybe, if the holographic recording is right, I can go back in time and warn my husband, tell him to leave the planet and take our unborn child with him."

Anin looked out into the broad landscape of Earth. They had left the whiteness of the Antarctic and were now travelling slowly over a blue and vast ocean.

After a few hours, they turned inland. As they spotted populated areas, the ship elevated to a height which would keep them off the primitive radar detectors below. They also slowed down and parroted the physical presence and frequency of a human air vessel. It wasn't just humans they had to stay invisible to, it was also Rumni and other species which had the technology to detect them.

"No one can detect us," Onelyet stated as a matter of fact. "My ship will shift and change as necessary for us to reach our destination without causing alarm to the local population or any other advanced species out there."

It wasn't long after that Cecilia shouted, "there!" Pointing towards a spark of light in a distant hill.

"I'm going back now, to tell them you are here." She said and vanished.

Anin and Onelyet both noticed that her absence did not cause any pain. They looked at each other, then at the point of light in the distance.

"We are close enough to her now that her leaving didn't affect us." Onelyet said.

"Good confirmation that we are in the right location." He said and contacted the Captain to reach the hill and make a safe landing.

They could have reached the hill in less than a second, but they kept to the velocity and signature of a human helicopter.

In reality, the ship was hundreds of times larger than a helicopter, but to the human eye and to all electronic and other detection systems, it was small and looked like a helicopter. At least it did while at a minimum of a thousand meters away.

It took them twenty Earth minutes to reach the hill.

Anin's heart was beating so hard his robe administered calming compounds into his bloodstream. He observed the Queen staying calm and collected and wondered how she managed it. The crew was having a hard time staying out of Source Bliss, so most of the systems were placed on autopilot.

They hovered above the light, which was a large bonfire. The ship scanned everyone on the hill. There was Cecilia, Francisco, Cecilia's two siblings, a Rumni shapeshifter that looked like a human female, and over three hundred other humans. The ship started transmitting the sounds of the gathering directly into the control room.

The large crowd was playing music and dancing in the manner he had watched humans on various planets during social gatherings and important occasions.

Suddenly, the dancing, music and singing stopped. Now only the fire crackling could be heard.

"I believe they are ready for us." The Queen announced.

Anin could hardly stand up himself, the excitement was such that Complete or not, he was unable to control his own state of Source Bliss.

The Queen stopped at the doorway, turned and reached for his hand.

"It's called love." She said, and her hand held his, his heart calmed down and he felt himself able to breathe once again.

The humans had created a large, large enough for the ship, landing pad. It was highly decorated with Anunnaki and human symbols of friendship and collaboration.

Both the Queen and himself put on their hats before exiting the ship.

Among the humans a collective gasp was heard.

Seven men and women, clearly Chiefs and leaders of their people, walked towards them. They were wearing full regalia, some of the symbols and materials indicating rank and lineage with Anunnaki historical relationships.

"Star Cousins. You are welcome here. Our Mother Returned has been born on our Earth, and she is here with us. She awaits you..."

At this point Cecilia had had enough of the entire ritual and ran fast through the welcoming group and into the Queen's arms.

The Queen fell to her knees, the tiny little human girl wrapped tightly around her. The Queen was not in Source Bliss but in absolute motherly happiness. This tiny impure and ugly little thing was her daughter. No test was necessary. And no one would come between them ever. They wiped each other's tears of joy, cried, giggled and laughed as their bond and link became stronger than anything known in the Universe.

Anin dropped all protocol and, taking his headdress off, held the Queen and her daughter in his arms. Tears run down his own eyes, and he felt embarrassed, mortified and happy about his crazy behavior. But he couldn't help himself. After having shared the Queen's memories, and she his, the bond he felt for and with her was greater than that of his own family. And Cecilia had become such an integral part of his life, he could not imagine life without her to protect and look after.

After a few minutes, one of the human leaders lifted his arms and everyone started singing, drumming, playing flutes and other instruments, and dancing once more. It was the best they could do to respect the intimate moment of reunion.

For the first time in his life, Anin actually felt peace and happiness. He would do anything for this woman. Lay his life down for her, his every thought and breath would from now on be hers.

Shocked at his own thoughts and emotions, he pulled away. The Queen, realizing what had happened, stood up, the child in her arms, and touched his forehead, his heart, and took his hand in hers once more. It was the acceptance of a Bonded man.

"You are Bonded to me Anin."

"But that cannot be, this is not my child by you, and I am Complete, I cannot be Bonded!"

"Bonding, like Source Bliss, is a natural and normal part of who we are. It was hijacked at a genetic level thousands of years ago to promote political, financial and genetic interests. A natural

Bonding happens mysteriously and without apparent cause. It used to be that the Bonding happened before any children were created."

Anin wanted to let go of her hand but couldn't. Was unable to. Didn't want to. Really did not want to.

The music around them continued, giving him a moment of privacy. A moment he really needed for himself.

His plans now had to change, they would be married, formally married, and they would bring up their children together. His baby not yet born, and Cecilia. And they would have children of their own. They would be a family.

As though reading his mind, the Queen turned to him, touched his face and said, "you are too young to bear children, Anin. You are little more than a child yourself. Your body and your mind are not yet mature enough to hold my full Bond. I cannot take you as my husband."

"I don't understand. I thought the Bonding was our joining. I cannot think of a future where you are not my wife. You cannot hold my age against me, I am a man and I feel the Bond from you too. I know this is real. You cannot turn away from me."

As if on cue, Cecilia pulled away from her mother and into Anin's arms.

"Mommy, we keep Anin. He is my Guard."

The Queen smiled. And nodded.

"Of course, we can keep him Cecilia. But the conversation Anin and I are having is about other things. But don't worry, he will never leave us."

The words were confusing, but they gave Anin a huge sense of relief.

He could understand the Queen's reluctance in taking him as her husband. His rank was nowhere near hers, and there was no longer any uncertainty that she was the Queen Regent. Anin also lacked her experience and maturity. But he was a fast learner, and he was Complete.

"Yes, you are Complete, Anin. And I am not. There are many things we need to address before making this important and lifelong decision."

Now he knew she was definitely reading his mind.

Her last words gave him the confidence to know that next to him stood his future wife. If there were things to address, problems to solve, and any type of barriers to their joining, he was the most talented person in the Empire to figure them all out.

A man started walking toward them. He was tall for human standards. Two children followed closely behind him.

Anin spoke, and his robe translated the words into various human languages.

"Francisco, Maria and Roberto. It is an honor to meet you all. Cecilia has spoken about you at length."

Francisco saluted him in the manner of an ancient religious order, now extinct, then turned to the Queen and knelt down in front of her. The Children stood nervously behind him.

The music came to a stop once more, and the seven leaders walked forward, standing next to Francisco and the children.

The next few hours were spent in formal exchanges of gifts and information with the gathered people, who were representative of many tribes in the region and beyond.

Anin, and the Queen, would have preferred to collect the child and leave immediately. But it didn't turn out that way.

Francisco introduced them to the Rumni female, who triggered various members of the Queen's crew to go into full defensive stance.

Anin took genetic samples of everyone he came across.

He knew it wasn't necessary, but his professional drive to collect data and information took the better of him.

Cecilia was definitely Onelyet's genetic daughter. Her siblings, however, were fully human although they had had huge genetic modifications. It explained their uncanny ability to communicate telepathically, as well as their capacity to see and understand things better than the other people present.

Francisco had a significant percentage of Anunnaki genetic material in him, which Francisco knew already. He also had a significant percentage of Rumni genetic material, which made Anin very curious.

The tribal officials and some of the other humans he came into contact with that night, had genetic markers he could trace back to several planetary systems in the galaxy.

Cecilia's siblings had waited until things quieted down before approaching Anin with their very important problem.

"You see, if we go home without Cecilia, it's going to be a huge problem. We need to come with you."

That was the boy.

"Our parents are really not that interested in us anyway, and people get lost in the mountains all the time. They won't miss us for very long."

That was the girl.

"In fact, I think, they will be glad to be rid of us. They can then be free to party without any worries at all." She continued.

"To be fair, I think they do that anyway," the boy added.

The children wanted to come with their sister and travel the universe in a spaceship.

Normally, he would not have taken notice or listened to children from inferior and unimportant races. Or adults, for that matter. But these were The Queen Returned adopted brother and sister.

She had grown up with them and having them around seemed to make her happy.

"I feel my job is done here, Cecilia is safely in your care now," Francisco began, looking at Anin and the Queen, "but taking all three children I think is a mistake. We definitely need to address Cecilia's absence to her parents, but I think that Maria and Roberto need to return home."

"These children are not going to fit into regular human life if left here to their own devices. Their genetic alterations are too great for them to have a normal and happy life among inferior… unaltered humans." It was Dr. Berit, who had been called to give her professional opinion about the nature of the genetic alterations in the children and had then stayed to observe them.

"Who did these alterations?" Anin asked.

"It's unclear, Sir," she began, "the markers and signatures on the alterations are very specific. If I didn't know better, I would say they were made by one of our own specialists."

"What do you mean our own specialists? Someone in our crew?" The Queen interjected.

"No, no one I know of here, but they do have our markers, as in, they were done using Anunnaki technology and knowhow."

Anin and the Queen looked at each other.

"Well, if you went into the past to put her in that family, it makes sense that you would travel further back in time and place a support system for her in that family too, in the shape of two siblings who would be able to communicate with her and keep her company." Anin said to the Queen.

"I wouldn't know where to begin." She responded.

"With the right instructions, these are alterations that could be programmed into one of our conception modules. It would then do all the work." The Doctor said.

"However, this doesn't address the fact that we have to leave now, and that these altered human children are now our responsibility." Anin stated.

Cecilia held her mother's face in her little hands and looked into her eyes.

The Queen nodded and smiled.

"We can reverse the alterations and send the children back. All memories and knowledge of us, Cecilia and their present adventures will be removed from their minds. The existence of Cecilia will also be removed from her human parents and everyone she has ever come into contact with. All evidence, physical or otherwise, will be removed from their house and lives."

The words came out as a statement, not an idea or suggestion.

Maria and Roberto both started protesting and arguing why that was a terrible idea.

"You will live a normal human life," the Queen said to them, knowing it was not going to calm them down.

The words came out of Cecilia's mouth, slowly, and filled with effort, "I will visit you all the time. One day I will come and fetch you and you will remember me again."

EPILOGUE

Roberto woke up, his cat Stardust, pawing at his chest. He looked over at the clock next to him, it showed 5:30 am.

"Want some food?"

The cat meowed.

"Ok." He said and climbed out of his tent.

The room was cold, and the house quiet. Roberto loved Sundays. He reached down to pick up his cat and saw his arms were covered in black writing.

"What the…"

An hour later his sister Maria and he were sitting inside his tent comparing notes. Literally. Both their arms and legs, and also their bellies and backs, were covered in writing.

"I'm telling you, it's someone's idea of a bad joke." Maria stated for the hundredth time.

"But this is my writing," he said, pointing at his arms and legs, "no one else writes like this. I have horrible writing. Plus, look, these bits on your arms have little hearts instead of dots. You are the only person I know who dots her 'I's with hearts."

"Yeah, this is definitely my writing."

"We have to copy it all to paper, before it fades."

"Maybe mom and dad brought some weird drugs home again and this time we took them?"

Roberto thought about this. It was actually the most logical explanation to their present predicament.

"Do you have something called anemia?" He asked his sister.

"No, and I don't faint either."

"And you remember nothing about a weird alien sister called Cecilia?"

Maria shook her head, no.

They spent the next few hours transferring the text onto a notebook. And then a few more hours searching the house for evidence of a third sibling.

Nothing.

At lunch time, their parents denied any use of drugs or administering of drugs, in the house that week. They also had no recollection of a girl called Cecilia.

In the afternoon, they walked over to their nanny's house to see if he remembered anything or knew anything about their mysterious writing or the existence of a girl called Cecilia.

Francisco and his wife Susie listened intently at their story, looked at the notebook and discussed the possibilities with them at length. They would keep the notebook and investigate the situation further.

The children felt listened to and left the house happy in the knowledge that they had allies in their investigation.

It was Monday the next day, and a school day.

Roberto woke up to the smell of bacon, and Francisco's voice calling him to the kitchen for breakfast. His cat Stardust still sleepy from a night of hunting, followed him out of the tent.

He got dressed and made their way to the kitchen.

"Do you remember your notes?" Francisco asked him the moment he sat down at the kitchen table.

"What notes?"

Francisco smiled.

"Your homework I mean. Do you have it ready for today's class?"

"Oh, oh."

It was twenty years later.

Roberto sat in his well-kept yard, smoking a cigarette and watching his hens, One of 8, Three of 8 and Four of 8, when a large light started coming toward him in the sky.

At first, he thought it was a missile and he had one of those life review episodes a person gets when they are about to die. "Who knew? It really happens." Roberto thought to himself as the memories crossed his mind. But the missile stopped suddenly then started moving again, this time slowly toward him, getting bigger by the second. It stopped again right above his yard. It was a massive spaceship.

A large transparent tube came out of the bottom of the ship and touched the ground in front of him.

His chickens ran out of the way.

He saw a person floating down the tube, then as the person landed on the ground, the tube opened up.

"Get in here! Quick!" A woman shouted at him. Roberto reached over for his glasses, "come on Roberto, snap out of it! We are needed!"

It was Maria, his sister.

Printed in Poland
by Amazon Fulfillment
Poland Sp. z o.o., Wrocław